Leyette

Hope you enjoy it

Best wishes

Drew Thomas.

WEIRD SEX

WEIRD SEX

Drew Thomas

Hart & Sole
LONDON

First published 1997 by Hart & Sole Ltd
211 Piccadilly London W1V 9LD

ISBN 1 900495 01 5

British Library Cataloguing in Publication data.
A catalogue record for this book is available from the British Library.

Printed in Great Britain by
Perfectaprint, West Byfleet, Surrey KT14 7JG

'It is in truth a most contagious game:
HIDING THE SKELETON shall be its name.'
George Meredith

'Reference GS163. I'm a slave in my late twenties, tall, dark and handsome, looking for a master - preferably over forty - who is well-versed in the art of control. A knowledge of leather, rubber, bondage and mild CP would be advantageous. I can't travel, but can accommodate in my secluded country retreat. Leave your telephone number and I'll get back to you respectfully. Once again, my reference is GS163.'

PROLOGUE

Five seconds before the crash, Michael was as happy as he could ever remember being. The wind blew in his face and rushed through his hair. He opened his mouth to shout, wanting to express the overwhelming feeling of mad abandon he felt. Ahead in the dark, the rear light of Terry's motorbike glowed red – a firefly leading the way. In the distance, the lights of the town glimmered like a thousand candles on the hillside. He breathed in, filling his lungs with the warm night air, the rarity of the moment intoxicating him, the sheer recklessness of driving at high speed in the pitch darkness.

One day almost two years before, standing on the docks at Piraeus, the same feeling had convinced him that he was doing the right thing. With barely enough money in his pocket to last a week, the thrill of having taken his life into his own hands by doing something wild, illogical and certainly not expected of him made him feel eighteen again. All he carried was a battered holdall containing a few pairs of 501s, five T-shirts, the obligatory Calvin Kleins and an equally battered copy of the Rough Guide to Greece borrowed from a library in Notting Hill. Faced with a seemingly infinite number of possible destinations, his dilemma was solved by the arrival at his side of a large-breasted Australian. Tara was the kind of girl who wasn't afraid to approach an attractive man and state her desires. Michael, although gratified that his new baggage-free persona was an instant success, convinced her that he would make a much better travel companion than he would a quick bonk and readily accepted her invitation to join her on the ferry to Naxos.

Within two days, their combined talents had landed them jobs in a bar on a beach and a small but functional room above a souvlaki shop. Three idyllic months of hard work and exhausting play made the traumas of Michael's past fade to the recesses of his mind. When the time came for Tara to continue her travels, it was mutually accepted that the time had also come for them to go their separate ways. Michael took his new found confidence with him on a ferry to Santorini, while Tara sailed back to Athens to catch a flight to Tel Aviv and new experiences.

Michael, having decided to allow fate to guide him, enjoyed the carefree life he found on each island he visited; when the time came to leave an island and move on, a new opportunity always arose to point him in the right direction. So here he was, nearly two years later, on Mykonos – an island he had previously decided to avoid. Fate, in the form of a Liverpudlian called Terry, had intervened and the last three months had been the happiest of his life so far.

The lorry came from nowhere, hurtling around a corner towards them. Terry swerved, his motorbike hitting the safety barrier as he was hurled into the ravine below. Michael swerved to the other side, losing control but managing to throw himself clear as his bike ploughed under the wheels of the oncoming lorry, the dizzy intoxication leaving him instantly. He watched in a daze as the lorry screeched to a halt and the driver jumped out. Death was in the air - he could feel it. Ignoring the searing pain in his leg, he ran to the edge of the road. The engine on Terry's bike was still running as it lay by the safety barrier, the headlight glowing ominously in the dark. He was sure death had come along again to shatter the new life he had made for himself. He might have left London, but he couldn't leave it all behind. Without giving it a second thought, he climbed down the ravine, falling over twice in his haste, making out Terry's crumpled form in the darkness. Death. He jumped as he heard Terry's voice cheerfully telling him that he was alright. The relief was overwhelming, but so was the feeling that this had happened for a reason.

The time had come for him to go home and face the past.

CHAPTER ONE

'Stand by studio and remember this is not a rehearsal... this is the real thing so good luck. Going in... five... four... three... two... and cue titles!' The titles rolled and the first ever edition of Clarion Television's flagship daytime show lurched onto the screens of the nation.

'Good Morning and welcome to "Family Values". My name is Tony Barkworth...'

'And I'm Julia Daley.' The woman beside him on the green suede sofa aimed a condescending smile at camera two, realising too late that the director had not yet cued her.

'For the next twelve weeks, we'll be with you every weekday morning from ten o'clock, bringing you news, reviews, star guests, competitions, discussions and much, much more...' Tony Barkworth could feel the cameras staring at him as if they had lives of their own. Their huge unblinking eyes seemed to be hanging on his every word, just waiting for him to make a mistake. Well, he'd just have to show them that he had got the guts to see this new challenge through. He had no choice...

'Yes Tony...' Unable to remain quiet any longer, Julia Daley launched her laboriously groomed persona at the camera, pausing momentarily to allow the director time to catch up with her. 'And we're not afraid to tackle those slightly *sensitive* topics are we, Tony?' Her husband glared at her, forcing his handsome features into a smile. After barely ten seconds on the air, she had already managed to steal one of his lines!

'Yes, Julia,' he paused to take a calming breath, 'we've got an exciting show lined up for you every morning, with subjects ranging from...'

'Male rape and incest to homosexuality and wife swapping. We're the couple who are going to hit you with the hottest topics, the most daring stories and the most risqué guests. Why, only next week we've got...'

'The pop star who's not afraid to bare her body as well as her innermost secrets,' Tony gabbled, trying to read the autocue before his wife could intervene, 'and the actor who defends his decision to marry...'

'His step daughter.' Julia beamed, delighted to have got the last word in. The director frantically searched for the next cue on his script and realised that this show was going to be one hell of an assault course.

*   *   *

Kathleen Barkworth suppressed a sob as she watched her son on television. She was more proud than she had ever been.

'Oh Anthony,' she sniffed into her lace-edged hankie, 'if only your father was still here to see you. I knew everything would be alright in the end.'

At fifty seven, Kathleen looked and acted ten years older. To say that she had lost her sense of purpose in life since her husband's death from cancer three years previously would have overestimated her ability to have recognised that she had one. If she had been honest with herself, which was not her custom, she might have asked some very fundamental questions about the reason for her existence, not to mention the opportunities she had wasted through sheer narrow-mindedness. Her marriage to a comparatively wealthy vacuum cleaner manufacturer at the age of twenty had lifted her from what might have been an interminably dull existence with an ageing mother and drunken father on a Northampton council estate. It had been like a dream come true at first, even if her husband had been twenty years her senior, but her life had gradually transformed itself into a nightmare as her childless state continued into their seventh year of marriage. The long-awaited arrival of identical twins at last gave her husband the heir he so desperately wanted and herself the excuse to sit back and wallow in the subconscious knowledge that she had done what was expected of her.

'I always knew you'd be the one to make something of yourself,' she sobbed, wondering how many of her neighbours on the Avenue were watching. 'I always knew you'd reward me for bringing you up so well...'

* * *

Crossing her legs in an attractive and, so she thought, sophisticated way, Julia Daley beamed at the camera and thought how well everything was going for her. Not that it hadn't taken some planning...

From the moment she caught sight of Tony Barkworth six months earlier, she decided that he was going to be her next husband. Whenever she set her mind on anything, whether it was a new hairstyle, name or career, she knew how to get it. Driven by little more than a need for self-importance and financial gain, she was a formidable enemy and impossible friend. The three years since her return to England from America had been spent relentlessly promoting her talents. Desperately aware that she was a virtually unknown television presenter on the wrong side of forty, she unashamedly called in a few old favours. Stopping inches short of blackmail, she wheedled her way into hosting an obscure show which ran twice a week on a satellite channel at four o'clock in the morning. Entitled 'Bubbles With Julia', the show asked viewers to request their favourite clips from well-known soap operas. She endured the comparative indignity of giving her name to a show whose highlights might be, typically, a burning motel, a gaggle of disturbingly masculine Australian women fighting behind bars or a jewel-encrusted wedding party having their shoulder pads blown apart by machine gun fire. She endured it because she knew that

14

something better lay ahead. In due course, it came to her attention that Clarion Television - the new franchise holder for the London area - was looking for a couple to host its planned daytime show. Julia decided that she would stop at nothing to get the coveted contract.

She knew it was within her grasp the moment she caught sight of the handsome but inexperienced Tony Barkworth at a studio party. The young journalist was clearly nervous about his television debut - a very brief slot on a short-lived consumer show. Seeing his potential, she introduced herself by slipping her arm through his. 'Don't worry.' The protective smile immediately put Tony at his ease as the next piece of her jigsaw fell into place. 'I'll be your Mummy...'

The rest had gone to plan. Their whirlwind romance, the marriage and all that went with it finally tipped the balance in her favour. What she had lacked as a single female presenter in her forties with an undeniably patchy track record was made up for by this partnership with a young, attractive man. As a married couple, they apparently fitted the bill perfectly. Not that she allowed her new husband any of the credit for her coup. In Julia's eyes, it had been all down to her. Tony was just a useful pawn. This was her big chance - maybe her last chance - to prove that she had indeed got what it took to be a successful television presenter.

It might have been a bit daring to wear Zandra Rhodes for the first show, but she was going all out to make an impression. The bright pink two-piece was certainly eye catching and the green tights and chunky emerald choker set off her eyes to perfection. She had been starving herself for months to get down to 'camera weight' and had spent much of the last two weeks at a health farm. She had caused trouble by turning up late for three production meetings and two rehearsals, but didn't let the fact worry her, convinced that Clarion needed her almost as much as she needed them. She knew where her priorities lay - it was appearance that mattered, especially when you were more than ten years older than your husband. Her figure was showing the benefit of the pounds, both spent and lost, and her perfectly manicured fingernails, sculptured blonde coiffure and glowing complexion made her feel on top of the world... or at least on the way there. She glanced over at her husband, handsome in his Armani suit but not totally at ease with his new image, as he introduced the opening item.

'Sexual abuse of children...' Pausing for effect and flicking back his newly styled hair, having been assured by Julia that it made him look sophisticated, he took on what he hoped was a meaningful expression. Image wise, Tony Barkworth was streets ahead of his wife. Thirty years old, just under six feet tall with jet black hair and vivid blue, dark-lashed eyes, his natural good looks were already making female hearts around the country flutter. 'Whether we like it or not, it is a subject that has become ever more familiar to us nowadays. What has happened to this nation which is meant to love its children? What has caused the apparently massive increase in cases? What is being done to combat this cancer eating away at our society? How does it bode for the future?' He paused again, rather pleased with his prosaic little bit of ad-libbing, but wasn't quick enough to stop his wife from continuing. She had suddenly realised that he was quite probably a good deal more intelligent than she was and wasn't about to let him have the chance to prove it publicly.

'It has been suggested that victims of abuse *never* fully recover from their ordeal. Today we are going to talk to three people who were sexually abused as children about the effect it has had on their lives.' Julia looked down at her pink stiletto court shoes and thought how elegant they looked as the camera panned out to show the three people sitting on the long sofa beside them. 'May I start with you, Sandra?'

'Yes... and we'd like to thank you for being brave enough to come on the show today.' Tony decided the human touch was called for, furrowing his brow and lowering his voice. 'Can you tell us when it all started?'

The slight, dark-haired woman looked straight at him. The researcher had told her that her views would be given a sympathetic airing. She hadn't expected this bright chat-on-the-sofa treatment and was currently regretting her decision to come on the show at all. She swallowed hard and took a deep breath.

'First of all - and I think I'm probably speaking for all of us -I'd like to stress that I am not here to recount all the details of what happened to me in the past.'

'Of course not,' Julia interjected, trying to keep the disappointment out of her voice. 'We all realise what you must be going through.' Sandra ignored the unscripted interruption and continued.

'I'm here in the hope that I can give some help to viewers who might be in a similar predicament, possibly thinking that they are the only ones in the world this has happened to. I'm sure there are people, both children and adults, watching today who are trapped in a tormented world of secrecy, not knowing where they can turn, what they can do about it. I want to let them know that they *aren't* alone and that there is something they can do about it.'

'So,' Julia said quietly, reaching over and putting her hand on the woman's leg in a comforting gesture, noticing as she did so what a particularly good job the girl at Champney's had done on her nails, 'how old *were* you were first sexually abused?'

*   *   *

Kathleen Barkworth decided it was time to make some coffee. She certainly didn't want to hear about the dreadful things they were obviously going to discuss. It quite surprised her that her son even knew about them. And to think of all the money they'd spent on a private education!

She walked towards the kitchen feeling that her enjoyment at seeing her son's success take shape in her own lounge had somehow been marred. There was a bitter taste in her mouth and she couldn't pin down the reason for it...

*   *   *

'So you're saying that it's possible for victims to live with their abuse for years and years without ever telling anyone?' Tony interrupted the therapist, their fourth guest, to clarify a point. 'What kind of effect could this have on them?'

'As I was saying,' the slim grey-haired woman hesitated to make sure she wasn't going to be interrupted again, 'many people have suffered from a form of abuse in the past, not necessarily sexual, and have never had the chance to come to terms with it, let alone tell anyone that it occurred. This can lead to deep-seated feelings of inferiority, insecurity, mistrust and an inability to form fulfilling relationships. As you heard a little while ago from Alexander, the hidden frustrations resulting from sexual abuse by his uncle when he was nine years old led to the failure of his marriage, the loss of his job and an almost total nervous breakdown. It wasn't until he admitted there was a problem and came to see us at the Ashdown Clinic that he was able to commence therapy and start living his life.'

'But surely there are still deep psychological scars that will never heal?' Julia decided she had been in the background for far too long. 'Alison·just told us that she still can't bring herself to trust a man... and that's more than twenty years after her father...'

'And that just about brings us to the break,' Tony announced ten seconds too early, throwing the control room into yet another panic.

*   *   *

Iris Devereaux' frown broke into a smile. She had been puzzling over the face on the screen for twenty minutes and had at last placed it.

'You might have changed your name,' she muttered to herself, 'but I never forget a face... even when it's been nipped and tucked 'til your ear's become your navel. I never forget one of my girls.' The old lady sat back, pleased that she had reached her eighty sixth year without losing her faculties. Seeing Julia's face on the television hadn't shocked her in the slightest. Her composure came from many years of expecting the unexpected and, more recently, longing for it. She had first set eyes on the girl almost thirty years

18

earlier. Thirty years. A lot of water had flowed under the bridge since then. So many things had changed.

She looked around her at the comfortable but dowdy furniture, the faded photographs on the walls, the yellowed theatrical posters. They had changed. Like her, they had aged; they belonged in the past. Even the street outside had lost its identity. Battersea used to know what it was and be proud of it. Now, everything was confusing. Most of the terraced houses on either side of hers had been bought by yuppies in the Thatcher years and made into 'desirable artisans' cottages' or 'faithfully restored townhouses'. It made her laugh. Everyone wanted to harp back to better times, wanted to strip doors back to pine that hadn't seen the light of day since it was a tree in Scotland, open up fireplaces and install 'coal effect' fires and make features of old wash stands. The old lady chuckled. You never caught them shovelling coal from the cellar, which had probably been made into a playroom for the children, or carrying hot water up the stairs in a jug. Oh no. 'Faithfully restored' meant having a reproduction Victorian bathroom - complete with bidet - and making the front garden into a parking space for the GTI. Mind you, there weren't so many of them as there used to be... and you hardly ever saw a Porsche in the area now, not since the recession had set in. Perhaps the new inhabitants of Sitatunga Road were getting a taste at last of the old days. Perhaps the houses were getting their own back and having a bit of a laugh at their new owners. Ye gods... how her mind was wandering!

Memories... they were all she had now. The old days had been good to her, there was no denying that, but she had known when to draw the line. She had got what she wanted out of the business - ten troupes of showgirls working all over the world, not to mention the speciality acts. And then there was the other side of the business...

Her girls had been the best. Oh yes... and she could remember them all. A lot of them still kept in touch. Some of her girls were grandmothers now. A few of them had gone a long way: she had seen more than one familiar face crop up on the stage or television and here was another. Yes, she remembered that face. She had always known that girl would go a long way, but had somehow thought it might be in the wrong direction. Perhaps it was.

She had known the girl had her sights set on higher things, known that she had the curse of ambition eating away at her insides. She had seen it before and seen it since, but usually it was accompanied by some degree of talent. It could either make you or break you, especially when it pushed you to heights you had previously only dared to dream of.

'Well, you've made it girl,' she mumbled as the adverts came to an end and the show started again. 'I just hope you like it now you've got there, duckie... I just hope you like it!' The tragedy was that they all thought they were doing something new, covering new ground, attaining new goals. But it had all been done before.

Iris was glad her own life was almost at an end.

*   *   *

'Welcome back,' Julia smiled icily. 'For those of you who have just joined us, we're discussing the subject of child abuse and the far reaching effects it has on its victims.' She adjusted the angle at which her legs were crossed, showing just a little more thigh before continuing. 'I'm Julia Daley, this is my co-presenter Tony Barkworth.' She paused again to emphasise the pecking order. 'With us in the studio today we have Sandra, Alexander and Alison, three victims of abuse at some time in their lives...' she paused long enough to let Tony think he was going to be able to deliver his lines and then snatched them away '...and Dr Naomi Lichtenstein, an expert in the treatment of victims of sexual abuse. Dr Lichtenstein... we've heard your views on the treatment and therapy of victims. What is your view on the treatment of offenders... those who commit these crimes? What is your view on current methods of treatment and do you agree with the currently controversial cases of convicted child abusers being treated within the community?'

'Er...' The doctor was lost for words, dazed by the speed at which the presenter had fired the questions.

'Oh well... while you decide what you think,' the corners of Julia's mouth twitched upwards as she realised she was in charge again, 'we'll move on to some footage which, incidentally, some people may find quite *distressing*.' She resisted the temptation to look at their guests on the sofa. 'We have managed to find an extract from an exclusive interview with a convicted child abuser who still maintains that what he did was not wrong...'

* * *

Clive Haynes had just switched on the television and his eyes opened wide as the face on the screen stared back at him. The last time he had seen that face it had been leering down at him in his own bedroom. The huge machete had appeared as if from nowhere in the middle of an otherwise unremarkable domination session and he had found himself staring death in the face. Thank God the telephone had rung. His attacker had jumped, Clive had kicked him in the groin and made a dash for the front door. He had run for all he was worth to the police station. The humiliation of it all was still fresh in his mind. The way the police had tried to fob him off at first, the way they had intimated that because he was a sexually active gay man he had as good as 'asked for it'. Only when it was discovered that his attacker was quite likely the man responsible for three particularly brutal gay murders had they changed their tune. He had suddenly become their best possible lead and was, for a while, taken seriously. The whole of the capital had been buzzing with the excitement of it all. Everyone had learned in great detail about his sexual habits and - in true English fashion - while lapping up the details greedily, many had been quick to criticise. Some had even condemned his lifestyle as due cause for the execution he had so narrowly avoided.

The police enquiries had led nowhere. No positive identification had been made as a result of his many hours spent with the police making up photo-fit images of the man he had let into his flat after talking to him on a telephone dating line. More than one article in the press had intimated that he had imagined the whole episode in an effort to seek attention. He had had to move house, leave his job and become a virtual recluse. It had even crossed his mind that he might really have imagined it all.

But now, two years later, his attacker was on the television. Any confusion that might have been there when describing him to the police evaporated as the disparate details in his memory came back re-embodied in a face. A complete face. A real person. He knew now, without a shadow of a doubt, that his sanity was intact. A great feeling of relief gave way to a renewed surge of gut-wrenching fear. There was nothing for it – he had got to pluck up the courage to go and talk to the police again.

* * *

'What the fuck do you think you're playing at?' Tony was fuming. Their first hour on the air had proved one thing to him and, no doubt, to the viewers: his wife was in charge.

'I don't know what you mean. I was only following the autocue. You know very well that they're relying on *me* to carry this show.' Julia smiled benignly as the make-up girl touched up her face with a huge powder puff. 'If you're not happy with the contract, I'm sure I can get my agent to go over it again with us.'

'What do you mean, *your* agent?' Tony was starting to sweat. It would be him needing the powder puff in a moment.

'Oh... I'm sorry darling. I keep forgetting that he's your agent as well. It's just that George and I go back such a long way. You'll realise what I mean when you've been in television as long as I have. No hard feelings? Love you!' Julia stood up and whisked off, leaving the make-up department to tone down her husband's flushed features.

Tony's life had never been easy and being married to Julia certainly wasn't going to make it any easier. He couldn't deny that it was her experience that had secured their contract and provided them both with an exceptional career opportunity, but was it worth it? Was he going to live to regret giving her the chance to dominate him openly and publicly? It had been like a dream come true when

22

it had first happened, but it was now looking as if it might, after all, be just another nightmare.

'Forty five seconds Mr Barkworth.'

Tony hurried along, not wanting to give his wife another opportunity to lecture him on professionalism.

* * *

As the show came to a close, Harvey Wolfenden heaved a huge sigh of relief. His career and credibility as a producer with Clarion rested on this show being a success. He had scoured the country for presenters and had only seriously considered Julia Daley, by no means his first choice, at the last moment. There was something about her, something that might just appeal to the legions of bored housewives at whom the show's slot was aimed. Her recent marriage to young struggling journalist Tony Barkworth had clinched the deal. To the viewers, they were quite likely to represent the epitome of the ideal couple. Julia on her own would not have kept their attention, but the knowledge that she had netted herself this young handsome husband made them all want to be like her. The publicity surrounding their phenomenal salary had more than justified the deal - they had been featured on more magazine pages than the Duchess of York's toes, ensuring healthy ratings for the launch.

What he had not bargained for, however, was Julia's remarkably high opinion of herself. She had made her presence felt from the moment she had stepped onto the studio floor. Not that he normally criticised strong characters. In the past, weak characters had angered him far more. People with great talents who allowed themselves to be walked over and their gifts to be exploited commanded no respect from Harvey Wolfenden. But with Julia it seemed to be exactly the reverse. His gut feelings had never failed him before and he knew he was going have a fight on his hands with this one. If the show was going to be a success, he needed to keep that bitch Daley under control.

* * *

The twenty minute delay before landing at Heathrow was a revelation to Michael. Far from being an inconvenience, it was a chance to relish the fact that, once again, he had made the right decision.

The plane circled low over the capital. It was a bright clear day and, for the first time, he could see his former playground in its entirety. The Thames – snaking through the metropolis like a glistening ribbon – seemed too still to be the massive tidal river he knew so well. He tried to remember the names of the bridges now they were neatly laid out below him. Tower Bridge looked like an intricately detailed model of the real thing. The trees along the Embankment looked like the green lichen he had carefully glued into place on his model railway many years before. Tiny cars moved slowly along the network of roads, more like clever finishing touches to the miniature city than modes of transport containing real people with real lives. Michael pressed his face against the window. From this distance, the buildings looked too precise to be genuine. It was hard to imagine that this was the same city he was familiar with from street level – the dirt, grime and irregularities ironed out as they presented themselves as part of the whole bustling being that was London. Battersea Power Station pointed its four white chimneys upwards – roofless, redundant, yet still firmly part of the city. It was all there as he had left it two years ago, but now it was more manageable because he was in a fit state to deal with the complexities of city living. London was the same, yet it seemed to have changed. No. He had changed.

Michael leaned back in his seat and smiled. He was home and he was going to have a good time whether or not he managed to take up where he had left off.

* * *

Julia stood on the white marble tiles in the huge hallway and observed her surroundings. Carved oak panelling, almost sinister in its ornate uniformity, spanned from floor to ceiling giving way only to a pair of lofty sash windows, one on either side of the solid oak front door. Heavy tapestry drapes, every inch carefully worked in delicate shades of green, hung in great drooping extravagant swathes, bashfully revealing their scarlet watered silk linings as they cascaded in folds to the floor. The late afternoon sun shot inquisitive rays through the bubbled panes of glass as the chandelier above the curving staircase glittered and winked in response, casting thousands of speckles of light over the warmth and opulence of the Georgian interior. The huge portraits on the wall smiled down at her almost condescendingly as she wondered whose ancestors they were. They certainly weren't hers. She looked towards the doorway to the dining room and frowned.

She and Tony had bought the house as soon as they had signed the contract for the show. It had been a bargain - a five bedroomed Georgian house overlooking the Thames in Barnes. All the furniture and fittings had been included in the price: a stately home filled with stately furniture to go with their new lifestyle. To Julia it represented achievement, position and status. The estate agent had told her that several famous and influential people had been interested in the property and this had made it all the more attractive to her. It had also been the only house they had looked at that came completely furnished and ready to move into. She had felt a little self-conscious going through the inventory with the agent - not actually knowing whether Chippendale furniture was better or worse than Parker-Knoll - but had hastily reminded herself that they had the money to pay for it. What else mattered?

Cuckoo Hall gave an initial impression of being a perfect and intact example of early Georgian domestic architecture. A trained eye, however, might have raised a few questions about its integrity. An American record producer had bought the house several years before and completely remodelled and renovated it. He spent huge amounts of money in an effort to put right the 'improvements' carried out in the sixties by a former owner, a pop star with an aversion to period detail, but a penchant for open-plan rooms, psychedelic murals and formica.

The record producer's insistence that the house must be returned to its former glory - regardless of cost - had taken his team of highly paid restoration experts all over the country in search of impecunious aristocrats. Many a stately home owed the continuing watertight state of its roof to the generous American and his ability to fix a price for anything. In order for the oak panelling at Cuckoo Hall to faultlessly meet at the edges, at least three notable families had been forced to resign themselves to the fact that having bare walls in the library, dining room or hallway was infinitely preferable to selling the lodge, taking Henry out of Eton or knowing what the weather was doing simply by looking at the ceilings in the west wing.

The result of all this ruthless bargaining and dismemberment was actually quite aesthetically pleasing, but the record producer soon tired of his creation, decided to sell it and moved on to refurbish a disused convent in Southern Ireland.

Being a newly successful and independent woman in her own right, Julia wanted to make her own mark on the house and set about having the dining room redecorated. The last three weeks had been constantly interrupted by the comings and goings of painters and decorators. Along with the imminent launch of her new show, the transformation of the dining room had given her a great feeling of anticipation. At last she had the chance to let her artistic creativity loose.

She had pored over countless copies of 'Homes and Gardens' and then 'The World of Interiors' when her new friend Serena Hesketh had told her that nobody with an income well into six figures ever read anything else. There were so many styles, colours and paint finishes. Would trompe l'oeil be too ostentatious? Would red lacquered walls really work? Should she import the furniture from Mexico? If she did, would it be statement or extravagance? What did one do about Georgian sash windows? She hadn't been sure if they were fashionable or not. They were certainly difficult to clean and the glass was old and full of bubbles. But, then again, why was she worrying about cleaning – she would hopefully never have to clean a window again in her life. Thank God Serena had gushed about how wonderfully intact they were and given her a clue.

'Be bold Julia. Let your imagination run riot!' Serena's words had taken root in her mind and given her courage. 'Don't let those prissy interior designers tell you what to do. Whose room is it anyway?'

Julia *had* been bold. She hadn't let *anyone* tell her how to have her room. And now it was finished.

She had finally got her inspiration from an Art Nouveau room featured in Hello magazine. Mellow oak panelling, intricate plaster mouldings, an authentic Adam fireplace and a polished floor, which together had formed the soul of the house and the only room that had remained intact throughout the massacre in the sixties, were ripped out and replaced with pink, mauve and blue walls, huge illuminated stained glass panels intertwined with geometric patterns in green, orange and purple, a matt black ceiling and tall, uncomfortable-looking chairs around a huge glossy black triangular table.

It was finished... and she hated it.

Why the hell was life so difficult? Surely it was meant to be easy now she had become successful? In the past she had faced and solved far greater problems than knowing whether or not it was 'daring' to mix antique tapestries with Colefax and Fowler chintz or Sanderson wallpaper. Life had been too full of other things to worry about. Back then she had envied people with beautiful homes. Back then she had had dreams - dreams which she was now living. The discovery that they might be too fragile to stand the test of reality was almost too much to bear.

She was jolted out of her reverie by the sound of the telephone ringing. Her heels clicked on the Italian marble as she crossed the hall eagerly. It was still a novelty to answer the old candlestick telephone; their number was ex-directory and they hardly ever got calls at home. Feeling rather like Joan Crawford, she lifted the ear piece to her ear, knocking one of her La Croix earrings clattering to the floor as she did so. *That* never happened to Alexis Colby. Trying not to sound flustered she spoke curtly into the mouthpiece.

'Hello?'

'Mrs Julia Barkworth?' The voice was husky and the line was bad. 'Hello... Mrs Barkworth?'

'I prefer to use the name Daley... Julia Daley. How may I help you?'

'Oh don't come all posh with me darling. Remember me? I remember you...' The line went dead.

CHAPTER TWO

Julia carried the bundle of newspapers into the dining room, hurled them on the table and grabbed the first one that came to hand. Her fingers frantically turned the pages of the Daily Sport. Her eyes opened in horror as they came to rest on the realisation of her worst nightmare. The Mirror had the same story ... and the Sun. Even the Independent had given her a few column inches. All the sordid details of her past life were laid out in black and white print for the nation to read. And photos... even colour photos. She stared in disbelief at the pictures. Who had taken them? She felt her brow prickle. How could it have happened when she had been so careful? This would be it: the end of her television career almost as soon as it had begun.

She looked again at a colour photo of herself bulging out of a bikini on a beach. My God... she looked so fat! She froze as the image turned to look at her and winked. No. She must have imagined it... and then it did it again. She watched in terror as the face... her face... rose up from the page and shrivelled in front of her eyes. The flesh was peeling away to reveal yellowed bone... and then the skull opened its mouth and laughed. It was a loud, raucous cackle of a laugh. She heard a little girl crying and bells ringing. So loud. The crying continued, but the sobs were now hers, great heaving sobs she couldn't control. And the bells were still ringing...

'What on earth's the matter?' Tony asked, turning the alarm off and the light on. Julia was so relieved that it had only been a dream, she threw her arms around him and hugged him tight. A split second later, the effects of the dream wore off and she pulled herself away from him, hauled herself out of bed and headed for the bathroom.

* * *

'It's not always this quiet... but I suppose there aren't that many people looking for a meaningful relationship at seven o'clock in the morning!' John was trying to make small talk with his new colleague. He hated the early shift. In fact, he wasn't too keen on the job at all. The novelty of showing a new guy how the system worked would at least make the time go faster. 'Right, what name are you going to use?'

'Sorry?' Michael frowned. Was he going to be able to take this job seriously?

'Your name... didn't they tell you to think of a pseudonym when you came for the interview?'

'Oh shit... I forgot all about that.'

'Never mind. You go and make the coffee – there should be milk in the fridge - and I'll think of one for you. I suppose I'd better show you how the computer works as well. Have you worked with computers before?' The telephone interrupted him. He glanced to see which light was flashing as he picked up the receiver. 'Good Morning. London Love Lines. How can I help you?'

* * *

The dream long since forgotten, Julia was launching herself on the floor manager who had dared to suggest she should swap places on the sofa with one of their guests. 'Well... I don't see what you mean. Who is this person anyway?'

'Look, Miss Daley, she's a magician. She's doing some quite complicated hand magic and we need the right camera angle on it.'

'Why should I throw myself off balance just because some silly old sideshow act can't cope with the pressure of television?'

'Look... I was only asking you as a matter of courtesy. Would you like me to bring Harvey down on to the floor to sort this out?'

He paused, hoping that the threat of bringing the producer into the frame would have the desired effect. 'As it is, I've got more to worry about than your inflexibility.' His courage now spent, he looked down at his clipboard and whisked over to the other side of the studio to make sure the sound engineers had overcome their problems. Efficiency was his speciality and the reason he was doing the job in the first place. Julia followed him with her eyes, but said no more. The studio was a mass of cables, lights, technicians and cameramen busily sorting out their own individual functions. To an outsider it would have looked like chaos, but she knew that everything was painstakingly planned and meticulously organised thanks to the efficiency of the expert crew. That was a word that had always annoyed her. Expert.

* * *

John took a long sip from his mug of coffee and looked at the new recruit. Maybe this one was going to turn out to be quite a laugh. He certainly looked alright: well proportioned, with a healthy look that probably came from hours spent at the gym. John felt a sudden pang of guilt – he hadn't been near the gym in ages – as he glanced again at Michael, who was busily getting to grips with the computer system. He looked about thirty years old and around six feet tall. His jet black hair and vivid blue eyes complimented his natural good looks. John sighed to himself. Was there a chance that a guy as good looking as Michael would look twice at someone like him – even if he was gay? He hadn't asked him about his sexuality yet. He rather hoped it would become evident without him having to ask or would arise in the course of the conversation. It could get a bit awkward if you just came out with it... and then there was the problem of how to phrase it. Did you say 'by the way... are you gay?' or 'I take it you're straight?' Either one was inclined to cause offence. Oh for God's sake, he'd come to work at a telephone dating agency. He was hardly likely to be easily embarrassed.

* * *

Tony sighed. Not for the first time, his wife had failed to read

31

the programme notes in enough detail and was now unashamedly exposing her lack of professionalism. The run-through was already well behind schedule thanks to the fuss she had kicked up over the positioning of their first guest. Now she was quibbling over the questions she had to ask their second guest - a Harley Street doctor. Neither guest had arrived yet and he wondered if they had any idea what - or whom - they were letting themselves in for. He could see the hitherto inert aggression starting to show itself as the lines on her face deepened slightly and the vein on her right temple began to pulsate. Instead of quietly going off to rectify her ignorance at the first opportunity, she had to try and prove that she was in full possession of the facts all along. Julia, he had come to realise, never backed down.

'Well, I still think they're rather strange questions to ask, but I suppose if I haven't got any choice...' her voice trailed off as she walked over to the sofa, martyr-like, wondering what the use of condoms had to do with surrogate motherhood.

* * *

'Right... how do you feel about being called "Troy"?' John had been wracking his brains for a name and the best he could come up with was the stage name of a stripper he'd seen the night before at the Royal Oak in Hammersmith. 'We tend to use slightly unusual names. They're easier to remember. Oh, my name on the lines is "Brad" by the way.'

' Troy...' The name rolled off his tongue nicely and he muttered it to himself for a while. Yes, he liked it. He looked around at the spacious office with its matt black furniture and flashing computer screens. Outside in Brixton High Street the traffic was beginning to build up. The sounds of revving engines and the aggressive blasting of horns reached their ears through the large first floor windows. Yes... this was all part of his new life. Part of a new life that was going to work. It was going to work because he was going to *make* it work. 'So... Brad,' he paused for a moment, realising that John was paying a little too much attention to every word he spoke, 'hadn't you better show me how this dating system of yours works?'

'Oh... yeah... sure...' John flushed, slightly perturbed but not displeased by the unerring gaze fixed on him. 'For a start... I don't know if you've seen any of the adverts in the papers? So you know about premium rate telephone numbers? People ring and listen to adverts other people have recorded...' His new work mate's nodding encouraged him to continue. 'So, when someone has rung one of the lines, listened to all the adverts and chosen one they like, they ring us here and quote a name and reference number. We look it up on the computer and either give them the telephone number of the advertiser or take a message to give to the advertiser later on.' He paused, wondering whether or not he was managing to explain it succinctly enough. He just couldn't stop looking at this guy's eyes. 'And because of a new ruling by the governing body that regulates all these lines, we now have to take the telephone numbers of all respondents... the callers in other words. Now, it's very simple once you know how to use the computer, so we might as well make a start. We operate the service for five different dating companies, so when the phone rings make sure you look at which light is flashing before you answer - they're all labelled. Then you access the appropriate service and you get a prompt on the screen asking for a reference number. See?'

'Do all the reference numbers begin with M?' Michael squinted slightly as he looked at the screen.

'No... M's for straight males, F is for straight females, C for straight couples, T for transvestites and transsexuals, L for lesbians and G...'

'Yes, I think I know what G's for...' Michael's eyes twinkled mischievously as he interrupted the rapidly blushing John.

*   *   *

Iris shuffled over to the armchair with her cup of tea and thankfully lowered herself into it. The clock said five to ten. Good. She would be in time for the beginning of "Family Values". It was the only thing that alleviated the interminable boredom of life at the moment. She had been awake for more than two hours and it had taken her all of that time to heave herself out of bed, get washed and dressed and butter a couple of slices of bread to have with her cup of tea. She had to laugh. Had life really come to this? Was it really possible that it took two hours to get herself out of bed, washed and dressed? Then the only highlight of the day was watching one of her girls on the box.

'Iris my girl... you're an old woman,' she muttered to herself as the realisation dawned on her, 'but at least you've done it all... or had a bloody good try!' She reached for the television remote control. Funny to think how she even took things like that for granted now. The mere possession of a television set was a major thing the first time it had come within the realms of possibility for her. Similarly, the advent of colour television had sent a wave of excited envy rippling through the population. Now, that too was taken for granted, just as life itself was taken for granted nowadays. There didn't seem to be the fighting instinct in young people. Perhaps it was just her age changing her outlook, but kids didn't seem to want a challenge. They wanted everything on a plate. They thought the world owed them a living. 'Oh, shut up you silly old bag!' she said out loud and chuckled again. It was no wonder old folks got put in homes by their families. No doubt she would have been if she had one. But she hadn't been the family type. Lord no, but at least she had realised it and had the good sense not to try. Just then she heard a key in the door.

'Iris? Are you up? Iris? Oh, there you are.' It was Trevor, her next door neighbour. 'Just thought I'd pop in before I go to work. Any tea in the pot?' He sat in the chair opposite the old woman and she grinned broadly, showing her yellowing teeth. It never failed to amuse her that a forty five year old man could still skip around like a teenager wearing things that in her day were only worn behind closed doors.

'What the bloody hell do you look like?' she cackled. 'I've not

34

seen so much studded leather since that high court judge's last visit in 1963!' She lost herself in a fit of laughter, almost losing her breath as Trevor looked on in amusement. 'And don't you dare ask for a name - I'm not telling!' she said with a sly wink.

'I wouldn't dream of it,' her neighbour said quietly. He was a large man with broad shoulders and a stocky build. A craggy but personable face sported a couple of day's growth of stubble. The leather to which Iris referred was worn in the form of shiny black chaps worn over faded Levi's and a battered black biker's jacket. It was one of many similar outfits, each one never failing to bring a smile to the old woman's face. 'And I would have thought you'd got past the stage of making comments about leather by now.'

'Oh... you know me... can't resist flogging a dead horse!' She stifled another laugh before continuing. 'Especially when you're wearing it!'

* * *

'Going in... five... four... three... two...' The opening titles began to roll as Julia rearranged the layers of purple crepe de chine around her knees, pleased with the way this new outfit left a bit to the imagination as far as her true dimensions were concerned. After barely a week of the show being on air, the weight had started to creep back on. At least this outfit looked as if it *might* be loose. What did it matter if half the folds of fabric were full? Tony shuffled a bit beside her and ran a nervous hand through his slicked-back dark hair as she caught his eye. Why the hell was the silly sod still nervous? God... if only he had the same coolness she had, they would be on course to be the most powerful couple in television. If only he would take more notice of what she said. Mind you, he was at his most attractive when he was nervous - just like a little boy ready to be instructed in the ways of the world...

'Will one of you fucking well introduce the show!' Harvey screamed through their ear pieces.

'Good morning and welcome to "Family Values".' Tony jumped in to cover his wife's mistake. 'I'm Tony Barkworth...'

'And I'm Julia Daley...' She came back to reality with a jolt in the nick of time. '...and we've got an action-packed show for you this morning.' Her heart pounded in her chest as she focussed all her energies on keeping up with the autocue. 'If you're into magic, we've got the one and only Abbie Cadabra who's going to be performing some mind-boggling tricks for us *live* in the studio. Our summer holiday competition starts today along with the first nominations for the "Family Values" Bride of the Year award. On a slightly more serious note, we'll be discussing the somewhat controversial subject of sex surrogacy...' Julia smiled outwardly but swore inwardly, reminding herself to insist that she had missed the first cue on purpose to test her husband's spontaneity on camera.

Harvey sighed and bit his lip. The stupid jumped up tart had almost messed up big time. If only she had a slightly lower opinion of herself, she might be some good. It was frightening to think that the goings on in this tiny studio were being broadcast live around the country. This dangerously ignorant woman had already taken advantage of the fact that she could use the show to express her own opinions. Why was it that good presenters were very rarely recognised as such? Probably because to be good they had to be virtually invisible: promoting their subjects rather than themselves. The tragedy was that the really good ones usually gave up because the very thing that made them special was their self-doubt, their need to be better and their desire to surpass themselves.

He sat back in the sanctuary of the control booth thinking that Julia, in her blissful arrogance, might just be the lucky one.

'And now - a lady who's always got something up her sleeve.' Julia smiled nervously. She had expected some sort of Butlins redcoat and was now faced with a breathtaking vision of voluptuous femininity. Dressed in a flowing creation of white satin encrusted with sparkling rhinestones, her crossed legs were elegantly revealed through a daring slash up one side. 'Miss Abbie Cadabra!' The magician delicately adjusted her white satin turban, camera one lingering for a moment on her large hands with their scarlet painted nails. 'Abbie... you've just got back from a highly successful tour of the Far East and are about to launch the British leg of your tour.'

'Yes Julia.' The voice was deep, husky and loaded with latent sexuality. Her obvious confidence in front of the camera unnerved Julia for a reason she couldn't quite put her finger on. 'It's quite a while since I worked in this country, but I'm looking forward to finding out what British audiences think of my particular brand of magic.'

'And what exactly *is* your particular brand of magic?' Julia condescendingly enquired, wondering how such a tall woman dared to wear six inch stilettos.

'Well... all magic is fundamentally concerned with appearance defying reality,' Abbie purred softly. 'So, before I've even done anything I'm something of a conjuring trick in myself... wouldn't you agree?' She looked over to the spellbound Tony for a response, but was disappointed.

In the green room, two of the researchers giggled as they watched the monitor, realising that the two presenters had no idea their first guest was a transsexual.

* * *

'Good Morning, Heart to Heart Dating... Troy speaking. How can I help you?' The line went dead and Michael replaced the receiver. John had warned him that this happened frequently. Two seconds later it rang again.

'Good Morning, Heart to Heart Dating... Troy speaking. How can I help you?'

'Er... yes... er... we... I mean me and the wife... want to record a message...' The caller went silent for a few seconds.

'Yes?'

'Well... what do we do?'

'Right...' Michael paused, silently praying that John would come back from the loo. He hadn't been shown how to record a message yet and was starting to feel the first tinges of apprehension, which disappeared immediately as he pulled himself together,

37

thought logically and took the matter in hand. After all, he had used the dating lines himself a couple of years ago. 'Now, which line would you like to go on?'

'Couples I suppose. You know... wife-swapping and all that.'

'And which area are you in?'

'Liverpool.'

'Liverpool.' Michael looked up at the chart on the wall. 'That comes under the north of England. So, let me take down your names... OK... Alan and Sheila... yes... and your dates of birth... no... no... we won't tell the callers.... no... it's just for the records.... right... thank you. Your reference number will be... alright then, I'll wait while you get a pen...' He was quite glad of the hold-up, since he had no idea where to find a reference number to give them. Rooting around in the desk drawers he found a clipboard with printed sheets on it. Heaving a sigh of relief, he heard the caller come back to the phone. 'Got your pen? Right... your reference number's C1012... yes... C for couple 1012. Now, I take it you've got a few details about yourself jotted down... you have?' He hastily fumbled with the controls on the recording device connected to the telephone. 'Good... well... you need to start with your names and reference number... yes... then some personal details... you know... age, height, looks... yes, whatever you like... and then a bit about the type of person - or people - you're looking for... and remember to finish with your names and reference number. Don't put the phone down... stay on the line until I come back to you.' Thanking his lucky stars that he had a good memory, he continued. 'Right, take a deep breath. I'll count you in and then it's all down to you...'

* * *

'I believe you're a member of the mysterious and exclusive Magic Circle?' Julia was trying to get the interview over as soon as possible. This woman was far too attractive for her liking. She carried on before Abbie had the chance to answer. But... tell me... isn't it a rather male-orientated organisation? Don't you find it a bit sexist? What's it like being a woman in a male profession?' The questions came like bullets out of a gun.

'Well, I suppose I am a bit marginalised... but I can't really complain because it was my choice wasn't it?'

'Er... I suppose so.' Julia couldn't help feeling she had missed something somewhere along the line.

'And you're going to do some magic for us now,' Tony hastily interjected, remembering Julia's argument with the floor manager. He could feel himself breaking into a sweat every time he looked at the voluptuous magician. There was something about her. He couldn't make up his mind what it was, but it was causing developments in his Calvin Klein underpants. 'So go on... surprise us.' Abbie privately mused that the most surprising thing was the fact that this couple had got the job in the first place.

'Well, first of all, I need something from you.' She paused, ran her tongue over her lips and re-crossed her legs, making sure the camera took in their full length and slenderness. Julia frowned at the amount of attention her husband was giving their guest and resolved to sharpen her tactics as Abbie continued. 'Have you got a little ring, Tony?' Her seemingly innocent smile didn't falter as she watched him blush.

'Here...' Julia almost shouted as she yanked off her wedding ring, 'have mine!'

'Oooh,' Abbie purred, 'that slipped off easily!'

* * *

'OK Alan, when you're ready... three... two... one...'

Hello... our names are Alan and Sheila and our reference number is C1012. We're a couple in our fifties... ' Michael was glad he had remembered to hold down the mute button. *I'm five foot six, fourteen stone, with ginger hair and a good sense of humour...* ' Just as well, thought Michael, stifling another giggle. *'Sheila is five foot nine, size sixteen, with very large breasts and a... a... a large appetite to match. We're looking for other couples or singles in the Liverpool area - age looks and colour unimportant - who are looking for a bit of adult fun. We've got a comfortable house and can accommodate. Our particular fantasy is for a man... or several men... to come and take Sheila out, give her what she's dying for and then bring her back to me all wet and sticky...'*

* * *

Julia frowned as Abbie dropped the gold wedding ring into a large test tube full of clear liquid, replaced the stopper and began to shake it vigorously.

'I suppose I'd better explain what I'm doing,' the magician nonchalantly commented, 'although it's basically quite simple. This is a very powerful acid which has...' She stopped shaking and held up the test tube in her long nailed fingers for the camera '... dissolved your ring.' Julia gulped as she saw that the ring had disappeared. Her mouth dropped open and she was uncharacteristically lost for words. Abbie smiled seductively and continued. 'Oh well, what's a little ring between friends? And for my next trick, Julia, I'd like you to feel in the right hand pocket of your lovely little jacket.' It might have been Versace, but this woman wore it as if it had come off the rack at Marks and Spencer. She watched Julia blush as her fingers traced the shape of the spare tampon in her pocket and then saw her expression change as she came across something unfamiliar that she hadn't put there herself. 'And what have you found?'

'A walnut,' Julia said in a quiet voice, holding the hard round object up for the camera.

'Now... if you'd like to crack it open for us...' Abbie handed her a set of nutcrackers '... perhaps you'd like to tell us all what's inside.'

The camera moved in closer as Julia fumbled with the nutcrackers and then exclaimed as a shiny object fell out of the cracked nut.

'It's my ring!'

'Actually,' Abbie grinned conspiratorially, 'it's just a good copy - but I think you'll find...' she looked sideways at Tony '...that it's far better than the real thing.'

* * *

'I thought you said you were on the way to work?' Iris looked over at Trevor, who was leisurely enjoying his third cup of tea. 'Although how they let you turn up at the library togged up in all that black leather I'll never know...'

'And I suppose you never went to work in anything remotely resembling black leather?' He had a twinkle in his eye as he asked.

'Well, I didn't go parading about in the street with it on!' She started and then realised what she was saying. Her wrinkled old face broke into a smile. 'They always came to me. Time and time again!'

'Dirty old bag. I suppose you're reminiscing about Mr Remington again!'

'Hmmm...' The old woman's smile widened as her mind went back more than forty years. She had been young then, well comparatively anyway, and could still turn a trick with the chosen few like Mr Remington. She still ached for him in her dreams. 'I always did like 'em big and black!'

* * *

'What on earth's the matter?' John had come back to find Michael sobbing uncontrollably. 'Are you alright... what happened?'

'No... I'm OK... I'm sorry!' He looked up, his face streaked with tears. John realised with relief that he was laughing. 'I just recorded a message...' He collapsed into another bout of laughter. 'I just didn't realise that short fat ginger-haired fifty year old people were into wife-swapping!'

'What?' John was a bit lost.

'Listen to it and you'll know what I mean... go on... you won't believe it.'

'I don't think anything will shock me any more. I sometimes think the whole population's at it. You haven't encountered the specialist lines yet. Do you know how many straight men have an overwhelming urge to have sex with a transvestite? Do you know

41

how many men want to be whipped into submission by a master or dominatrix? No? Well that's the least of it. You'd be amazed the uses a cheese grater can be put to. I hope you've got a strong stomach.'

* * *

'So...' Julia brought herself back from a little daydream ready to pick up the interview with their second guest where Tony had left off. She observed the doctor on the couch and decided he was boring, but infinitely preferable to the glamorous magician who had stolen rather more than the limelight. He was a tall, distinguished looking man in his early sixties with a strong hint of breeding in his voice. He had been a cosmetic surgeon in Harley Street for many years, but had recently changed his field of speciality to one which had sparked off a big story in the tabloids the day before. Needless to say, the entire subject had escaped Julia's attention. '... I understand you are making vast amounts of money from a profession many would see as immoral...' She read the words from the autocue without really digesting them. '... but defend yourself by sticking to the argument that sex surrogacy...' She paused. Wasn't the show about surrogate motherhood? '...is a much needed way of solving some of the sexual problems of the nation.' Julia was confused, but couldn't resist adding her own pearl of wisdom. 'Personally, I can't see that sex has much to do with it. I mean, it's not even necessary with artificial insemination and all that is it?' The doctor's bewildered look gave her a slight hint that she might have slipped up a little. He interjected rapidly to prevent her from complicating the matter any further.

'Sex surrogacy developed as a result of the increased need - or at least increased recognition of the need - for sex therapy. The more we become sexually liberated, the more problems seem to bubble to the surface in that area.' The doctor paused and looked over at Julia. 'Wouldn't you agree?'

'Oh... er.... yes.' She was still desperately trying to work out what exactly the subject of their conversation was. She'd have to have harsh words with the researchers about this. Fancy them not letting her know beforehand. Tony cleared his throat and took over again. 'So... just in case any of our viewers are still in any doubt as to what is actually involved in sex surrogacy, can we just recap?'

'Of course. As I was explaining, the increased need for more efficient ways of working out sexual problems led me to realise that there was very little chance of a patient being able to solve his sexual problems by just talking about them to *me* or to any other doctor or therapist. With this in mind, we have developed a system of treatment through which the patient can actually work out his problems, in comfortable surroundings at our country house clinic, with a surrogate partner.' The doctor's pause gave Julia time to butt in.

'What do you mean by that exactly?' She didn't notice Tony sigh and cast his eyes upwards.

'As I was saying,' the doctor continued, 'the patient has the chance to overcome any sexual hang-ups he may have in the most practical way possible as well as trying out various techniques which we may suggest as part of his treatment. After all, how can you expect someone to practise your advice if they have no-one with whom to practise it? Our sex surrogates are fully trained to understand all the problems that may arise.'

'So... are all your patients men?' Julia asked rather bluntly. The penny was threatening to drop. Tony was desperately trying to think of questions to ask their guest in order to prevent Julia from showing herself up again. Why she couldn't have read it in the papers like everyone else was beyond him, but he wasn't ever going to change her. Unless, perhaps, he could get her a surrogate brain.

* * *

'Oh come on girl,' Iris chuckled. Trevor had gone to work and left her to watch the show in peace. 'You of all people should know a pimp when you see one!'

* * *

'You'll know what I mean when you've been here for a few

43

months.' John was trying to explain his feelings about the job to Michael. He was getting to like his new colleague more by the minute. And he seemed to fit in so well. 'It's having to deal with sex all day... especially some of the kinkier stuff... it tends to put you off it altogether.'

'Really?' Michael was a little incredulous. 'You mean completely?'

'Well,' John decided not to burn his bridges and rephrased his last statement, 'it's just that you get an impression of a such a large proportion of the population having such diverse sexual problems and perverse sexual preferences - like that one with the wellies and pneumatic drill - that you begin to wonder what it's all about and whether it's safe to let your urges rule your life.' He stopped for breath, surprised by the depth of what he had just said.

'I think I know what you mean,' Michael said slowly, 'particularly with regard to all the more way out stuff. In a way, the more sexually liberated society becomes, the more is expected of an individual. In our case,' he didn't shift his gaze from John's face, 'the fact that we've admitted to differing from the norm in being gay could lead to greater all-round sexual deviance becoming a way of life. By the sound of some of the titles of these 'Specialist' gay lines, it's possible to find just about anything you want - Leather, Denim, Masters, Slaves, Watersports, Rubber, Torture, Uniforms - the list goes on, but I don't honestly think *anything* could put me off sex altogether.'

* * *

Tony shifted uneasily on the sofa, resigned to the fact that he had no control over his wife. Julia's brow furrowed as she unwittingly prepared to dig herself in deeper.

'So men are paying five hundred pounds a session to come and have sexual intercourse with your girls?'

'I wouldn't have phrased it like that myself.' The doctor remained calm. 'I would prefer to say that they are paying for the therapy, which incidentally has a very high success rate.'

44

'Well, if you ask me it's just legalised prostitution!'

'My dear,' retorted the doctor, 'you're clearly an expert on the subject.'

CHAPTER THREE

'Oh my God! Listen to this one!' John was working the early shift with Michael again and had found himself looking forward to coming to work. The usually dreary early morning tube journey to Brixton had, for once, held a ray of hope.

'Oh yes... go on. What's he into?' Michael was still experiencing the novelty of his new occupation.

'Gay master. Probably not at all what he seems, but then again who is? Here goes.' He rewound the tape with a feeling of purpose. Knowing that Michael was interested in the job gave him an enormous amount of pleasure. A mundane task had become a teaching experience. He pressed a button on the recording machine and a deep voice boomed out into the quiet office.

'*Eric - reference number GM935. I'm a master in my fifties. Location: West London. Height: six foot. Weight: fourteen stone. I'm seeking a genuine slave for regular sessions in my fully-equipped games room. You must be under thirty, slim, clean shaven and totally submissive. Experience with leather, rubber and bondage would be an advantage, but inexperience is no problem as long as it's accompanied by a willingness to obey me completely. If you fit the above requirements, get my number from the office and call me. Nuisance callers and telephone fantasisers need not apply - I don't suffer fools gladly. Once again, the name's Eric, reference GM935.*'

'The sad thing is he's probably a traffic warden from Isleworth.'

John grinned, using the opportunity to put his hand on Michael's shoulder.

'Well,' said Michael pensively, 'I hope he gets what he wants.'

* * *

'Mummy Marilyn?' The little girl's accent, although American, was becoming more English by the day.

'Yes Zoë?'

'Well... you know it was Mother's Day?' The child paused with a spoonful of Weetabix halfway to her mouth. Milk dripped onto the table, but she didn't seem to notice. 'I know that you're my Mummy now... but what I've been wondering is...' she paused again as she noticed the puddle of milk running into her lap.

'What love?' Marilyn could feel a difficult question coming and thought of the huge carefully made card that had been waiting for her on the kitchen table the morning of their last day in America - the day she had heard of her own mother's death. The irony was still fresh in her mind. Thank goodness Zoë had been there. Her heart went out to the little girl every time she looked at her: the huge brown eyes and curly blonde hair would be enough to melt the hardest heart even without the loving personality behind them. She still, after more than five years, couldn't understand or forgive what the child's natural mother had done.

'Well,' the seven year old took a deep breath and started again, 'what I've been wondering is... where *is* my real mummy? I mean, I know Daddy's in heaven... and the angels are looking after him... but where did my real mummy go... and who's looking after *her?*'

That, thought Marilyn, was a very good question. If the past was anything to go by, she was probably looking after herself - as always putting her own interests first. Thankfully, the telephone rang.

'Hello.'

'Marilyn, it's Max.' The voice on the line was unmistakably public school. 'I've got some work for you. Actually I'm in a bit of a spot – another girl's let me down. How are you fixed today?'

47

Marilyn looked down at the little girl. School finished at half past three and she would have to be back in time to pick her up. But she needed the money.

'What time?'

'About twelve o'clock. There are eight of them. The usual fee. Cash of course. It'll take two hours at the most. Please Marilyn, I'm counting on you.'

'I'll call you back in five minutes.'

'I'll be waiting.'

Marilyn sighed as she put the receiver down and ran her fingers nervously through her long dark hair. Today of all days she had been looking forward to having a peaceful day, but it wasn't every day she was offered the chance of earning that kind of money. And it was the little girl's birthday soon.

'Come on young lady - it's time you were ready for school.'

*   *   *

Julia beamed at the camera as Tony introduced the day's first studio guests. They were a variety of people who had all, at one time or another, experienced the disappearance of close relatives. Inspired by the unexplained vanishing act performed the previous week by a London businessman, the first part of the show was about missing persons and the effects on those they left behind. The researchers had rounded up this motley crew whom Julia found most distasteful, but at least controllable. One of them had even kept her anorak on at Julia's suggestion. True to the old television adage, she felt glamorous and sophisticated. Crossing her legs and leaning towards the first guest, like a bird of prey eyeing up a helpless mouse, she turned up the corners of her mouth to give it the appearance of a smile.

'So... Glenda.' Her eyes moved up and down the nervous woman next to her on the sofa. Her smile remained, even if the feeling behind it had never existed. 'Your husband disappeared in the middle of breakfast over a year ago...'

*   *   *

'Treading on thin ice a bit aren't we duckie?' Iris snorted at the television screen. 'What goes around, comes around!'

* * *

'Hi - my name's Paul, reference G2935. I'm a married bi guy in my early thirties looking for similar bi or gay guys in the London area. I'm comparatively new to the bi scene and would prefer to meet fairly inexperienced guys so that we can explore our sexuality together. A bit about myself: I'm nearly six foot tall with dark brown hair, blue eyes and a lean muscular build. I work out at the gym a couple of times a week, play squash and swim regularly. If you think we might have something in common, please leave a message for me at the office and I'll get back to you as soon as possible. I live in the Clapham area at the moment but will be moving very shortly. I'm willing to travel anywhere in the London area. Once again, my name's Paul and my reference is G2935... that's G2935.'

'OK Paul, that'll go on line in the next day or two,' Michael said cheerfully. He was beginning to quite enjoy the job. 'Please remember to call us every few days to collect your messages. Thanks for calling. Bye.' The caller rang off. 'He sounded alright. Lives in Clapham. I'm moving into a flat there tomorrow. I wonder if he lives anywhere nearby.'

'God, I can tell you're still new! After a while you'll be sick of the sound of all of them. I suppose it's like working in a sweet shop. Once you've tasted everything, the inclination goes!' John laughed. 'So you're moving tomorrow? Well, Clapham's quite convenient for here I suppose.'

'It's a great place actually... and I've got another part time job starting on Thursday at a bar in the West End. It's all happening this week!' Michael exuded happiness as he organised the clipboards and tapes.

'Where do you live now, then?' It was the first time John had dared to enquire into his new work-mate's lifestyle. He didn't want to be too blatantly interested in case it got Michael's back up and blew his chances of getting any closer.

'Oh... just a cheap bed and breakfast place. I only got back from Greece last week and it was the best I could find in a hurry.'

'Whereabouts in Greece were you?' John was getting more intrigued by the minute.

'All over the place, but I finished up in Mykonos.'

'You lucky sod! Whatever did you want to come back for?'

'Well, I'd been away for two years and I felt ready to come back and take up where I left off!'

* * *

Marilyn, having telephoned Max to tell him she would be there at twelve, had taken Zoë to school and rushed into Sainsbury's for the week's shopping on the way back. There was just about time for her to have a bath. It would help her to relax. The child's innocent question had unnerved her more than she had realised. How could she ever tell her what her mother was really like? How could you tell a child she had been deserted? She picked up a pile of freshly ironed clothes and carried them upstairs on the way to the bathroom. Since having assumed the role of mother to Zoë, she automatically combined tasks. At first it had been a necessity - juggling her television career with the child's needs and demands. Now it was habit.

It had been strange at first living in her mother's house again after all these years. Although it was the house in which she had grown up, she had never envisaged herself living in it again. Now that she was, it seemed the most natural and inevitable thing in the world. Life seemed to be springing constant surprises on her, but it kept her guessing. She put the clothes in Zoë's room - the room that had been her own when she was a little girl - and smiled at the photographs on the wall. There was a picture of her at Zoë's age with her mother and a big shaggy dog. Twenty five years ago. It had been all smiles then. Her mother had always made sure she was happy. Knowing that Mum was always there had kept her going through some of the darker periods of her life, wherever she was, whatever she was doing. But now she wasn't there any more... and she missed her more than she would ever have thought possible. If only she had known, she would have come home from the States earlier. But her mother hadn't wanted to worry her. As always, she had convinced everyone, including her only child, that she was fine. But even she couldn't beat the cancer that was slowly and painfully eating away at her.

A tear rolled down Marilyn's cheek as she leaned over the bath to turn on the taps. She squirted a bit of Zoë's bubble bath into the tub and tried to think happy thoughts. That was what Mum had always said: 'Think happy thoughts and they'll blossom into a smile... think nasty thoughts and everyone'll see a little black dog on your shoulder.'

* * *

Clive Haynes sat quietly watching the television considering his sanity. It was true that people became obsessed with celebrities. There was the man who shot John Lennon, for instance, or the guy who became infatuated with Jodie Foster and went on to shoot Ronald Reagan. Perhaps the attack had unhinged him and he was now focussing all his anger and insecurity at this face on the screen. Perhaps he was losing his mind. But deep down he was sure of his sanity - and he was sure that he was right.

* * *

'And, Eileen, you have no idea why your husband disappeared suddenly after twenty years of marriage?' Tony looked straight at the large, homely-looking woman on the sofa, his expression showing her that he cared, that he really wanted to know what she was thinking.

'No, Tony, I 'aven't. We was quite happy... always 'ad been. There was always plenty of food on the table. The kids always 'ad what they wanted. Alan always went to the local of a Saturday to play darts with 'is mates. 'E 'ad a good job with the electricity board... been there twenty one years...'

'So there wasn't any particular reason why he might want to run away?' Julia decided to get her oar in before Tony got too much air time. Besides, she was getting bored. 'Was there anything he'd always wanted to do? Hopes? dreams?'

'What d'you mean?'

'Well... don't you think he might have felt a bit trapped?'

'Trapped?'

'I mean this in the nicest possible way... but don't you think he might have felt that his life was going nowhere?'

'Where's it meant to go then?' Eileen didn't like this woman and wasn't about to be trampled all over by her. 'What would the world be like if everyone did what they wanted? Life's no picnic... there's work to be done and kids to feed.'

Julia decided that she'd had enough of Eileen and moved on to the third guest, a slim, unassuming man in his late twenties sitting with his knees together looking nervous.

'Adrian...' she flashed a smile at the camera, 'life hasn't been easy for you either has it since your wife vanished, leaving you with two young children? I believe you had to give up your job to look after them and consequently lost your house. Apparently no-one has seen her since that day?'

'No... it was a Tuesday.' Julia waited, wondering what difference it made what day of the week it was. This was certainly the most dreary show they had done so far. 'It was the day before our third wedding anniversary... and I came home from work to find a note saying that the kids were at my mother's and my dinner was in the oven.' Julia had to bite her glossy lower lip to stop herself from giggling.

* * *

Marilyn agonised for a few minutes over what to wear and then plumped for a tried and tested outfit that showed off her figure but didn't make her feel uncomfortable. She very rarely bought clothes nowadays, her finances being limited, but those she did buy were good quality. She couldn't pretend that things had been easy since she'd become mother to Zoë, but it had been her choice. The little girl had given her life a purpose... and she loved her as if she were her own. She enjoyed having to be careful with money, having to search for clothes which were good quality but affordable.

She looked at her reflection in the mirror and quickly applied a bit of make-up, careful not to overdo it. The overall effect was quite pleasing; she always found that the less time she spent getting ready, the better she looked. She liked to give Max the impression that she was a composed, controlled young woman who could pick and choose what she did rather than a single mother grateful for a bit of pin money. But she couldn't really complain about Max. He had always treated her well, even when she had had slight qualms about what he wanted her to do the first couple of times. Anyway, she had got over that quickly enough. It was all in a day's work now.

*   *   *

'What were you trying to do out there? Haven't you got any compassion for those people?' Tony was angry. Not for the first time, Julia had taken over the whole show and given him the feeling that he had no control.

'Compassion? For them? As far as I'm concerned they deserved to be deserted. Wouldn't you have wanted to get away from a life with any one of them? But I suppose that's a stupid question to ask you... you've never been able to make any decisions of your own. Where would you be without me?' Julia's eyes flashed as she spat the words out. Tony didn't answer. 'Well? I thought that'd make you think. You have to fight for what you want in this life and if that means making sacrifices...'

'Alright, alright, I get the message.' Tony knew when he was beaten. And so did Julia.

*   *   *

The black XJS zoomed past in the opposite direction, coming dangerously close to Marilyn's battered Mini as it did so. Unshaken and unimpressed, she smiled as she watched the car recede into the distance in her rear view mirror. It suddenly occurred to her that most of the human race spent a great deal of its time trying to go somewhere very fast.

'Drive a bit slower... you might enjoy the journey,' she muttered sagely.

* * *

'And that brings us back to where we started – the mysterious disappearance from his Middlesex home of the highly successful and extremely wealthy businessman, Nigel Parton.' Tony was glad there was a commercial break coming up. Julia had been getting more and more irritated, restless and rude as the show went on. For some reason, she had been more scathing than ever with the guests. He could almost feel Harvey's breath on the back of his neck. It wouldn't do to upset the producer after only a week on the air and he knew that some of Julia's comments hadn't gone unnoticed. 'Kidnapping has been virtually ruled out since there have been no ransom demands. His distraught wife says he had no particular worries and was a devoted family man.'

'Obviously!' Julia smiled sarcastically as Tony salvaged his caring look and continued.

'Perhaps a logical explanation will one day present itself... but perhaps his disappearance will always remain a mystery.'

'And don't forget to join us again tomorrow morning,' Julia chipped in, obliterating Tony's dramatic pause. 'We've got fertility expert Dr Leslie McManus here in the studio talking about the agony facing couples who can't have children. You'll have the chance to phone in and talk to the doctor about your own personal problems.' She smiled, relishing the prospect.

'And there will be a special make-over for the three lucky winners of last week's Asian phone-in competition by make-up expert Surita Sidhu.' Tony tried to look suitably socially aware. 'Also, we have image consultant Beryl Crabtree with tips for the lady with the fuller figure.' He sneaked a glance at Julia's waistline. Noticing his far from subtle glance, Julia pursed her lips and ignored the scripted end to the show.

'So, ladies, if you're...' she paused, trying to think of the right words to use, '...darker skinned or... fat... I mean overweight... there might be a ray of hope for you.' She could feel herself blushing. 'Until then, from all of us at "Family Values"... bye bye.'

As the credits rolled and their smiles faded, Julia pounced on the young Assistant Floor Manager as he passed by clutching his clipboard.

'Darren... the water wasn't cold enough and the coffee was lukewarm. I know we're having to struggle with limited resources,' she stopped and looked straight into his eyes, 'but I think you could be trying a *bit* harder, don't you?' As she quickly moved on to find something condescending to say to the sound technicians, Darren decided that if *anyone* was trying it was Julia. How he wished she would just drop dead in her designer dress - which, he couldn't fail to notice, didn't hide the fact that her bottom had dropped - and leave him to comfort her husband. Now *there* was something to dream about...

* * *

The Surrey village epitomised perfection. All the houses were architecturally perfect. All the gardens were perfectly landscaped. Even the ducks on the village pond were perfectly white. In fact it was all a bit too perfect, Marilyn decided. Like a seemingly blissfully happy family or a flawlessly beautiful face, this chocolate box village was just too good to be true.

She steered the car between a pair of stone gateposts into a gravelled drive lined with pleached limes. A large Queen Anne manor house surrounded by verdant green lawns loomed in front of her, its large windows staring out at the world: unblinking, yet revealing nothing about the many people who had lived, loved and died behind them. Everything about the house and its grounds exuded an aura of inherited wealth and long-established stability. There was no evidence or hint of the industry that she knew kept it going.

The Mini's little wheels crunched to a halt at the bottom of the steps leading to a huge front door. Marilyn's heels clicked on the old limestone steps as she noticed for the first time that the lichen-encrusted stone portico was decorated with a curious mixture of cherubs and skeletons. It really was a beautiful house; she had found it quite awe-inspiring the first few times she had visited, but now it amused her to think that such a stately old home could harbour such a business. Mind you, they probably weren't the first strange goings-on it had seen in its lifetime and probably wouldn't be the last. She pulled the iron bell pull beside the heavy oak door and waited. Bells jangled deep in the bowels of the house.

* * *

'Do you need a hand moving tomorrow?' John was getting quite brave. 'Just let me know if you do. I'm not working or anything in the afternoon.' He was trying to sound casual.

'Thanks,' Michael smiled gratefully, 'but I really haven't got a great deal to move - just a couple of bags.' He didn't miss the look of disappointment on John's face. 'But you must pop round sometime.'

* * *

'Tony... I hate to have to say this,' Julia's tone belied her words, 'but you were a bit sickly sweet again. You've got to be more forceful. You don't want the viewers thinking you're queer do you? Tony? Are you listening to me? Tony!'

'Yes?' Her husband sighed and looked up from his copy of the Daily Mail.

'Did you hear a word I said?'

'Why... was it worth listening to?' He muttered and went back to his newspaper as Julia stormed out of the dressing room, almost colliding with Darren who had been hovering outside the door. The boy had heard every word.

* * *

'Marilyn! Punctual as ever. Come in.' Max flashed his leg-weakening smile and ushered her into the lofty hallway. He looked as handsome as ever, his six foot frame in perfect shape, his dark hair casually styled but perfectly placed. He wore his loose-fitting but perfectly-tailored suit like a model and she wondered, not for the first time, how old he was. It was difficult to tell; he could have been anywhere between thirty and forty. 'How was the traffic?'

'Not bad,' Marilyn smiled, 'except for a maniac in a Jag almost running me off the road a mile or two back.'

'Oh... not a black XJS?'

'Er... yes.' She could feel herself blushing. 'Why?'

'It was probably my wife. She seems to forget that we don't actually own the roads!'

'I really am sorry... I didn't realise. I mean...' It was quite a surprise to her to hear that Max was married. She had never heard mention of a wife and had assumed he was a carefree, if rather successful, bachelor.

'Don't worry about it... I don't.' His eyes showed that he meant what he said and she relaxed again. 'Now, are you in a tearing hurry to get started or shall we have a coffee first?'

* * *

Darren watched Tony and Julia leave the studio and head for their car. He wondered what they did when they were at home. They were a strange couple and he somehow couldn't imagine them having a life outside the studio. They almost seemed made for daytime television. She was as hard as nails and epitomised the vision of what many housewives wished they could be. He represented what most housewives wished they could have. These qualities made them immediately familiar and human, identifiable with the viewers, yet slightly out of reach. And it wasn't only housewives who lusted after Tony Barkworth. Darren felt a familiar stirring in his groin and rushed off to the toilets to sort it out.

* * *

'Have you finished your coffee?' Max hovered by the scrubbed pine kitchen table as Marilyn nodded and got up. 'Shall we make a start then.' He led the way out of the kitchen, down a passageway and out into a courtyard. It was a fresh, clear day and the sun's rays made the old flagstones glow. Max had rebuilt and restored the stable buildings surrounding the courtyard and was immensely proud of them. Marilyn could see this in his eyes as he led her towards the door of the old tack room. From the outside, it could still have been a stable block. Inside, although there was still a comfortable rustic air created by the exposed brick walls and heavy wooden beams, it was clearly a high-powered business environment. A young blonde receptionist looked up and smiled as her boss walked in. Marilyn could feel the buzz of unseen activity all around her.

'Hold all calls for the next two hours please Zara,' Max said quietly but firmly. 'Absolutely no disturbances.' The girl acknowledged his instructions and went back to a call she had put on hold.

Marilyn followed Max through a maze of corridors until they came to a door carrying a 'Strictly No Admittance' sign. He turned a key in the lock and stood aside to let her enter the padded room.

* * *

'Tony. I think we ought to get a new car.' Julia decided to strike while the iron was hot and take advantage of having her husband's undivided attention while they were driving home. The metallic silver XR3i screeched to a halt at he realised at the last moment that the traffic lights were red.

'What on earth do you mean? This one isn't a year old yet!'

'Yes... but it really doesn't go with our image now, does it? A Ford was all very well when we weren't in the public eye, but in view of our current position... well... it's a little bit common,' Julia whined.

'And you don't need to give me three guesses as to who's filling your head with these ideas,' Tony blurted out. 'First the house, then the dining room... now a new frigging car. God bless Serena Hesketh and all who ride in her!'

'Tony! How dare you? She's my friend - and she's coming to dinner tomorrow night with her husband, so you'd better be civil.'

'Oh God, no. It's one thing re-decorating the dining room, but I didn't think you were actually going to use it!'

'There's no point talking to you when you're in one of these moods,' Julia hissed. 'If you're not careful, you might have to do without your Monday treat…'

* * *

'Right, what shall we do first?' Max settled himself into a large leather chair. It amused Marilyn to see how consistently businesslike he was: completely unselfconscious, unapologetic and unaffected. 'What do you want to start with? Domination, Watersports, Naughty Schoolgirl, Sex-Starved Housewife? You know the kind of thing – "My husband's away and I can't do without it any more…"' He grinned. 'Or how about Licking Lesbians or Forced Cross Dressing? Any preferences?'

'Look, Max, I don't mind where we start, but can we get on with it. I've got to be back to pick Zoë up from school.'

* * *

'Tony… it's for you… it's your mother!' Julia shouted into the kitchen where Tony was looking for the paracetamol. 'Tony!'

'Yes… yes… I'm coming.' He took the receiver, doing his best to ignore her frown. 'Hello… Mum?'

'Anthony… I thought you might have rung by now… but I suppose you're very busy.' Kathleen had decided it was time to be a part of her son's new-found fame.

'Yes, very busy.' Tony had never had much to talk about with his mother.

'Actually, the reason I am ringing is to find out whether you've heard from your brother. He rang to say he was on his way back about a week ago, but I haven't heard anything since.'

'No. I haven't heard from him.' Tony paused as he remembered the last time he had spoken to his twin and then continued in little more than a whisper. 'I doubt that I will either.'

'What was that? Anthony?' Kathleen didn't like the offhand way her son was treating the conversation,

59

'I... er... I said I'd let you know if I hear from him.'

'Right! I suppose I'd better let you get on with your busy life then.' Tony didn't miss the resentment in her voice.

'Bye Mum.'

* * *

'You're working the early shift again tomorrow aren't you?' John asked hopefully as he picked up his bag and put the strap over his shoulder.

'Yeah,' Michael replied casually, 'and then I'm going straight over to Clapham to my new place.'

'Oh yes, that's right. Well don't forget to let me know if you want a hand.'

* * *

The heavy velvet curtains were drawn allowing only a few stray rays of sunlight to fall across the white lace coverlet on the large brass bed. Flames danced across the coals in the grate, creating a warm glow to the self-conscious authenticity of the over-furnished room. A woman wearing a long white night-dress knelt in front of the fire, trying to give the appearance of looking deep into the flames.

Suddenly, the heavy mahogany door burst open and a man wearing full hunting pink and carrying a riding crop entered the room. The woman looked up and shrank back in terror.

'I'm sorry, master... I know I shouldn't be in your bedroom, but it is a cold night and... and... it's so cold in the servants' quarters.'

'So... you have ideas above your station, do you? We'll soon see about that!'

'Sir! I beg of you... please don't tell the mistress. She'll throw me out in the street and... and... I'll starve to death!' The woman threw herself at his feet, clutching at his shiny leather riding boots. 'I beg of you... I'll do anything you ask...'

* * *

'Housewife, take one. Three... two... one....' Marilyn moved closer to the microphone, almost brushing it with her lips as her smooth honeyed tones carressed Max's ears. 'Hi... I'm glad you've called, because I've been *dying* to tell someone all about what happened to me yesterday. You see, I'm a housewife and spend most of my days on my own in the house while my husband's away on business. He's much older than me and is usually so tired when he gets home that there's little chance of any satisfaction for me... if you know what I mean. I'm a full-blooded woman, for goodness' sake! There are times when I think I'm going to die of frustration. But yesterday... well... yesterday was something else. The day started off normally enough. I got up at seven thirty to see my hubby off to work and then tidied up around the house, not even bothering to get dressed. I was just wearing a pink silk dressing gown. It felt good as it brushed against my firm young breasts as I moved around making the bed, hoovering the stairs, loading the dishwasher. Well, it was then that the doorbell rang. I'd totally forgotten that the window cleaner was coming... '

Max smiled. Marilyn's recordings were always good; she was a natural. It was thanks to voices like hers - and his own ability to recognise the potential of the premium rate telephone network - that he was now turning over close on three million a year.

* * *

The riding crop came down on the woman's buttocks, which were now exposed as she lay on the imitation tiger skin rug in front of the fire.

'Oh master!' she cried out in distress, 'don't be so hard on me. I'm only a poor servant girl. Have mercy!' Crack! The crop lashed against her bare flesh once again and she screamed in agony.

'Hard? I don't think you know the meaning of the word,' her master barked out from his position above her as he undid the flies on his riding breeches. 'Let's see what you can do with this!'

* * *

'Right, can you take it from "Is that a chamois leather in your pocket, or are you just pleased to see me?"' Max put his headphones back on and looked down at the mixing desk. He enjoyed the fact that he managed nearly all the recordings himself. There were advantages to taking an almost obsessive interest in the specifics of his business: if he didn't, he wouldn't have met Marilyn. 'Three... two... one...'

*　*　*

The riding boots and long white night dress lay discarded on the floor.

'Shall we do the naughty schoolgirl next week?' Julia asked, almost forgetting that it was Tony's treat not hers.

CHAPTER FOUR

Waking before the alarm call, Tony was reminded of his days at boarding school and realised that it would probably be the only peace he would get all day. He looked over at Julia's sleeping form and thought how old she looked with her face squashed against the pillow. The bags under her eyes were almost black, her nose was shiny and her mouth, surrounded by hundreds of tiny lines, was open. This unpleasant sight was accompanied by the ugly sound of her snoring.

It had occurred to him several days after their hastily arranged wedding that he knew very little about his new wife. She had made such an impression on him that he had not seen any need to know more about her than was immediately obvious. Julia Daley had literally swept him off his feet, impressing him in a way no other woman had ever done. He couldn't deny that she had changed his life completely, but he still didn't feel that he really knew her. Somehow, he had always imagined having a blissfully happy marriage with a house in the country and a few children running around. Perhaps he was being unrealistic in even expecting happiness. Was anybody happy? He had previously been naive enough to think that success and happiness went hand in hand.

He looked again at the sleeping form next to him. What was going on in her mind? What was she dreaming about now? She hardly ever referred to her past. It was as if she only lived for the present and the future. That was what had made him curious. After all, he still had contacts; the past was there to rake up when the need arose. But the source of her motivation still puzzled him - what *really* drove her to be who she was?

He got out of bed quietly and tiptoed to the bathroom to have a long, uninterrupted shower.

* * *

Clive Haynes heaved himself out of bed and surveyed his body in the full-length mirror. It was a long time since he had been able to look at himself and like what he saw. The last two years had seen him sink further and further into oblivion and further away from himself. He looked ten years older than his forty years. Through self neglect, his once firm body was flabby and out of shape. Along with his physical fitness, his personal life had suffered and, subsequently, his career. He didn't need a psychoanalyst to tell him where it had all started going wrong. But now he was at last feeling some sense of purpose, because he knew who was responsible. But Clive knew that he was the only one who could do anything about bringing him to justice. And he could feel that his chance to do so would be coming very soon.

* * *

'And I'd like to offer a warm welcome to our first guest this morning, fertility expert Dr Leslie McManus.' Julia smiled, manoeuvring her face into a radiant, if artificial, vision a million miles away from the gorgon-like mask Tony had woken up beside. The doctor smiled, completely at ease with Julia's obvious attraction to him. After all, this happened every day of his working life. It looked as if this foray into television could prove to be a good move after all.

'If you're among those unfortunate people *desperately* trying to have children,' Tony paused to smile and then straightened his face as he realised it wasn't quite appropriate, 'stay tuned, because Dr Leslie McManus might be able to shed a ray of hope on your plight.' He put his hand on the doctor's knee, not wanting to be left out of the adulation, then snatched it away in horror.

'Leslie,' Julia leaned towards the doctor sandwiched between them, 'you've brought happiness to many women over the last few years...'

*   *   *

Marilyn put the vacuum cleaner back in the cupboard and flicked the switch on the kettle. She always felt better if she finished the housework before she had her first coffee of the morning. It had occurred to her that she ought to get a full time job now it looked as if she and Zoë were going to stay in the country permanently, but today she was quite happy to be a housewife. Besides, she had no idea what she was capable of doing. Having achieved moderate success as a continuity announcer on a cable television channel in Los Angeles, she knew that she no longer possessed the drive and energy to do it all over again. Things had been different when she had first arrived in America: she had needed to prove herself and give her life a purpose. Then Zoë had unexpectedly come into her life. Her priorities had changed and she didn't regret it for a moment.

Television was now purely something for entertainment – no longer the powerful force that had once driven her. She wandered across to the old set in the corner and turned it on, blissfully unaware that the screen was about to reveal an all too familiar face from the past.

*   *   *

Tony felt humiliatingly inadequate in the presence of this god-like being who was apparently able to provide the solution to the fertility problems - not to mention fodder for the sexual fantasies - of a large proportion of the female population of the country. On top of that, he seemed to really believe in what he did. Sincerity oozed from every inch of his perfect body. He was currently in the middle of a discussion with Julia about infertility problems often being psychological.

'So... Leslie,' Julia pulled her stomach in again and leaned even closer towards the doctor, lowering her eyes in a coquettish manner, 'you're saying that some women who *think* they want children, are actually subconsciously stopping themselves from conceiving.'

* * *

Harvey drew in his breath in exasperation as he heard Julia once again unashamedly repeat what the doctor had said in an attempt to seem intelligent. Her flirtation had not escaped him either. 'If that hard-nosed bitch can get the hots for him,' he muttered to himself, 'He'll be a definite hit with the female viewers.' Harvey made a mental note to investigate the possibility of a regular slot for the doctor.

* * *

Iris Devereaux chuckled at the television screen as she watched her former protégée putting all her assets on show.

'Make the most of 'em, duckie. You know what happens to goods when they're in the shop window!'

* * *

'So, what you're saying is,' Tony decided to resort to his wife's habit of repetition rather than staying in silent exile on the sofa, 'that nowadays there is no need for women to automatically think that first time motherhood is out of the question just because they have reached forty.' He looked pointedly at Julia.

'Oh, that's a comfort,' Julia chirped cheerily to the camera before shooting an icy sideways glance at her husband. 'Of course, I've never wanted children - with my busy lifestyle it wouldn't be fair on them - but if I did...'

* * *

Marilyn, still reeling from the shock of seeing Julia's face on the screen, gritted her teeth and kicked the nearest chair as she heard the words spoken so flippantly.

* * *

'Trevor - reference GM565. I'm 45, 6'3', 15 stone, well-toned, muscular, hirsute. I'm looking for submissive males, 30 years old and under, who are in need of firm direction. I am a dominant father figure who will take you in hand, give you a firm beating, and

show you what your body is for. Trevor - reference GM565.'

'Yep... that sounds good. You should get a good response.' Michael had quickly learned how to put callers at their ease and help them to record good messages. 'Yes... I've got your telephone number here on our records and that'll be given to anyone who enquires about your message. Just wait for that phone to start ringing! Bye.'

'Getting a bit familiar aren't we?' John was trying, unsuccessfully, to hide his jealousy. 'I thought you were going to give him your telephone number then!'

'I don't need to,' Michael teased. 'I've got his!'

* * *

'Don't you think we could have discussed the matter of your not wanting children before you told the nation?' Arguments in the dressing room were a regular occurrence now, but this time Tony was really annoyed.

'Oh... I didn't realise it was a subject that concerned you.' Julia went back to the task of choosing earrings for the drive home.

'So you don't think I've got any say in the matter?'

'Well, quite frankly, no. It's not you who'd have to endure that dreadful bovine state for nine months, the excruciating pains of labour, not to mention the resulting stretched fanny, sagging tits, sore nipples and,' she paused for effect, looking at her husband and thinking how pathetic he looked, 'a shitty-nappied brat screaming to be fed at all hours of the night. I'm a career woman not a brood mare!' With that she pulled the door open, narrowly missing the swift departure of Darren who had seconds earlier had his ear pressed to it fervently wishing he was capable of childbirth.

* * *

Kathleen Barkworth sat in front of the hairdresser's mirror with her head swathed in towels and surveyed her rather podgy face. But, she reflected, nobody looked their best when they had just had their head in a sink, for whatever reason. Anyway, she didn't care at the moment. She felt on top of the world because the girl who had washed her hair was a fan of Tony's. Well, not a fan exactly. When pressed, she'd admitted to having seen him on the cover of the TV Times, but to Kathleen that was as good as an admission of infatuation.

'I suppose you can see where he gets his good looks from, can't you?' she twittered.

'His father, I suppose!' said the girl, who had had quite enough.

* * *

'Are you sure you don't need a hand?' John was watching Michael staggering out of the office with two large holdalls and a rucksack.

'Yes, I'm sure. Thanks for the offer though.' Michael smiled over his shoulder, determined to manage on his own.

'What are you doing tonight? I'm going to the Fridge if you're interested.' John was determined not to give up that easily.

'The Fridge?'

'Yes... you know... the club up the road here. It's *the* place to be on Tuesdays and Saturdays.'

'Well,' Michael looked pensive for a moment, 'I haven't been to a club since I was back.'

'I... I can get you on the guest list if you like. A friend of mine works on the door.' John felt breathless in anticipation of doing Michael a favour.

'Great... thanks. I'd appreciate that.' Michael was already halfway down the corridor.

'Er... I can't remember what your real name is. I can't get them to put just "Troy" on the guest list!'

'Oh yeah... my name's Michael... Michael Barkworth.'

* * *

'What time's this bloody dinner party then?' Tony sank into a chair and fingered the remote control for the television.

'Bloody eight o'clock!' Julia snapped, 'and don't think your sulking impresses me. Being quiet all the way home in the car isn't going to make me suddenly give way and have a baby. Did I ever hint to you that I wanted kids? No! Did you ever tell me you wanted to be a father? No! Have we ever...'

'All right... all right! I get the message. Who's coming to dinner, anyway?' Tony's head was aching... really aching.

'Serena and her husband.'

'Is that all? Two people and it's a "dinner party". Mind you, I suppose you've got to justify spending all that money on the dining room. Beats me why we need a dining room when you've upset all my friends and seem to have conveniently mislaid all your own. Well... you'd better get your pinny on and start cooking!'

'Don't be ridiculous! I've hired a wonderful Cordon Bleu trained girl recommended by...'

'Serena?' Tony interrupted. 'Who else? What is it with that woman? You spend a week with her at a fat farm and ever since she's been running your life for you. Perhaps it was her who decided you didn't want children...'

* * *

Darren carefully cut the picture from the front of the magazine and stood back as he decided where he was going to stick it in relation to the other fifty or so already on the wall. It had started as an idle attraction, but had quickly exceeded that stage. It was nothing like his fixation with Jason Donovan and Philip Schofield, not to mention his rather bewildering crush, all those years ago, on Olivia Newton John. He was in love... in lust... seized by an obsession... with Tony Barkworth.

* * *

Julia decided to ignore Tony's mood and hope it would go away while she had half an hour under the sun bed. She wanted to look 'casually expensive and lightly tanned' tonight - a look she had just read about in Cosmopolitan - to make a good impression on Serena's husband. The sunbed had been installed in one of the guest bathrooms under a big palm tree next to a large Edwardian roll-top bathtub. It looked strangely out of place but, as Julia entered, it wasn't alone. She dropped her bathrobe on the floor and planted her dimpled buttocks on the cold perspex of the tanning machine.

'Half an hour,' she said to herself, 'and I'll feel sixteen again...' realising with a jolt that it was nearly thirty years since she really *had* been sixteen. She lay on the hard surface and flicked the switch, wondering why everything to do with the pursuit of beauty held a degree of discomfort or pain. As the glass tubes above her face illuminated instantaneously before she had a chance to close her eyes, she was suddenly and overwhelmingly reminded of her first visit to the dentist. That light shining into her face... her mother's voice telling her to sit still and be a good girl. Forty years ago. The warmth and light pervaded her body as the ultra violet rays burst into action. She closed her eyes. Her mind wandered and she remembered. It had been a lovely day and she had been happy. She had had a whole morning off school and had been allowed to go into some very grown-up shops with her mother, but the dentist had hurt her and she had cried. All she needed was her mother to reassure her. 'Mummy.... please hold my hand...' But her mother had slapped her hard and told her to sit still. 'Don't make a fool of me. It's not going to hurt!' But it *had* hurt. She had been so frightened that she had been sick down her new dress and sandals. The dentist had been nice and said it didn't matter and helped to clean her up, but her mother had grasped her hand, marched her down the cold wooden stairs, pulled down her pants and smacked her bare bottom. 'How dare you show me up like that? And don't think I'm ever going to buy you a new dress again if that's the way you're going to treat it!'

*   *   *

Michael staggered up the steps at Clapham Common tube station and breathed in the smell of the traffic. He put his bags down on the pavement and surveyed his surroundings. All the buildings, apart from the station itself, were tall and discoloured. Brightly coloured and irregular shop fronts gave way to drab brickwork and dirty windows as the eye moved upwards. Generations of pigeons had left their mark on every possible ledge and their progeny were following suit unabated. Several shops were closed down and boarded up, others were clearly in need of a facelift. Everywhere people bustled about their business -buying, selling, browsing, talking, arguing. The place was dirty, even dilapidated in parts. It had more than a tinge of decay. But it was just perfect.

He couldn't quite put his finger on the reason for it, but he had a feeling that this place was going to be a good influence on him. The posters plastered over the bus stop, none of them complete, formed an unwitting collage of contemporary culture in their tattered and disparate togetherness. Just over the road, the green common stretched almost as far as the eye could see. Grass and trees, traffic and noise, shops and people. Perfect.

* * *

Julia awoke with a start as the switch on the sunbed clicked off. She had been having the strangest dreams. Tony's remark about friends had been dangerously close to the truth. All through her life, she had made acquaintances rather than friends. She had got to know people in order to use them or sleep with them - or sometimes both. Now things seemed to have changed. At last she had got the glitzy career she had been striving for for more years than she dared admit. She had got a big house in a fashionable part of London. She had netted herself an attractive younger husband. But where was the social life to fit in with all this? Where were the friends with similar big houses and careers? She wanted parties in the country, soirees in town and invitations to balls. Why weren't people clamouring for her company now that she was famous? Hopefully this dinner party would be a start.

It had only recently dawned on Julia that she needed friends more than anything in the world. But where did you find them? Serena Hesketh had popped up next to her in the jacuzzi at Champney's and she had decided to hang on to her for all she was worth. She pulled on her bathrobe and wandered downstairs to find her husband. Here I come, she thought, all tanned and beautiful.

71

Here she comes, he thought, all red and sweating.

* * *

'At school...' Zoë paused with a look on her face that told Marilyn she was about to tell her something she had been bottling up for a while, 'Claire Shackleford said if I hadn't got a Daddy it meant I was illiterate. I said I wasn't 'cos I had a Daddy and he went to heaven... and that anyway I might have another one soon who's even better... 'cos my new Mummy's much better than my old one...' The child stopped and looked up at her guardian. Marilyn was lost for words and felt a lump form in her throat. In her dreams, she wished she could provide Zoë with a father. In reality she knew it was highly unlikely that she would allow anyone else into her life. But where was the harm in dreaming?

An image began to form in her mind as she pondered on her ideal man. The image became a face and it was a face she recognised.

* * *

'What did you say that's called?' Julia was hovering around the caterer in the kitchen.

'Beef Wellington,' the girl said patiently, wishing silently that the batty cow would run along and arrange the napkins or something.

'Are you sure that's the right thing to serve at an intimate dinner party?' Julia's nerves were getting the better of her. This was the first time she had ever invited people to dinner in a home of her own.

'Well... it was good enough for the Duchess of York last week,' she replied, shamelessly namedropping without a hint of truth, knowing that it would be the only way of shutting up this nightmare of a hostess. At least most her other celebrity clients in Barnes had the common sense not to challenge her knowledge of etiquette.

* * *

The sun shone but the air was cool as Michael made his way along the pavement. He caught glimpses of different front gardens as he passed each gateway in the tall privet hedge. Some were tidy and ordered, others overgrown and littered with overflowing dustbins or old bicycles. At last he came to the one he was looking for. He pushed open the small gate and walked up the brick pathway, grinning at the laboriously tidy patch of lawn surrounded by well-chosen, perfectly pruned shrubs. He could almost feel the three storey Victorian terraced house looking down on him knowingly. It was already beginning to feel like home. Putting his bags down on the doorstep, he pressed the third bell and waited in front of the blue painted door.

'Hello?' A male voice answered through the intercom.

'Hi... it's Michael.'

'Come on up.' The lock buzzed and he pushed the door. Inside the hallway was strewn with unwanted letters, newspapers and leaflets that had obviously found their way through the letterbox. The walls were painted white but had become discoloured and stained, especially where they joined the scuffed skirting boards. Someone had obviously made a vain attempt at brightening it up by putting a vase of dried flowers on a little side table. Michael wrinkled up his nose at the faint smell of cats rising from the purple carpet as he climbed the stairs to the first floor, his bags bashing against the anaglypta wallpaper. The door to the flat was open and he walked in, breathing a sigh of relief as he dumped his baggage on the floor inside.

'I got here as soon as I could,' he said, as the flat's owner came out of the bedroom. 'I hope I didn't keep you waiting?'

'No. I don't fly off until late tonight.' Simon Massey was about thirty five, technically well-built and handsome, but with a curiously uninteresting face. 'The phone is due to come back on any minute - in your name - and all the other stuff is in order. Just pay the rent directly into my account as we agreed. I'm sure I can trust you - your references were positively glowing!'

Michael had seen the flat advertised in 'Capital Gay' the Thursday before and had come to view it the same day. The location had attracted him - just a few minutes from the tube and overlooking the common. He also wanted to live south of the river for no other reason than that he had already lived in West and North London, as well as a brief stay in the East End. The tried and tested never appealed to him as much as the new and different.

There was nothing very remarkable about the first impression the house itself gave. The hallway in its communal shabbiness told the same story as thousands of similar pieces of no man's land in the capital, giving no hint at the nature of the flats carved out of the divided body of the once-grand residence. Michael's open mind had, however, been rewarded once he had crossed the threshold of the first floor flat. It opened straight into a large living room decorated in a way Michael had come to recognise as typical of a gay man living a 'straight' existence during the day. Simon Massey was an accountant and betrayed no stereotypical clues to his sexuality. His release from his professional restraint was clearly seen in his private surroundings. The room was divided by a gothic screen probably saved from a condemned church which lent it a curiously religious air. A large kilim-covered sofa sat in the window bay beneath the perfectly pleated raw cotton roman blinds. The original Victorian fireplace formed a backdrop for a collection of carved wooden figures, clearly African, and a huge curved sword hung on the wall above. The honey-coloured walls gave the room a warm, comforting feeling, enhanced by semicircular glass light fittings. Behind the screen, a marble-topped dining table with wrought iron chairs sat beneath a huge metal lantern, probably Indian, shedding a red glowing light from the holes in its grey metal.

Michael had decided to take the flat within seconds of walking through the door, before he had seen the slightly disturbing touches like the fully-dressed shop dummy behind the door in the bathroom and the stuffed parrot hanging upside down from its perch in the kitchen. Whatever anyone wanted to say about the decor, he liked it. He wouldn't have to make excuses for it to himself or anyone else because he hadn't chosen it. Like many other things in his life, it had chosen him.

'I'll just show you how everything works and leave you to it,' Simon offered cheerfully. 'I hope you don't mind, but I've left everything except my clothes. That's the advantage of letting to someone gay - you're not going to be shocked by the contents of my cupboards!' He laughed and then set about showing his new tenant the controls for the central heating. He had explained previously that he was going to Switzerland for six months to work and wanted someone to look after his prized possessions as much as he needed the rent. Michael was pleased that he obviously projected such a trustworthy impression.

* * *

The doorbell rang and Julia virtually flew into the hallway screaming for her husband, who was already there with his hand on the door knob. The guests were ten minutes late and she had been worried they weren't going to arrive.

'Serena! Darling, you look wonderful!' Julia gushed, pushing in front of Tony and opening the door to her friend. Her eyes wandered to the man behind her and took in his breathtaking good looks. He was tall, strikingly tall, with dark hair and a very angular but well-proportioned face. Dr Leslie McManus suddenly lost the number one slot in Julia's list of male targets.

'Julia!' Serena gushed in return, planting a kiss on each of her friend's cheeks. She might as well have been wearing her clothes inside out, so loudly did they speak of the expensive shops they came from. Her dark hair had obviously been styled that afternoon and her make-up was flawlessly applied to her large-boned face. The long salmon pink silk shirt hung in effortless elegance over a small jet black camisole top and black leggings drawn in tightly at the waist by a broad leather belt with a large silver clasp at the front. Julia stood in her equally expensive but scarcely flattering Jean Muir dress and silently cursed herself for not having anticipated her friend's ability to outshine her. She hadn't dared to think that it was acceptable to wear anything other than a dress for a dinner party. Serena greedily and correctly read her thoughts. 'What a *charming* little dress!' And then, stepping inside, she gestured behind herself without looking. 'Julia Daley, Tony Barkworth, this is my husband Max Hesketh.'

*   *   *

Michael walked around the flat and gently touched things as he passed them, happy in the knowledge that it was all his... at least for a while. The fact that he had only got the flat for six months made the sensation even better. He wouldn't have the chance to tire of it, constantly thankful that he had found such a place on which to centre the next chapter of his life. The moment his landlord walked out of the door, he had been unable to resist the temptation to look in the cupboards. So far he had discovered an extensive collection of curiously titled videos - 'Long Hard Drive', 'Policeman's Truncheon' and 'G.I.'s Initiation' being among them. There were stacks of imported magazines and, at the top of the wardrobe, a collection of leather harnesses, whips and a pair of chaps. He grinned as he thought of the accountant leading his double life and was thankful, not for the first time, that he had come to terms with his sexuality; he was the same person morning, noon and night.

*   *   *

'You were a journalist?' Max, although bored and frustrated with the company, thought he ought to make an effort. 'What sort of stuff did you write?' Tony, delighted to be asked about his pre-Julia days, launched into an account of his undistinguished journalistic career. Max pretended to be interested.

'... and you may have seen a big piece I did a while ago for the Mail on Sunday about those premium rate telephone lines.' Max suddenly didn't have to pretend any more. Tony was relishing in the captive audience he had found and continued. 'I exposed a big scandal involving a telephone dating company.'

'Oh - what company was that?' Max looked earnestly interested and Tony's tongue began to loosen further. The Chateau Neuf Du

Pape was slipping down nicely. It had been a while since he had felt as light-headed as this.

'A big set-up called Diamond Communications. They operate under various names: "Mansearch Dating", "Heart to Heart", "Adult Contacts", "London Love Lines"... that kind of thing. They've got a load of those dirty story lines as well. You know... "Saucy Suzie'll Blow Your Mind". Mind you, I don't suppose you'd have come across that kind of thing, would you?' Tony laughed, 'Anyway, it's a huge company, massive turnover. You wouldn't believe how many people phone those lines.'

'And what was the scandal you uncovered during your *in-depth* investigation?' Max had a glint in his eye. 'Sex for sale? Satanic orgies? Paedophilia?'

'Er... well.' Tony was taken aback. His 'scandal' was going to look pretty tame now. 'I managed to bribe a couple of their operators to say that most of the recorded messages from people wanting to make a date were fake. It caused a lot of trouble for the company and grew into quite a big story. I suppose it appealed to the general public's sense of horror at anything to do with sex... not to mention their telephone bills.' Having conveniently omitted the subsequent embarrassment caused by the story - the upshot of which was a court case and the newspaper having to make an apology and pay damages to the company - Tony suddenly remembered his manners. 'And what do you do for a living, Max?'

'Oh... I'm surprised you didn't know.' Max paused and smiled. 'I own a company called Diamond Communications.'

*   *   *

Being unable to decide whether to wear denim, leather or a mixture of the two, Darren sat on the edge of the bed with his head in his hands and turned his thoughts to which bar or club he would go to for the evening. He didn't really want to go out at all, but he had to do something to take his mind off Tony Barkworth. Maybe he would even meet someone who would bowl him over and provide an alternative subject for his daydreams. Somehow he doubted it. Why did he always go for men he couldn't have? Is that what made them attractive to him? He pondered, just for a second, on what his life was all about... and then decided to wear lycra.

* * *

'More coffee Max?' Julia leaned over the table with a cafetiere in her hand, confident that she had made an impression on her friend's husband.

'No thanks Julia, I've had quite enough,' he replied, meaning it, having discovered that there *was* a woman he despised more than his wife. 'Actually, Tony, I believe my main client is on your show sometime this week?'

'Oh? Who's that?' Tony had realised that he was no match for Max and suddenly felt very small.

'Barry Sugden. He owns the Daily Nation. I run all his dating and story lines for him. Very powerful man.' He paused a moment and then smiled wickedly as he added, 'I must tell him it was you who covered that story. I'm sure he'll be fascinated!'

* * *

The taxi drew to halt in the busy Brixton street and Clive paid the driver. No ordinary taxi ride, this was a significant step in his attempt to pull himself together and put the past behind him. A queue had already formed outside the club and he pulled his black leather jacket closer around himself to prepare for the chilly wait. Two years. Yes, it had been more than two years since he had been out at night. This was a major step forward.

* * *

'Don't ever expect me to socialise with those dreadful people again!' Max was angry but thankful that they were at last on the way home. 'I can't imagine why you want to associate with them.'

'They're on television.' Serena summed up the reasons for her friendship with Julia and slumped back into a drunken sleep as the car sped homewards.

* * *

It didn't take Michael long to unpack his few belongings and stow them away in various cupboards and drawers. He put a framed photograph of a man on the bedside table and smiled sadly to himself.

'I've come a long way, Peter, I've come a long way,' he muttered and then pondered on what to do for the night. Maybe he *would* pop down to the Fridge for a little while...

* * *

Clive felt almost human again as he bought himself a drink and surveyed the rapidly filling club. A converted music hall, it was one of the largest venues in the capital and attracted a crowd varying in age as much as appearance. Any traces of night club chic and sophistication had been ripped out in favour of bare plaster and scaffolding. Stark visual effects produced by lasers and projected images gave the whole place a surreal edge and provided a foil for the noticeably muscular and well-honed physiques shamelessly peeping out from ripped denim and close fitting lycra. He couldn't help noticing that the 'clone' look of the eighties - moustaches and black leather - had been almost completely replaced by the new cropped and body-conscious look of the nineties. Fifty year old men mixed with those barely over the age of consent. There were girls there too. Not the usual 'fag hags' associated with gay clubs, they were young people intent on having a good time and well-informed enough to know where to get it. It was evidence of a community now confident enough to strip away any pretences of conformity and develop what was exposed underneath, both physically and mentally.

And he had been letting it all pass him by.

* * *

'Bollocks!' Tony nearly spat, he was so angry. 'How can you say it was a successful dinner party when that bitch was sniggering at us all the time?'

'I think you're just in a mood because her husband showed you up,' Julia sneered. 'I don't know what happened, but you certainly looked embarrassed at one point.'

'Oh, forget it!' Tony went to the table in the hall and picked up the car keys, 'I'm going out to get some fresh air!'

*   *   *

The atmosphere in the club was humid and close. Darren's lycra top was sticking to his body and sweat was pouring from his brow. He had been dancing solidly for nearly two hours, but it hadn't got rid of his all-pervading obsession. God... he needed some water. He should have known better than to take an E.

Clive looked at his watch and thought it might be time to make a move. He was pleased with what he had achieved, but was now tired. Perhaps he would have just one more drink before he left. Turning in the direction of the bar, he nearly collided with a boy in lycra.

'Sorry!' Darren looked him up and down and decided not to pursue the apology any further, then stopped dead in his tracks like a rabbit caught in the headlights of a car. His mouth dropped open. Clive instinctively followed his line of vision and froze too.

Totally unaware of the impact he had made on his audience of two, Michael pulled open the door and walked out into the foyer. He had had a really good night. As he walked out into the still busy street, the fresh air lashed his face and filled his lungs. The overwhelmingly sexual undertones in the club had awoken sentiments in him he had almost forgotten existed...

*   *   *

A finger pressed the doorbell at a basement flat in Maida Vale.

'Yes?' a deep voice asked through the intercom.

'It's me,' the young man on the doorstep replied, his knuckles whitening as he gripped the holdall tightly.

'OK - push the door.' He heard a buzz as the door was unlocked and pushed it, a deep seated feeling of excitement and trepidation playing havoc with his insides. Finding himself in a dark hallway, he looked around anxiously for the source of the voice. A masked head suddenly popped out from a doorway.

'Take off your shoes and come in... and call me "Sir"!'

'Yes sir.' He walked into the room and took a deep breath. The walls were painted black and the only light came from a dim red lamp in one corner. In this half light he was just about able to make out the shape of a small narrow bed covered in black PVC and various chains, shackles and whips hanging on the walls.

'What's in the bag?' his host demanded. Now his whole body was visible it became apparent that, as well as the leather mask, he was clothed completely in leather: black leather trousers, heavy black boots and a harness made of black leather straps and rings. He was tall, around six foot, and thick set. A solid wall of hirsute muscle. 'I said, what's in the bag, boy?'

'Oh... just some spare clothes in case... well... I didn't know... Sir!' He remembered just in time to address his host correctly.

'Now - I don't want any messing about! Let's see what you're made of. Get your clothes off... now!'

He hurriedly obeyed and soon stood completely naked. The leather-clad man circled around him, eyeing him as a prospective buyer would look at a bullock in a cattle market. His jowly face broke into a lop-sided smile.

'Hmm... not bad. At last a slave who doesn't exaggerate about himself on the telephone.' He put his hand out and touched his guest's buttocks. 'Yes, nice firm butt. What d'you say, slave?'

'Nothing... sir.'

'Good. That's the way it should be. Don't speak unless spoken to. Understood?'

'Yes sir!'

'Now, lie on the bed and let me show you what *I'm* made of. Yeah... that's it.' He undid his heavy leather belt and unzipped his fly. 'What does it look like from underneath... eh?' His large semi-flaccid penis was inches above the reclining man's face. 'I said what does it look like, slave?'

'Magnificent... sir! Far too good for the likes of me... sir.'

'Well, we'll just have to see how good you are, won't we? Open your mouth. I said open your mouth!' His penis was virtually erect by this point as he straddled the slave's face, his sweaty testicles brushing against the man's lips. 'Lick them... slave... lick them. Lick my balls... aaah... yeah... aaah. Lick my cock.... yeah... lick it! Yeah... more... aaah! Take it in your mouth... that's it... aaah... more!' The man nearly gagged as the huge organ was repeatedly jabbed down his throat. He could hardly breathe and any air he *was* getting smelt of stale pubic hair. 'All the way in slave... make me happy... make me happy... make your master happy!' Suddenly it was all too much. He pushed against the massive body on top of him in a frantic attempt to breathe. As the penis slid out of his mouth he heaved a sigh of relief and took in great mouthfuls of air. 'Oh... so we're going to misbehave are we, slave? Do you know what happens to slaves who disobey? Do you?'

He was dragged to his feet and then made to lie face down on the bed. Crack! A searing pain shot through his body as the whip struck his buttocks. Crack! The second lash was harder. Crack! 'Are you sorry slave? Are you sorry? Say "Yes Sir"!' Crack! Crack! Crack! 'Say "Sorry Sir"!' Crack! 'Say "Have mercy on me, Sir"!' Crack!

A large hand rubbed the now tender buttocks and laughed; it was a deep, throaty belly laugh. 'So... you see what happens to slaves who disobey me... and that was just the start!' His fingers probed between the reddened buttocks and then jabbed at the soft opening as, in a flash, the 'slave' leapt up, taking his 'master' by surprise. Picking up the whip, the 'slave' struck the back of the older man's head with the handle, knocking him to the floor - momentarily unconscious - and then reached for the holdall he had left by the door. In a fraction of a second he was standing over his 'master' holding a large, curved, broad-bladed knife. He laughed at the almost comical sight below him. This strong, menacing wall of muscle was now lying unconscious, face down with his leather trousers still around his knees.

Suddenly he moved, regaining consciousness by the second, groaning, looking over his shoulder, still in a daze, trying to remember what had happened. The look in the eyes behind the mask turned to one of terror as he saw his 'slave' holding the knife, laughing. It was the laugh of a madman.

'Now who's in control? Now who's got to be punished? Now who's going to DIE!' The razor sharp knife plunged between his buttocks as he let out a heart rending scream. Blood spurted from the wound as the knife went in deeper and then from his mouth as his scream died. The pungent smell of excrement filled the slave's nostrils as he pulled the knife out. 'You can't hurt me now, Daddy, you can't hurt me now...'

CHAPTER FIVE

Michael let himself out of his flat and walked down the stairs. It was a new day and he was going to start his new job. He opened the door, grinning at the hideous stained glass which blocked out nearly all the natural light when it was closed, and looked out at the fresh green grass of the common on the other side of the road. It was a bright, sunny morning and a slight breeze was rustling the leaves on the trees. He breathed deeply as he let the door close behind him and strode off down the road, feeling a deep-seated sense of wellbeing pervading his body and senses. His excursion the night before had made him realise that he really belonged in the capital. Although, on the surface, London held no mystery for him, it was as if he was discovering it all over again. And there was so much to discover.

It was no doubt due to the changes in his own character that had come about as a result of the two years he had spent in Greece. When he had left London at the age of twenty eight to fly off into the unknown, it had raised a few eyebrows. Some of his friends had said that he was running away - that the death of his long-term lover had affected him more deeply than he was letting on. The fact that he had left behind a good job with a decent salary and excellent prospects had disconcerted the more conservative amongst them.

'It's in my nature,' he had said at the time to his close friend and mentor Sebastian. 'When things are going badly, I stick with them until they get better. When they *are* better, what's left to fight for? I need to stimulate my survival instincts or I'm not going to get through this. I have to do it my way.' Sebastian had frowned, so Michael had added 'Anyway, I'm a Capricorn - what do you expect?' Sebastian had given in - and started to wonder what was expected of him as a Scorpio.

Michael remembered feeling that he was going to achieve so many things, remembered the feeling of excitement in the pit of his stomach as the plane had touched down in Athens. All the obstacles to overcome were like pure oxygen to his system. Which island should he go to first? Where was he going to stay? What if he couldn't find work? He had no contacts over there - how was he going to fit in? Within a week he had found an idyllic island, a fantastic apartment overlooking the sea, a job in a local bar and had made more friends than many people encounter in a lifetime. But it had all served its purpose - even if he hadn't known the particular purpose at the time. He now knew that he didn't need a job with a title and material possessions to be what he was. He didn't need to hide behind anything. He was who he was. Alone, except for a rucksack, he had conquered new territory, climbed new heights and grown within himself.

Now here he was on familiar ground, in a city he had previously thought held no more excitement, starting all over again. And he loved it. As he jumped down the steps into the underground station two at a time, he glanced at an advertisement for life insurance and grinned. 'DON'T LET LIFE TAKE YOU BY SURPRISE' it said. Why not, thought Michael, it's what keeps me going. What had he called it each time he had been down to his last handful of drachmae? He remembered the term with a smile: 'Living on the knife-edge of insecurity.'

*   *   *

'And today, on "Family Values", we will be discussing the problem of homosexuality in the family,' Tony smiled sympathetically at the camera, 'a problem affecting more of us than we'd perhaps care to admit. But does it need to be a problem...'

'Yes,' Julia butted in and then squinted at the autocue, 'or is it our attitudes that are wrong? Is ignorance still causing families to split apart?' Tony tried to ignore her caring expression and concentrate on his own.

'Also we have our *new* resident health expert. Dr Leslie McManus,' Tony saw his wife's body tense as he mentioned the doctor's name, 'this time talking about the pros and cons of genital cosmetic surgery...'

'And don't forget our cookery expert Diana Hennessy,' Julia interrupted, wishing she was able to control her blushes, 'who'll be showing us how to whip up a delicious liver casserole in under half an hour!'

* * *

Marilyn looked at the bill from the undertaker and sighed. Life, as ever, was expensive. In this case, though, it was death that was proving to be almost beyond her means. Her mother's funeral, which had taken place just over a month earlier, had now got to be paid for and she wasn't quite sure how she was going to do it. Her savings had been severely depleted in recent years by the extra expense of paying a childminder to look after Zoë while she was working. What remained had been just enough to pay for them to get back from the States. She still kicked herself for not having come back sooner, but she had called her mother at the hospital and had been assured that she was showing signs of recovery. The very day she and Zoë were leaving, the hospital had called to say she had died peacefully in her sleep.

* * *

'Homosexuality,' Julia said carefully, 'is a term ever more common in daily conversation. But how tolerant are we of people whose sexuality differs from the norm? This morning we're discussing the effects homosexuality can have on the family, the problems it can cause and what can be done to avoid it.' In the control booth, the director put his hand to his forehead in total exasperation. Tony managed a forced smile and followed on.

'One of our guests today is Father Declan O'Shaughnessy, a self-confessed gay priest.' Camera one held on the smiling friendly face of the plump Irishman. 'We are also pleased to welcome Dan Daniels, who is editor of 'OutRight' - a leading gay publication - along with Sheila Duncan of the Christian Union of the New Trinity - an organisation still forthrightly opposed to homosexuality in any form. Finally...' Tony didn't quite know what expression he should use to avoid contravening the rules of daytime television etiquette when introducing a transvestite nun, 'I'd like to welcome Sister Insatiable of the Sisters of Perpetual Indulgence.'

Julia beamed at the camera, knowing that this was going to be controversial. Maybe she wasn't keen on queers, but if they boosted her ratings, they were welcome on her show.

*   *   *

Michael got off the tube at Leicester Square, relishing in the fact that he had got a whole hour to kill before starting work. The thrill of knowing a new challenge lay just ahead brought with it a sense of purpose that eradicated any possibility of feeling guilty about wasting time. Like a child set loose in a playground, he thrust his hands into the pockets of his Levi's and trundled off towards Soho. He sauntered past shops and news stands offering magazines which would once have excited him, given him a quick thrill because they were forbidden. He grinned to himself as he remembered the thick brown envelope hidden under the bottom drawer in his bedroom when he had lived at home. The contents had kept alive the conviction that he wasn't the only one with his inclinations, that one day he would be able to satisfy his urges. Of course, that was all in the past. Now he knew what he wanted and how to get it.

Old Compton Street was alive, vibrant and buzzing as he drank in the atmosphere. In only two years, things seemed to have come to life - they were more real, more happening. Three gay café bars had opened during the time he had been away and several more were apparently planned. The area was becoming something of a gay 'village'. The icing on the cake was that his new way of life

87

would allow him time to explore it all at his leisure. Once again it struck him that the pieces of his life seemed to be falling into place rather well.

He walked past the shaded windows of one of his old haunts, a somewhat packed and seedy gay pub, not unaware of the admiring glances coming from a couple of old queens just inside the open door. Grinning to himself, he nonchalantly quickened his pace, darted in front of a taxi, turned a corner and walked into a bright and airy café. To an average passer-by, it looked like a fashionable but wholesome place to stop for coffee or lunch, but Michael knew otherwise. He quickly found himself a seat by the window and browsed through the snack menu. A young, attractive waiter was at his side in an instant. This, thought Michael, was a million miles away from the sleazy image conjured up all those years ago by the forbidden magazines. Bright, clean and healthy. Trendy, but not affected. Not dark, definitely not sleazy, but unmistakably gay.

* * *

'Marilyn.'

'Max!' Marilyn's morning suddenly became more bearable, but a hint of anxiety crept into her thoughts. 'I'm surprised to hear from you so soon. Were those stories I did the other day okay?'

'Oh yes, they were great. But that's not what I'm calling about.' His friendly tone almost allowed her hopes to rise in an unexpected direction. 'I remember you telling me you were something of an expert in Tarot and Astrology... or am I mistaken?'

'Well, I don't profess to be an expert, but I do know a fair bit about it. Why?' Her curiosity was definitely aroused.

'I don't really want to talk about it on the telephone. Are you free tomorrow? Can you come over at about eleven? I think it would be worth your while.'

* * *

'So you're trying to tell me that you can see nothing wrong with the way you lead your life? I just pray that God has mercy on your soul. He is there for everyone. He sees everything.' Sheila Duncan's opinions were in full flight. 'Just remember next time your carnal urges threaten to overcome you that He still *wants* you. I'm not pretending that I'm perfect…'

'Too damn right you're not!' Dan Daniels cut in. 'I expect "sex" to you is what the coal comes in. Get a life, woman!'

'I think what the young man means,' attempted Father O'Shaughnessy, 'is that we have had enough of people trying to make out that we are abnormal. All we want is tolerance and acceptance.'

'And how am I meant to tolerate something I find totally abhorrent and disgusting,' Sheila twittered.

'The same way we have to put up with your bigotry,' Dan muttered under his breath, unable to take any of it seriously. He had taken too long coming to terms with his sexuality, getting to like himself as a person, to let this woman or anyone else preach to him about what he should or shouldn't do.

* * *

'More coffee, Marjorie?' Kathleen blurted out. The bone china cup rattled on its saucer as she wished she had chosen another morning, any other morning, to ask her friends around to watch her son's show. They usually chose such interesting subjects. Why oh why had they chosen this one? It was bad enough having to think about sex at all, but sex between men…

* * *

'Don't I know you from somewhere?' The question came from a man at the next table.

'I don't think so, but I've got no objections to rectifying that. I'm Michael.' He put his hand out to shake the stranger's hand. 'I've got to go to work in a minute, but maybe I'll see you there – "Crews" in St. Martin's Lane.'

'Maybe,' said his new acquaintance, 'but I'm sure I've seen you before. I never forget a handsome face. See you around.' He got up and walked towards the door leaving Michael smiling to himself. No matter how often it happened, it was still an ego boost when a good looking man chatted him up. Not that he had an ego problem anymore, but everyone liked a compliment now and again. Anyway, it really was time to go to work. It wouldn't look good to be late on his first day. He paid his bill, leaving a good tip for the waiter, and headed back down Old Compton Street. As he passed a newsagents, he couldn't help catching sight of a copy of TV Times on the rack outside. He grinned to himself at the picture of the beaming couple on the cover. Two years ago it would have made him feel jealous, made him think he hadn't achieved as much as he should. Thank goodness all that had changed. Now he could deal with other people's achievements – even his brother's - without measuring them against his own, without feeling inadequate as a result. He could even feel happy about it and fortunate - fortunate that he hadn't lost his identity in the way Tony had. Forcing himself to keep the sadness that threatened to creep into his thoughts at bay, he wondered if it would ever be possible to repair his relationship with his brother. Why should he feel guilty? He put it out of his mind and quickened his pace. He was definitely looking forward to his shift behind the bar. Today was going to be a good day.

* * *

'Sex is for procreation within the sanctity of marriage and for *nothing* else!' Sheila Duncan was on her hobby horse again, safe in the knowledge that God was with her.

'And where does that leave us?' asked Sister Insatiable calmly. 'Celibate?'

'Well, you *are* a nun!' Julia got a word in at last, delighted that she had made a joke.

'Precisely!' Dan Daniels interjected. 'I must have underestimated your understanding of the Sisters' cause. You've hit the nail on the head!' Julia, lost for words yet again, looked over to her husband.

'And this is where we have to pause for a break,' was all Tony could offer.

* * *

'Ooh, they certainly get to the heart of the matter don't they Kath?' Marjorie was having the best fun she had had since Kathleen had confided in her twenty years earlier about her husband's penchant for wearing ladies' underwear. The strain of keeping the secret had nearly killed her, but this was making up for it. 'I never knew your Tony knew so much about... you know... that sort of thing.'

'Nor did I, Marjorie. It must be all those television people he mixes with.' Kathleen was finding that she had marked reservations about the influence this new career was having on her son. She had prayed more than once that Michael would get over the phase he had been going through, but for Tony to go off the rails as well...

'Well, I think I missed the point.' Betty wasn't going to be excluded from the conversation, even if she was a bit hard of hearing. ' But in my day, nuns never wore make-up.'

* * *

'Welcome back to "Family Values", where the topic of conversation is homosexuality and its effects on the family. Dan Daniels, editor of 'OutRight', has brought along some extracts from a video he has been promoting entitled "The Gay Man's Guide to Safer Sex". Now, Dan, perhaps you would like to enlighten the viewers on why you think this video is so important.' Julia smiled her 'woman of the world' smile and pointed her chin at the leather-clad young man, glad that she had got the show back on an even keel.

'If you think I'm going to sit here and let pornography be promoted under my nose,' Sheila almost shouted, 'then I'm afraid...'

'Please Sheila!' Tony put his hand up in an attempt to pacify her. 'We're here to discuss this calmly and openly as adults. Dan is going to tell us about this informative guide to...'

'Sodom and Gomorrah! If this is what the world has come to...'

'Please, please my dear,' Father O'Shaughnessy muttered, 'let the boy tell us about it or we'll never know.'

91

'Thank you Father,' Dan said quietly. 'As Julia was saying, this is a new video, approved by the Terence Higgins Trust, aimed at helping gay men achieve more from sex while reducing the risk from HIV and other infections. As we all know, ignorance is dangerous,' he paused, looking pointedly at Sheila Duncan, 'and the more we can do to let men know what puts them at risk and what doesn't, the nearer we will get to stopping the spread of the virus.'

'Wouldn't abstinence be more effective?' Sheila blurted out.

'Ooh no love,' said Sister Insatiable, adjusting his wimple, 'it just makes the heart grow fonder!'

* * *

'And what the bloody hell did that achieve?' Trevor was annoyed. 'I can't think why you watch this crap!'

'Language Trevor! Remember I'm an old lady.' Iris was amused that he had let the show irritate him.

'Old lady? If you're an old lady, I'm Greta Garbo!' he snorted,

'Well, you do walk a bit like her sometimes when you're not concentrating...'

* * *

'Hello again!' Michael looked up from pulling a pint to see the stranger from earlier smiling at him. He had known that the guy would take up the hint he had dropped and call in to see him at work. The strange thing was that he really didn't care that much whether he did or not. Yes, the man was attractive. Yes, he felt attracted to him. Yes, he liked to know that he still had 'pulling power'. But he wasn't necessarily going to take it any further. Michael had very rarely taken anything when it was offered to him on a plate. 'A bottle of Sol, when you've got a moment,' the man continued, 'and one for yourself.'

'I'm allergic to lime,' Michael grinned, banking on the fact that it was safe to flirt because he had still got to work for hours. Anyway, this chap *was* seriously good looking. 'But maybe I'll risk it if you tell me your name.'

'Bruce.'

92

'That's five fifty then please, Bruce.' Michael took his money and smiled to himself as he rang it up on the till. It was strange how accomplished he felt as a barman. Career wise it was a step down. It was hard work, the hours were long, the bar was noisy and full of smoke, but he loved it. He gave Bruce his change, thanked him with a wink and moved on to another customer.

He caught sight of one of the murals on the wall opposite - a series of life-size semi-nude sailors which gave the bar its name and realised that he was as much a part of the place as they were. He and his fellow barmen, all in faded Levi's and lumberjack shirts with the sleeves cut off, contributed to the overall image of the place. It was a busy night and he was hardly in a position to stand around idly thinking about life and its meaning, but one thought never left him - that he was, quite possibly, the most fortunate person in the place.

'Two pints of Budweiser *when* you can be bothered!' an angry voice, belonging to an even more angry face, asked loudly through the seething mass of pectoral muscles, biceps and faces. It was nice, Michael mused, to see people out enjoying themselves. He loved it when customers were rude, because he never lost his cool and it *really* got their goat.

'Two pints of Fosters then?' he asked the angry face.

*   *   *

'The one time I needed you - the *one* time you could *actually* have been of use helping me control those... those... *perverts* - what did you do? I'll tell you what you did, Tony Barkworth. Nothing!' Julia stomped out of the dressing room.

'Life's a bitch,' Tony mumbled to himself, 'and then you marry one.'

*   *   *

'Aren't you going to be late for work?' Iris changed tack. Trevor was still sulking about her comment on the way he walked. It had been a joke, but she couldn't deny the fact that he did mince a bit.

'Yes, I'd better be going.' He picked up his black leather jacket and stood up to put it on. 'Have you seen my stilettos anywhere?'

'Oh, don't get sensitive on me. You're meant to be a big leather master.' Iris looked at the accentuated and well-rehearsed figure of masculinity standing in front of her. 'Don't tell me you're going to let an old bag like me upset you.'

'I'm sorry.' Trevor smiled at last. 'It's just that I work hard at being a real person - or at least being the *same* person all the time. I see these stockbrokers and accountants slipping into their rubber and leather on a Friday night - even though they've been in pinstripes all week - and I feel sorry for them. I just want to be *me*. I wouldn't like to think that I'm trying to be something I'm not.'

'As long as you're happy and you're not hurting anybody, you don't need to keep justifying yourself.' Iris was sorry she had upset him.

'Well,' the glint had returned to his eye, 'I only hurt them when they want me to!'

* * *

'And for those of you who missed his first appearance on the show, I'd like to introduce Dr Leslie McManus.' Julia made a good impression of oozing pleasantness as she beamed at their next guest who had been a definite hit with the female viewers if the faxes and telephone calls received at the studio were anything to go by. 'Now, Leslie, you're here to reveal the secrets of female genital cosmetic surgery – a subject of which most of our viewers are probably totally unaware.'

'Yes.' Tony realised there was a real danger of being pushed out of the limelight by the expert medic. 'There's been a lot of publicity surrounding the revolutionary operation available in America which... er .... shall we say... enhances the dimensions of a man's pride and joy, but what about women who may be unhappy about the state of their... er...' For once Julia didn't interrupt and watched gleefully as her husband blushed the colour of her scarlet Jaeger mohair two-piece. Luckily Leslie McManus came to his rescue.

'Yes... a lot of women have undergone surgery to parts of their bodies previously thought of as unchangeable.' Camera two zoomed in on the doctor's perfect features, allowing Tony a brief respite in which to cool down.

'Can you be a bit more specific, Leslie?' Julia asked enquiringly, still watching her husband squirm out of the corner of her eye.

'Well... one of the most commonly-requested operations in this field is what we call perineorrhapy - tightening of the vaginal walls. It's nearly always requested by women in their thirties and forties who have had children. Then there is liposuction on the mons pubis - the pad of fat above the vagina covered in pubic hair. This, incidentally, is the most purely cosmetic of the surgery available. It is also possible to trim the labia minora - the small inner lips of the vagina.' He paused for a moment, noting Julia's fascination and Tony's continuing discomfort. 'But the most bizarre surgery available - to my mind anyway - is the repair of the hymen.'

*   *   *

'Bugger me!' Iris exclaimed from her armchair. 'Talk about locking the stable door after the horse has bolted...'

*   *   *

'So you mean it's possible for a woman to have her virginity surgically restored?' Julia asked, wide-eyed. 'Is there much call for that?'

'Oh yes,' Leslie continued, 'mostly from young Muslim women who have tasted the freedom of the Western world but have to appear to be intact on their wedding nights.'

'And is it expensive?' Julia couldn't resist finding out, despite the fact that she was meant to be asking about the psychological aspects of the topic.

'It varies... but the operation would usually cost between one and two thousand pounds.' Leslie could see that she was completely fascinated by the idea. 'But the point we haven't touched on yet is that there are dangers involved in having these operations

95

available.'

'What... you mean they can go wrong?' Julia asked gleefully.

'No, I wasn't referring to that side of it. My concern...' he paused in a caring fashion for a moment, '... is that some women may transfer what is essentially a psychological problem into a non-existent physical one. Particularly in the current era of sexual liberation and all it entails, there is an increased pressure to have a beautiful body and know how to use it to satisfy your partner. Many surgeons insist on counselling prospective patients to make sure the problem really is physical.'

'But surely,' Julia leaned over towards him again, her fingers gently brushing the fabric of his trousers, 'if a woman wants something altered and can afford to pay for the operation, whose business is it apart from hers?'

* * *

Marilyn slammed the iron down on the ironing board and sighed. She had just about got used to seeing Julia's face on the screen, but it still worried her that a woman like her was in a position to express her views to the nation. In other ways, though, she felt sorry for her.

'You can pay to have your life tightened and trimmed as much as you like,' she murmured to herself, 'but the best things always happen by accident.'

* * *

Michael smiled to himself as the simple action of restocking the fridge with bottles of beer jolted his memory. Mykonos... a bar by the harbour... night after night of bustling holidaymakers in search of sea, sun and sex. Oh yes, there had been as much of that on offer as he could handle. A plentiful supply made it easier to abstain. He grinned. Despite the atmosphere in which he was working, he still felt smugly immune to the incessant exchange of sexual electricity all around him. He was glad, he reflected, that he didn't have to base his whole life around sex. No, he could handle his sex drive - most of the time. But there were still those times when that little

devil inside him - or was it inside his trousers - got going and then
there was no holding him back. He shook his head and thought that
there were times when he even shocked himself. Oh well, as long as
it didn't happen too often…

* * *

'You've got to learn to control your embarrassment on screen,
Tony,' Julia twittered as she searched in her handbag for a nail file.
'You don't want the viewers thinking you're unprofessional do
you?' Her husband remained silent, keeping his hands on the wheel
and his eyes on the road ahead. 'Do you?'

'Do I what?'

'Oh… I don't know why I bother trying to help you!' There were
times when he totally exasperated her. 'If you're going to go all
silent on me and disappear into yourself, there's nothing I can do.'

'I know.'

* * *

'Just in case you decide you might want to use it, here's my
number.' Bruce had slipped back into the bar while Michael was
busy serving customers. 'Speak to you later.' He turned and was
gone before Michael could say anything.

* * *

'Mummy Marilyn!' Zoë walked out of the classroom carefully
clutching a little parcel. Her eyes were shining and Marilyn
marvelled at the child's enthusiasm. 'Look … it's for you. We just
finished them today. Claire Shackleford's one exploded in the kiln,
but mine came out perfectly.' She held out her offering and Marilyn
took it.

'Can I open it now?' She could see the other mothers going
through similar motions. Zoë nodded furiously and watched open-
mouthed as her guardian gently peeled back the brown paper. Inside
was a little blue-glazed clay bowl with meticulously scalloped
edges. Marilyn could see the care and attention to detail that had
been poured into the creation of the little object and felt a lump
form in her throat. 'Oh Zoë… it's the best thing I've ever been

given. Thank you darling!'

'It's a popery dish,' Zoë informed her proudly, waiting eagerly for a reaction. 'You know... you put dried flowers and things that smell nice in it.'

* * *

'Hello Julia... I watched you again today. I suppose you think you've made it...' It was the same gravely voice on the end of the line filling her with dread. A feeling of nausea rose from the pit of her stomach. Thank God Tony wasn't there. She didn't want him getting involved in this. 'So successful, but you could lose it all if a few of your secrets just happened to get out. Wouldn't it be a shame to end your career when it was only just beginning...'

'What do you want? Tell me... tell me! I'll get it for you. *Just leave me alone*!' For the second time that day, Julia felt out of control. 'I don't know what it is you know... but...'

'Why are you upset about it then? If you've got nothing to hide, what is there to fear?' The line went dead.

* * *

Michael was tired. Ten hours behind a bar was enough to wear anyone out, but it had been a good day as far as tips were concerned. And he was happy. It may have only been his first day at a part-time job, but it was another achievement. He put his key in the big old front door and pushed it open. Home. It really did feel like home, even though he had only just moved in. He trod lightly on the stairs so as not to disturb the people in the ground floor flat and let himself into his new domain. As he flicked a switch, the red bulb in the Indian lantern cast a glow over his living space and the gothic arches threw macabre shadows. He stripped off his boots, shirt and Levi's in the kitchen, walked through to the living room and flopped onto the kilim-covered sofa. He reached for the television remote control. It was great having all these mod cons - and it was great to be able to feel justified in lounging around and taking advantage of them. He had taught himself not to feel guilty for taking time to do nothing. The first time this realisation had struck him marked a milestone in his personal growth. But he couldn't ignore the nagging thought at the back of his mind that things were going a bit too well. Wasn't it at times like these that a big grey cloud used to appear on the horizon?

He flicked somewhat disinterestedly through the channels and wondered why there was never anything worth watching when he had time to do so. Getting up to go to the kitchen for something to eat, he noticed a card poking out from the pocket of his discarded jeans. Bruce. A smile came to his face. There was no harm in giving him a ring.

*   *   *

The telephone rang again and Julia hesitated for a few moments trying to decide whether or not to answer it. Surely he wouldn't ring twice in one evening? If only Tony was back from wherever he had gone off to. If only she wasn't sitting in this big house on her own. She lifted the brandy glass to her lips again and reached gingerly for the receiver.

'Hello?'

'Julia... it's Serena. Just ringing to say thanks for last night. We both...' she paused, remembering the mood Max had been in on the way home '... enjoyed it tremendously!'

'Oh, glad to hear it. I'm just having a little drink... why don't you go and get one? I hate to drink alone!' Julia simpered.

'Oh, alright then... hold on a moment.' Serena clattered off as Julia waited with her ear to the receiver, imagining her friend in her huge house - her ancestral home... to the manner born. More than anything in the world, Julia found herself wanting to be Serena. 'Hi... I'm back. So, what kind of day have you had?' Serena thought of her own uneventful life and envied Julia for having a purpose. 'How was the show? I really must watch it sometime.' She couldn't possibly admit that she sat glued to the television every morning.

*   *   *

'Come in... come in!' Bruce was beaming from ear to ear as he opened the door to his apartment. 'I wasn't sure if you'd call, but

99

I'm glad you did.' He moved back to allow Michael to come in. 'As a matter of fact, if you hadn't rung tonight, you'd have missed me. I've got to go abroad on business tomorrow and I won't be back for a while. Can I get you a drink?' He wandered into the kitchen as Michael surveyed the flat. It was smaller than he had expected from the outside - evidently converted from one room of the huge house it was in. An open staircase led up to a galleried sleeping area and bathroom. The kitchen was tucked away underneath. Compact and stylishly furnished, it seemed to echo Bruce's lifestyle. For the first time, Michael realised he wanted to know more about him.

'Yes, I'd love one. What have you got?'

'Beer, whisky, vodka... you name it. I suppose it makes a change for someone else to be getting you a drink?'

'Yeah... I suppose it does. Mind you, it was only my first day on the job.'

'Well, you certainly look the part. But that's enough about work. What are you into?' His directness took Michael by surprise.

'How do you mean?'

'You know... what do you like to do in bed? Who's your ideal man?'

'Er... I don't really know. It might sound like a bit of a cop-out, but it depends on the occasion... and the mood I'm in.'

'So you're single?' Bruce's no-nonsense manner was impressive, but not altogether welcome.

'Yes... yes... I have been for a couple of years now.' He thought suddenly of Peter and wasn't sure that it had been a good idea to come here. Could anyone ever replace him?

'So am I. It's the way I like it really, even if my mother does keep asking when I'm going to take Mr Right home to meet her!'

'Your mother? You mean she doesn't mind about...'

'No, she loves it. It makes her feel she's being "socially aware" or whatever they call it. Mind you, I can't see her being very impressed with me taking a different man to meet her every week!'

* * *

Marilyn rooted around in the cupboard and finally found the packet of pot-pourri she had been looking for. She wanted Zoë to see that she was using the dish when she came down for breakfast in the morning. The piece of lovingly-crafted pottery meant more to her at that moment than any other possession. Not for the first time, she pitied Zoë's natural mother for what she was missing.

* * *

'That's it... aaah... yeah... aaah...' Bruce freely expressed his enjoyment at their lovemaking. Their clothes were strewn up the staircase and on the floor of the bedroom. The complete lack of pretence and artifice in the situation gave Michael a feeling of liberation. Any hint of regret at having come over had disappeared. The bed creaked as they writhed together in well-matched passion.

'Aaah... I'm going to come!' Michael was losing control.

'Let it go... let it go.... yeah.... yeah.... aaaaah!' Bruce shouted as his body tensed and then relaxed in unison with Michael's. They lay in a satisfied heap on the bed.

Bruce grinned as he reached out for something to mop up with, not realising that it was Michael's T-shirt.

CHAPTER SIX

'Shit!' Michael sat bolt upright in bed and reached out to switch on the light as the alarm on his watch bleeped annoyingly. Bruce rolled over beside him and opened his eyes.

'What's the matter?' He looked over at the clock.. 'It's only five thirty for goodness' sake.'

'I've got to be in Brixton at six. I told you last night, but I think your mind was on other things!' Michael grinned as he searched for his underpants and found them draped over the bedside lamp. 'Don't get up... I've got to dash!' Bruce looked on in mild amusement as Michael ran around the apartment gathering his clothes.

'I'll be back in about ten days. Call me...' he shouted, as Michael disappeared out of the door.

*   *   *

Tony yawned as he walked into the bathroom to find Julia with one foot up on the lavatory waxing her legs. He grimaced at her rear view - rolls of fat spilling over her pink lace panties - and found himself reminded of a Sumo wrestler. Not feeling quite up to dealing with this sight at such an early hour, he quietly retreated to use another bathroom. Julia's squeals of pain reached his ears as he ran a bath and braced himself to face another day.

*   *   *

Michael shivered as he ran along the road to Charing Cross station. He swore under his breath as he realised he had left his bomber jacket in Bruce's flat. There was no way he had time to go back for it. He felt in the pocket of his jeans and breathed a sigh of relief at finding his wallet and keys there. Another disaster averted, he thought calmly. And it gave him a good excuse to call Bruce again. While he couldn't decide exactly what he thought about his new acquaintance, the fact that he was going to be away for ten days gave him the chance to think about it as his leisure. No rush, he thought, as he hurried down the steps to the underground station.

* * *

Tony felt a bit more in control of his life as he flicked his dark hair away from his face and splashed some Givenchy on his freshly shaven cheeks. The after shave made his skin tingle as it permeated the pores. He stretched his arms out and clapped his hands together. A bath always made a world of difference. Julia looked at him with blood-shot eyes as he walked back into their bedroom. She was in her underwear, fully made up, obviously trying to decide what to wear. Considering how dreadful she looked first thing in the morning, he mused, she didn't make a bad job of herself. The weight problem was, however, becoming more evident by the day.

'What do you think?' she asked earnestly, standing up and holding out her arms. 'I've lost three pounds since Monday.'

'Yes... I can see,' he lied, watching the way she smiled to herself at his recognition of her efforts. There were times when he genuinely felt something for her. She was really as insecure and scared as he was. He just wished she could admit it and let them forge ahead together.

'You're not going to wear that are you?' She eyed the lightweight suit from Kenzo he was taking out of the wardrobe. He had chosen it himself and had been looking forward to wearing it. 'No.... no... far too young for you. I can't think why you bought it!'

* * *

It was just before six as Michael leapt up the escalator at Brixton tube station and emerged into the daylight again. He dashed across the road, narrowly avoiding a double decker bus and a cyclist, and ran as fast as he could to the entrance of the office building. The ageing security guard, who had grown accustomed to his face by now, opened the door and looked totally nonplussed as Michael hastily greeted him and then ran up the stairs two at a time.

'Nice to see a young chap so eager to get to work,' he muttered to himself, wishing he had the energy, not to mention the motivation.

John was tidying up the office from the night shift as he burst in, gasping for breath.

'Hi Troy... I mean Michael,' John said brightly, 'you're a bit late.' He took a closer look at Michael and frowned. 'What's that awful mess down the front of your T-shirt?'

* * *

Beryl Handsworth felt in the pocket of her coat for her bunch of keys and marched purposefully down the steps to the basement flat. This was always a good one to start with - Mr Hefford lived on his own and there was never much cleaning to do, even though she only did it once a week. A quick run around with the hoover and a bit of a dust and a polish were all it usually needed. The kitchen and the bathroom were never really dirty, not like some. Oh no. Some of them thought they were so clever with their big jobs and their big cars, but she'd seen the other side of them; kitchens encrusted with the leftovers of Chinese takeaways, bathrooms looking as if people didn't train their kids to aim straight anymore, overflowing cat litter trays... If only she had more clients like Mr Hefford, her life would be a lot easier.

Turning the key in the lock, she pushed the door and walked in. The flat was unusually warm and she wondered if the central heating had been left on, but that wasn't like him. He was usually very careful and methodical - everything was always in its place. She sniffed. There was a dreadful smell in the air, as if something had gone off. Beryl wrinkled her nose and went to investigate. The second door leading from the hall was ajar. Now *there* was a strange thing. That room was always firmly locked. She had assumed that it was an office or something and had never had occasion to worry about it.

'Mr Hefford?' It had suddenly occurred to her that he might be at home. That would account for the heating being on, although it wasn't cold outside, not like it had been the other night. 'Mr Hefford? Are you there?' She pushed the door open and froze in terror as the light from the hallway shone into the black-painted room.

*   *   *

'The rising tide of violence,' Tony announced as if it was the title of a new film. 'What is its cause... where did it come from... whom is responsible?'

'Yes,' Julia said, trying to keep her eyes still as she read the autocue. 'Does it begin at home? Has the disintegration of family values led to this sad state of affairs?'

'Let me introduce our first guest today,' Tony gushed, 'Leading historian and anthropologist Dr Henry Wilkinson. Henry...' he paused and smiled briefly at the camera as the historian winced, 'you apparently have the opinion that things aren't in fact as bad as we think. How on earth can you think that? What about... er... um...' Tony wished, not for the first time, that he had stuck to the script as Julia butted in.

'Let the doctor speak. *He's* the expert, after all.'

'Thank you,' Henry Wilkinson was bitterly regretting having agreed to come on this travesty of a show. He could have written a thesis on the social hang-ups of this couple already... and he couldn't begin to speculate about their sexual behaviour. 'I think you are referring to my view that there is not, in fact, a "rising tide of violence" as you so dramatically put it, but an increased trend in reporting it, discussing it and searching for its cause. As with anything, there are natural fluctuations, but we can't honestly say that the level of violence is any higher now than it was in, say, the nineteenth century. To be honest, it's a lot lower.' He paused to allow the presenters to show their shared ignorance. 'One of the problems of today is the sensationalisation of certain violent crimes and incidents by the media which can then result in subsequent similar happenings which wouldn't have happened otherwise.'

'You mean like copy-cat crime?' Julia felt she had been quiet for far too long.

'Well, I suppose so, but I was meaning it in a rather broader sense. It coincides with the argument that children become violent as a result of watching incessant violence on television. Many will disagree with me, but it is true that violence breeds violence. In letting children watch it, we are to a certain extent condoning it. In reporting violent crime in great detail, we make it something worthy of attention. Most people, at some time in their life, crave attention.' He paused again, looking at the two presenters. 'So what do they turn to when all else fails?'

'Oh,' said Julia, glancing desperately at her programme notes, 'and I suppose that explains the particularly sexual nature of a lot of the violence nowadays.' She hoped it did. Otherwise she was lost.

'Well,' Henry continued, 'that is a slightly different matter and an exceedingly fascinating one. We must all have noticed the recent trend for *talking* about sex and sexual matters. You can hardly open a newspaper or turn on the television without being faced with someone's view on new positions or methods of achieving an orgasm.' He paused again, watching Julia blush. 'The main problem with this, I believe, is that we - as a nation - are not able to deal with sexual intercourse as a concept. This is probably a legacy from Victorian times, but is still very much with us. Since it has become fashionable, and indeed sometimes obligatory, to discuss all this openly and supposedly without embarrassment,' he glanced sideways at Julia again, 'the pressure on those who still can't deal with sexual intercourse in its many forms has increased tenfold.'

'I don't quite grasp your meaning,' Tony said without thinking.

'No,' said the doctor, 'I didn't think you would.'

* * *

'He's got *you* sussed, love!' Iris had switched the television on to see what Julia was up to and was, as usual, enjoying the spectacle the husband and wife team were making of themselves. It had quite taken her mind off the latest bills that had been thrust through her rusty letterbox. Who cared about bills anyway? She would soon be beyond all that. She looked again at the screen and saw Julia trying to be sophisticated. She shook her head and clicked her tongue against her dentures. 'If I've said it once, I've said it a thousand times - you can't make a silk purse out of a sow's ear!'

*   *   *

Serena awoke with a tremendous hangover. She looked up at the delicate muslin drapes around the ancient four poster bed - so white, so pretty, so pure. They seemed to be mocking her as she lay in self-inflicted agony and ran her tongue over the residue left in her mouth by excesses of rich food and alcohol. If she were a wealthy woman in a soap opera, she thought to herself, she would wake up with her handsome lover beside her and roll over towards him, lips pouting and nipples pert, for a bit of early morning erotic exercise. Serena's lips were crumpled, her breasts sagging and her breath acrid and foul tasting. It was probably just as well, for his sake, that her husband wasn't anywhere to be seen.

As she moved to sit up, it felt as if someone had dropped a concrete block on her head. Why oh why did she have to drink so much? She gave up the idea of sitting up and put her head back on the pillow. By the looks of it, Max hadn't slept in the bed with her at all. His nights in the spare room were getting more and more frequent. Maybe she would be able to bring him round later. Somehow she couldn't convince herself that this would be easy. If only she could get rid of this hangover. A bit more sleep should do it. She slid her hands back under the covers and realised she had wet the bed.

*   *   *

'Good Morning... National Datelines. This is Troy speaking, how can I help you?' Michael was on his own in the office. He had consulted the rota and was meant to be working with someone called Edward who hadn't yet materialised. He was quite enjoying his own company.

'Er... my name's Marjorie. I've got a message on your lines and I'd like to take it off if possible.'

'No problem. What's your reference number?'

'Oh... just let me see... wait a minute.' Michael laughed to himself as he imagined the woman fumbling in her handbag. 'Here it is. F279.'

'And your date of birth?'

'Don't be personal!'

'Look - I need it to make sure that really is your reference number. Otherwise, anyone could ring up and cancel your message.'

'Oh... I am sorry. I thought you were being nosey. It's the fifteenth of January 1935,' she said quickly. 'And to save you adding it up I'm fifty eight!'

'Right, just a minute while I check it out.' Accessing information on the computer was second nature to him now. 'Yes... I can take that off line for you within the hour. If you don't mind me asking, why do you want to cancel it? Didn't you have any luck?'

'Ooh no... quite the opposite. I found just the man I was looking for. I think it's a wonderful service you're offering.'

'Glad to hear it. Thanks for using National Datelines.'

'Thank you love. Bye bye.' She rang off leaving Michael laughing to himself. He couldn't really picture a fifty eight year old woman getting a blind date on the telephone. It intrigued him to think of it... she could almost be his mother! Unable to resist the temptation, he put on the headphones and accessed her message from the bank of audio data.

'I'm a widow in my fifties seeking a younger man - around thirty five -for a mutually rewarding and satisfying relationship. I'm fit and active and enjoy walking, theatre and cinema, as well as eating out and maybe staying in with a bottle of wine. My friends tell me

I'm still attractive and I'm known for my high spirits and like to live life to the full. If you think you might be the man for me, please get in touch - my reference number is F279.'

Another satisfied customer, he thought to himself.

* * *

'What do you mean? Are you trying to tell me that he was looking down his nose at us?' Julia had assumed one of her puzzled expressions and was, quite frankly, not all that interested in what her husband was telling her during the commercial break.

'Not exactly, Julia, I just think he was sending us up. It might be an idea for us to spend a bit more time studying our subject matter in future.'

'I'm not going to let some stuck-up psychologist tell me how to conduct my bloody show. I bet we earn more than him anyway'.'

'Nice and quiet please. Coming out of the break now.' The floor manager's voice made them both look up and realise their next guest had already joined them on the sofa. 'Five... four... three... two...'

'And welcome back to "Family Values". I'm Tony Barkworth...'

'And I'm Julia Daley and...'

'With us on the sofa is Barry Sugden - a man who describes himself as a media magnate, but is better known in the press as a porn king.' Tony shifted nervously on the sofa, hoping that Max hadn't told their guest about his journalistic foray into the world of telephone dating. Camera two picked up the short, fat man sitting with his legs apart and a rosy-cheeked grin on his face.

'I'm also one of the richest men in the country,' he croaked smugly.

* * *

Marilyn sat nervously in the waiting room at Max's office. She wished now that she had asked him what this meeting was about. It hadn't seemed like a big deal at the time, but now she wasn't so sure.

'Do you mind if I put the television on?' It was a petite blonde girl who broke the silence. She had been sitting in the corner reading a magazine and Marilyn had hardly noticed her.

'No, not at all. Please go ahead.' The screen came to life, revealing a close-up of Julia Daley talking to the dumpy little guest. The blonde girl suddenly became animated.

'Ooh... I'd like to slam my fist right in that ugly mouth of yours!' she mumbled at the screen, her face contorted into a painful grimace.

'Do you know her?' Marilyn was surprised.

'No, I'm talking about him! Barry Sugden. I knew he was going to be on. I suppose I must be a bit of a masochist wanting to watch it. Smeggy little git owes me over a grand.' She paused for a moment, noticing Marilyn's somewhat bemused expression. 'Sorry... I got a bit carried away there. Anyway, I'm Vikki. I'm a photographer. I'm down here to sell photos. You know... for adverts. What are you here for?'

'Oh... I do voice-overs.' Marilyn wasn't sure what to make of this bubbly little blonde bombshell and wasn't going to impart her own life story in return. 'Who *is* this guy then?'

'What? Barry Sugden? Where the hell've you been for the last few years?'

'America,' Marilyn answered succinctly, making Vikki giggle.

'That told me, didn't it! Seriously, though, he's fast becoming a household name.' They both looked at the screen again where Julia was engrossed in a conversation with Sugden about the house he had just finished building in Essex.

'Yeah, it's a scaled-down version of Buckingham Palace... new bricks of course... with an indoor swimming pool, gym, sauna *and* an Egyptian jacuzzi.'

'What on earth do you do with twenty five bedrooms?' Julia asked wide-eyed.

'I could tell you!' Vikki sniggered. Marilyn was still a bit lost.

'What does he *do* then?'

'In his bedrooms?'

'No... why is he becoming a household name?'

'He's a porn king. Along the lines of Paul Raymond, but far more sleazy. Made his first million ages ago selling tits and bums videos as hard core - advertising titles like "Girls With Animals" and sending out films of a girl with her top off throwing a stick for her dog. Apparently, very few people ever complain about that kind of thing. I suppose they're too embarrassed.'

'So what's the big deal?'

'Oh... he's got a newspaper now - if you could call it that -called the Daily Nation. Full of sex scandals and "my grandmother's an alien" type stories, but it sells like hot cakes. Max runs all the lines for him. Anyway, recently he's been trying to buy several regional papers. It's caused a bit of a stir because he could become the next Rupert Murdoch. The implications are quite far-reaching. As one MP said last week: "The moral fibre of the nation is at risk!" They both looked back at the television screen as Julia finally finished talking about the gaudy details of his house and reluctantly let Tony move onto more serious matters.

'You have vehemently defended your motives for acquiring the regional newspapers you have bought, assuring the readers that they are not going to be inundated with topless women and stories of sex scandal...'

'Not unless they want it!' Sugden was getting more smug by the moment.

'He really makes me want to throw up,' Vikki said pointedly, 'D'you know what he said to me when I went to his office to get the money for a load of photos he'd used? He said that if I wanted to be paid I should get on my knees under his desk like a good little girl and...'

'No!' Marilyn didn't want to imagine what the contents of this fat little man's underpants were like.

'Yes... it's apparently standard procedure for all his models. I must be the only female photographer he's ever encountered, so I suppose he thought I ought to do the same.'

'I take it you didn't...' Marilyn stopped herself and blushed. She had been enjoying the gossip.

'Too bloody right I didn't. I need the money, but not that badly! Oh... and back to the subject of all those bedrooms, d'you know that he has a bevy of girls he keeps pregnant?'

'What?' Marilyn couldn't believe what she was hearing.

'Yes... he can apparently only get it up properly for women who are heavily pregnant. They stay in a separate wing in his house... greased up and ready for when he gets the urge.' Vikki was in her element, but Marilyn was beginning to feel rather sick.

'Has he got loads of kids then?'

'Well... no. That's the strange thing about it. There isn't a nursery in his house...'

Max suddenly appeared in the doorway, seeming taller and more healthy-looking than ever.

'Marilyn! Lovely to see you. I must say you're looking rather well. Vikki... Alex will be out to see you in a moment. Marilyn, come through please. There's someone I want you to meet.' He ushered her into his private office where a distinguished-looking middle aged man was waiting. 'Marilyn this is Harvey Wolfenden. Harvey this is Marilyn Mitchell.'

* * *

'Well, I don't see what the problem is. He wanted to talk about his new house, so I did. I must say, it sounded quite nice. Who cares whether or not he buys all the bloody newspapers in the country? That's not the kind of thing our viewers want to hear about.' Julia had had enough. Her legs were still stinging from the waxing session and now Tony was trying to tell her that she had messed up the interview with the media magnate. 'And what's wrong with Essex, anyway?' Grabbing her Gucci handbag, she delved inside for the car keys and threw them at Tony. 'You'll have to drive home on your own. I'm meeting Serena in town. She's helping me choose furniture for the conservatory.'

112

* * *

Washing down another Nurofen with her second glass of wine, Serena eyed the firm buttocks of the departing waiter. Her eyes then moved up to her reflection in the large gilt-framed mirror on the wall opposite. She had squeezed herself into a black Versace suit in attempt to at least *look* good for this shopping spree even if she felt like death. As a result - with her scraped-back hair and large dark glasses - she looked like a drag queen doing a Jackie Onassis impression. So what, she thought, taking another gulp. She glanced at the menu again, wishing that Julia would hurry up and arrive. Julia. A smile formed on her lips and she purred inwardly at the power she had over her friend. Power to make her buy the most hideous and expensive things. Power to make her almost think she liked them. Her smile faded. It was the only power she had left...

* * *

Max could see Harvey was impressed with Marilyn. The way he had relaxed and sat back in his chair betrayed the fact that he felt at ease with her. He was currently explaining his new project.

'I'm basically looking for a competent and reliable astrologer who sounds good on tape for the premium rate lines... that's where Max fits in,' he was going to continue by telling her about the possibility of a regular spot on his television show, but thought against it. There would be plenty of time for that when he'd seen and heard what she could come up with. She certainly looked the part, her long dark hair falling almost to her shoulders, the finely chiselled features of her face forming naturally into a smile. 'I'm toying with the idea of interactive tarot lines as well. I believe you are something of an expert in that?'

'Yes... it's my speciality actually.' Marilyn saw Max breathe a sigh of relief and commended herself for daring to be immodest.

'Well, "the proof of the pudding's in the eating" as they say, so I think the next step is for you to do a week's star forecast for the twelve signs. Can you do them by Saturday?' It was only two days away. She sensed that he was testing her and nodded demurely.

'Good. Is it alright if we meet here Max? We can do a trial recording then. Jolly good. Eleven o'clock on Saturday morning then. Must dash. Goodbye.'

*   *   *

'Where are we going first? I'm relying on you to find me just what I want for my conservatory.' Julia smiled as she spoke, but was secretly still reeling from the shock she had received when the bill arrived. She would have disputed it if it wasn't for the fact that she had to pretend that spending money came as second nature to her. She couldn't let Serena - with all her breeding and wealth - think she was penny pinching. 'I've got the credit cards... let's hope you've got the ideas'.

'Oh yes,' said Serena meaningfully, her dark eyes flashing, 'I've got lots of ideas...'

*   *   *

Clive froze as he listened to the news item on the radio.

'... *the body of a man was found early this morning in a flat in Maida Vale. The deceased has not yet been named, but he is thought to have been dead for over twenty four hours. Reports emerging from the scene, although not officially confirmed, state that the victim was a single white male in his early fifties and that he was brutally attacked and murdered in his own home whilst participating in some bizarre sexual ritual. Police are eager to talk to anyone who may have been in the Sutherland Avenue area in the early hours of yesterday morning. And now to the sport news...*'

*   *   *

Michael pushed open the door of his flat and realised he was completely exhausted. He needed to go to the supermarket, but felt grubby and unwashed from the night before. He ran his fingers over the stubble on his chin and looked down at his stained T-shirt. What he needed was a long soak in a hot bath. Just then he noticed the light flashing on the answering machine. He pressed the button and waited.

'Hi Michael... it's Cliff here from 'Crews'... I know it's short

114

notice, but can you work tonight at six? Give me a call when you get in.' Oh well, it was good to be in demand.

* * *

'No... no, you want something *far* more bold than that. What about that trellis design with the grapes and marigolds?' Serena was having a lovely time advising Julia on fabric for the wrought iron furniture she had eventually chosen. 'Yes? I somehow thought you'd go for that.' Nobody had ever asked for her opinion before. She felt respected and in control. 'How about a little drink to celebrate?' The longer she could put off going home the better.

* * *

Michael arrived in the West End to find the bar very busy. There were certainly no visible signs of a recession as far as the gay community was concerned. The time flew by when he was rushed off his feet and he liked the sense of achievement - albeit simple - which arose from dealing efficiently with his new job. Life, he thought as he pulled yet another pint while reaching behind himself for a couple of bottles of beer from the fridge, was being particularly good to him.

'Hello stranger!' The voice was familiar and he swung around to see his old friend Sebastian standing at the bar. 'Fancy finding you here.'

'Where have you been? I've been trying to get in touch ever since I got back but you'd moved and that woman at your old flat said... sorry mate, that's six twenty.... she said you hadn't left a forwarding address.' Michael was so excited to see his old friend, he almost forgot that he was still working. 'A Pils and a Budweiser? Coming up!'

Sebastian spent the whole evening leaning on the bar filling Michael in on the happenings of the last two years. In a way, it seemed to Michael that many more years than just two had passed since they had last met, but in another way they were able to take up where they had left off.

* * *

Detective Inspector Ratter sighed and leafed through the pathologist's report on the Maida Vale murder for a third time. There was very little doubt in his mind that the gay serial killer - long since relegated to the 'unsolved crimes' department - had struck once again. The report revealed details that pointed strongly to this murder being the work of the same man. A trace of semen found at the scene of the murder was being analysed in the laboratory. He had a feeling it would match up with those from the past and prove the point. But what had made him strike again after more than two years? What had made him strike in the first place?

He shifted uneasily in his chair and ran a hand through his greasy hair, adding to the flecks of dead skin on the shoulders of his dark blue jacket. He pondered on the telephone call he had received that morning from Clive Haynes - a man he had personally fobbed off more than once. He had a gut feeling that this case was about to hit the headlines in a big way, highlighting his very public failure to catch the killer two years earlier. If only someone else could have dealt with it. It wasn't true that he didn't like gays. No, not as long as they kept themselves to themselves and didn't go near children...

* * *

'...from your letters I thought you'd found the perfect way of life in Greece. I'm surprised you ever came back.' Sebastian, an out of work actor, had long since become cynical about life and was almost - in a well meaning way - hoping that Michael had lost his unnerving optimism. 'What happened to your new way of life?'

'I brought it back with me!' said Michael, laughing as he saw Sebastian's face fall.

'But what about all your drive and ambition and need to prove yourself?' Sebastian wasn't going to give in that easily.

'What about it? I just found that I was looking too hard for a solution to the riddle of life. It was here all along.'

'Anyway,' Sebastian stood up to leave, 'I've got comps for a show at the Vaudeville. Must dash. Call me soon.' He slapped a card with his telephone number on the bar. 'Oh... I almost forgot.

Your brother got a big break didn't he? Who'd have thought he had it in him? Naff show... but even I wouldn't sniff at the salary! Just as well for you that no self-respecting homo watches daytime telly or you'd never get any trade!'

* * *

'Do you mean to say you're going to do absolutely nothing about it?' Clive Haynes gripped the receiver more tightly as he got closer to losing his temper. 'Why hasn't he been arrested yet?'

'It's not quite as simple as that.' The voice at the police station was reticent. 'We can't go storming in and arrest this man just because you say he pulled a knife on you two years ago...'

'*Yes,* but he's killed again and you've got to stop him!' Clive was near to hysteria.

'I won't deny that there has been speculation that this recent murder could be connected with the three gay killings in 1991. At the moment we're having a profile made up of the killer from the evidence.' He was bluffing now and Clive knew it. 'And if it in any way points to this Barkworth man being a possible suspect...'

'If? How can you say "if"? Would you be taking the same stance if it were heterosexuals being murdered? I suppose we've got to wait until *another* man gets murdered before you'll do anything about it...'

* * *

Julia paid the cab and staggered through the gates of Cuckoo Hall. Searching for her key, she realised she was happy... but her happiness owed more to alcohol than general wellbeing. Unlocking the door and giggling as she struggled to turn off the burglar alarm she wondered why Tony wasn't at home. Damn! She had hired some new costumes to try out - the show the day before had inspired her. Oh well, he had probably gone out in a mood because she wasn't at home being a dutiful wife. A thought suddenly occurred to her and she reached for the telephone.

* * *

When Michael finally arrived home, all traces of tiredness had evaporated. The busy shift behind the bar had stimulated him, not to mention the unexpected arrival on the scene of Sebastian. Along with the drinks he had consumed with the other barmen after the bar had closed, the day's events had proved to him that he was on the right track. The alcohol was coursing through his veins and he felt in the mood to go out again. Where had he put those telephone numbers?

* * *

'Yes?' The voice on the intercom was deep and masculine.

'Trevor?' The young man on the doorstep sounded uncertain.

'Good chap! Bang on time. Come in - just give the door a shove.' A loud buzz sounded. The figure on the doorstep clutched his holdall and pushed the door.

* * *

'No bishop... I beg of you... respect my vow of chastity!' Julia grovelled on the bedroom carpet in the nun's habit she had hired that afternoon. 'My body is a temple of God and no man must... er...' she paused for a moment, lost for words, '...no man must shove his thing up my shrine!'

* * *

The room was dimly lit and sparsely furnished. A shaded lamp in one corner shed its dingy light on an exercise bench strewn with an assortment of leather straps.

'Let's get down to it then! Where do you want to start?' Trevor got no reply and changed tack. 'Oh I see... the silent type. Well, you'd better do *exactly* as I say. I don't like to be disobeyed. Get on your knees!'

* * *

'Oh bishop... what would Mother Superior say if she could see you now? Aaaah... mmm!' Julia groaned in ecstasy as the mound under her habit moved up and down, 'Oh yes... aaaah... yes.... aaah... yes bishop...stick your holy tongue up my... aaaaaaah!' She lost control momentarily and slid down the wall against which she had been standing. The habit rode up as her legs splayed out on the

118

floor. Forgetting herself for an instant, she grasped the head that was still exploring the depths of her sanctuary and pushed it further in. 'Oh yes, bishop, your holiness is quite.... aaaah... quite overwhelming!'

* * *

'Let's see your cute little smackable arse then! You've been a naughty, naughty boy! Pull your shorts down for your master. Yes... that's more like it. Oh yes... oh yes...' Slap! The leather strap swiped at the smooth flesh of the exposed buttocks. Slap! 'Oh yes! Daddy's going to make your cheeks so red... so red... and sore!' Slap! 'Tell Daddy you're sorry. Say it. Go on.... say it!' In the half darkness, a hand reached for the holdall. 'Tell Daddy you're...' Trevor froze as he saw the knife.

* * *

Julia sat propped up against the wall with her wimple askew and her now sticky habit pulled up round her waist. She watched the 'bishop' drawing heavily on a cigarette as he leaned back against the sofa.

'It doesn't seem right for a bishop to smoke,' she said, then suddenly saw the funny side of it and giggled like a schoolgirl, 'even if it is after sex with a nun!'

'Well,' said Dr Leslie McManus, 'we don't all have to practise what we preach!' Their mutual laughter was interrupted by the telephone ringing.

'Hello?' Julia was brusque, wondering who would ring after midnight.

'Don't get snotty with me, darlin'. We've got things to talk about.' Her face fell as she heard the deep voice at the other end of the line. 'Just remember I'm watching you... watching you with your posh friend and your interior designers. But I remember the old days...'

* * *

Iris was just dozing off in her chair when she heard a door slam. Bloody neighbours! She heaved herself up and wandered to the window. It was probably Trevor up to his late night tricks again. She admired his energy. Only a gay man could carry on behaving like a teenager well into his forties. She leaned closer to the glass and her suspicions were confirmed. Here was one of Trevor's 'friends' just walking out of the front gate. The light from a street lamp shone on him for an instant as he walked onto the pavement and the old woman's eyes opened wide.

'Bugger me!' she exclaimed as she recognised the departing night visitor. *'He's* a dark horse and no mistake!'

CHAPTER SEVEN

Michael awoke just after nine. The sun's rays were shining through a crack in the curtains right onto his face. He slowly eased himself out of bed and walked naked to the bathroom. There was no need for him to get up yet as it was his day off, but he felt like getting outside and breathing in the fresh air. He needed to reaffirm life's values and reassure himself that he knew what he was doing. The shower aimed needles of hot water at his lithe, tanned body. He put his head under the gushing stream and felt better immediately. Perhaps he should go to the gym for a quick work out. Yes, a quick jog around the common and then off to the gym for an hour or two. That would be a good start to the day.

* * *

'And our next guest this morning is a lady who has just seen a single she recorded more than fifteen years ago hit the top ten all over again.' Tony paused and looked across the sofa at the alluring and beautiful half-caste woman. Her smile seemed to illuminate the whole studio as he continued. 'Shanelle... it's very nice to have you on the show. Now, as I just said, your single "Stand On Your Own" has reached number five in the charts this week. It was a huge disco hit in the late seventies. I remember it well from my schooldays...' He paused again and looked sideways at Julia. 'Ironically, though, in spite of its title, the original success of this song marked the beginning of your descent into a life of drug-induced despondency and despair, didn't it?' He leaned over closer to the singer with an understanding look on his face, eagerly awaiting the heart-rending story she was about to pour out.

'No.' A puzzled look had crept over Shanelle's ebony features.

*   *   *

'Slipped up a bit there, didn't he?' Marjorie loved to sail close to the wind and this morning, as she sipped coffee from Kathleen's dainty bone china, was no exception. 'Never mind, I suppose we all make mistakes!'

'Yes,' said Kathleen pointedly, 'like you letting the whole neighbourhood know about your... your... affair...' her voice trailed off in disgust.

'Oh Kath,' Marjorie watched her friend wince at the casual abbreviation of her name, 'you're so old fashioned. Just because my new man is a bit younger than me...'

'A bit? He could be your son!' Kathleen had been enduring it long enough. She couldn't be seen to be supporting this kind of behaviour.

'Oh stop exaggerating! Jason's thirty nine. What about your Tony and his wife? She's no spring chicken is she? What bothers you is the thought that I'm still able to have a sexually satisfying relationship...'

'If you're going to stoop to that level...' Kathleen flushed bright pink. It was bad enough that she'd mentioned sex, but to mention it in the same sentence as her son!

*   *   *

Gasping for air as he completed his two thousand metres on the rowing machine, Michael reached for a towel and mopped his sweating brow. So far this had been a good workout and it hopefully meant that the rest of the day would go well. He had discovered a long time ago that a healthy body meant a healthy mind and vice versa, even if he did have his little relapses...

*   *   *

'Er... so... Shanelle, it must have been a big surprise for you to find your single suddenly catapulted into the forefront of the pop

122

world out of the blue.' Julia decided to have a go at salvaging their credibility. Either the researcher had been having a laugh at their expense or this woman was a bit strange.

'No... not really,' the sultry singer drawled quietly as she looked Julia up and down with her dark, almond-shaped eyes. 'Jesus told me it would happen.'

* * *

The water was cool and bracing. Michael had the swimming pool to himself and was glad of the fact. While being naturally gregarious, when he came to the gym he wanted to be able to work out and swim without any interruptions. That was why he had chosen this particular one. It was well equipped, efficiently staffed and not frequented by over-developed, muscle bound hunks obsessed with their bodies. Nor was .it full of sex hungry men looking for a quick pick-up. If he wanted that kind of thing, he was quite well aware of where to find it. When he came to the gym he wanted to work out.

His body cut through the clear water as he completed another length, lifted himself out and headed for the changing room. There was a lone man in the showers who looked up as he came in.

'Good work out, mate?'

'Not bad,' Michael replied amiably. In a gay gym, it wouldn't have been possible to talk to a naked man in the showers without it meaning something. A careless look could speak volumes. He slipped off his trunks, grabbed his towel and stepped into the tiled area, turning the gushing stream of hot water onto his body. He felt more deserving of this shower than the one he had had at home earlier on, because he had done something to deserve it. Yes, a good workout was definitely a step in the right direction...

'Nasty bruises on your backside, mate! What you been up to?' His shower companion's observation shattered his reflective mood.

* * *

'And I believe you're going to sing for us now...' Tony ventured, his nerves virtually shattered.

'Am I?' Shanelle asked, a look of wide-eyed surprise on her face. Tony thought his heart would stop, then watched as her features suddenly broke into a grin and her eyes twinkled. 'Yeah... 'course I am.' She leapt up and skipped over to the microphone as the music started.

*   *   *

'Hello...' the voice on the telephone was husky and muffled. 'I've got a message for Detective Inspector Ratter.'

'Hold the line please...'

'No... no... tell him he'll find the body of my latest victim at number fifteen Sitatunga Road.' The line went dead.

*   *   *

Iris watched with increasing interest as yet another police car drew up in the street outside her house. She certainly couldn't complain about being bored today. It had taken her an hour or two to stop chuckling about the way the singer had run circles around Tony and Julia on the show. She still couldn't be sure whether or not the singer was doing it on purpose, but it had made good viewing. It was without much surprise that she noted the gradual deterioration of the two presenters. Julia, in particular, seemed unable to stand the scrutiny of daily exposure: the harder she tried, the more cheap and inept she appeared.

'Pity you ever lost that poshness you 'ad when you first came to us,' Iris had commented that morning. 'Only, I suppose you never realise what you've got until it's all gone and used up. Ten years on the bash is enough to make anyone common.' And now it seemed she had found herself a husband who was a fairy, she mused, remembering the fleeting glimpse she had caught the night before. Oh well, the business was full of them...

She watched the policemen getting out of the car and wondered, not for the first time, what was going on. There wasn't usually much call for police in Sitatunga Road. The odd burglary from time to time caused a bit of a stir. And there had been that incident with the man at number thirty two with the raincoat. No, this was decidedly odd and uncommonly exciting. The three men walked up the path to the house next door. Trevor. Maybe Trevor had done something. Naughty boy. What had he been up to?

* * *

Marcia Napier sighed as she looked out of her kitchen window at the front garden of which her husband had been so fond. She reached to the back of the cupboard for the gin bottle and poured herself a large measure. Paul had been gone for four days and it didn't look as if he was coming back. She wandered over to the fridge to get some ice and looked at her daily planner on the wall above it - the wall with its carefully sponged paintwork. She smiled as she remembered the loving care with which her husband had decorated the flat: fitted cupboards, concealed lighting, shelves everywhere. A place for everything and everything in its place...

She looked again at the planner. Tonight was Paul's squash night. Last night had been allocated for training at the gym. Tomorrow night there was a round table meeting. Paul. Her whole life revolved around him - making sure the appropriate clothes were washed and ironed for his various activities, ensuring his meals were ready on tine so that he wouldn't be late for anything. She sat down gently on a reproduction wheelback chair and put her glass on the table. The table had been one of Paul's 'finds' at Camden market the year before. Every item in the flat had been searched for, carefully chosen, well looked after. Their life had been well ordered, well balanced and perfectly happy... or so she had thought.

He had at least had the decency to tell her to her face rather than leaving a note. No, that would have been just too much to bear. But somehow she had hung on to the belief that he would come back. For the last few days she had jumped every time the telephone rang and rushed to the landing every time someone came through the front door, willing it to be Paul, praying that it would be him.

She took another swig of gin and wondered what she was going to do now the purpose of her thirty seven year old life had vanished.

* * *

125

Michael sauntered guiltily into the video shop on Battersea Rise and nervously winked at the young man behind the counter.

'You've... er... got something put by for me to collect.' He nervously glanced over his shoulder to make sure he was still the only customer in the shop. 'The name's Barkworth.'

*   *   *

'Shit!' Julia wasn't having much luck with her new hobby. She had always imagined that flower arranging was something women just 'did' when they felt like it. Surely there couldn't be that much to it? In the dim and distant past she remembered watching her mother gathering great armfuls of flowers from the garden, arranging them around the house with an apparent lack of effort and modestly taking no credit for it with disclaimers like 'Oh, really, it was so easy... I just threw them in a vase.'

Julia's first creation had, so far, cost her well over a hundred pounds. The flowers had all looked beautiful when they had arrived - great billowing sprigs of misty white gypsophylia, large yellow chrysanthemums, massive pink gladioli and intriguing red bird of paradise flowers. Individually they had been lovely... but now she had chopped, tugged and tweaked them into an 'arrangement' in a big old Chinese vase they looked ugly and artificial. She stood back and frowned. Her mother's critical voice drifted into her mind. 'No... no... no... you just haven't got what it takes have you? I know we can't all be good at *everything* but in your case we haven't found *anything* yet!'

*   *   *

Michael ran his fingers over the unmarked video case hidden inside his leather jacket as he closed the big old front door behind him, a feeling of wicked excitement beginning to creep through him. He knew that he shouldn't be pandering such desires, but there were times when he just couldn't help it.

His foot was on the first stair when the door of the ground floor flat opened and the tear-stained face of a woman peered out. 'Oh... I'm sorry,' she said quietly, 'I... I thought you might be somebody

126

else.'

'I don't think we've met.' Michael looked at her and wondered what on earth could be the matter. She was, he estimated quickly, about thirty five years old, not unattractive but clearly very distraught. Her dark hair looked as if it needed a wash, her face was red and puffy and her eyes bloodshot. 'I live upstairs... my name's Michael. Are you alright?'

'Yes... yes. I mean... no...' Her voice trailed off as the tears began to flow again.

'Would you like to come up for a drink? You look as if you could use one.' The video would have to wait until later. He felt his excitement subsiding.

'Are you sure?' She looked so grateful that Michael immediately berated himself for even considering that a video could be more important than helping a neighbour in distress.

'Of course I'm sure,' he said cheerfully, 'and who am I having the pleasure of entertaining in my humble abode?'

'Marcia... Marcia Napier.'

* * *

Gerry Ratter carefully picked his way through the room. Forensics would be there any second. He shuddered. It was eerily similar to the last murder: the same type of flat, the same kind of guy, the same pieces of equipment lying around and... he took a breath and wished he hadn't... the same murder method. He held a handkerchief up to his nose to try to keep the acrid smell from his nostrils. Thank God they had found this one so soon. He didn't like to imagine what it would have smelt like in here if the body had been left for a few more days. The telephone call... now there was a mystery... why would the killer want to help them? Maybe he was playing with them... cat and mouse. The news would break soon enough and the whole capital would know there was a serial killer on the loose.... and it was up to him to catch him. He moved as fast as he could towards the front door. He needed fresh air... space.

* * *

127

'Did you know the guy who lived here before?' Michael asked, wondering whether or not Marcia had encountered a homosexual before. He was relieved that she had at last begun to relax and was looking a bit more like a human being. She had poured her heart out to him, which he found a little strange since she had only just met him. The poor woman obviously had no-one else she could talk to. He couldn't even begin to imagine what she was feeling inside Fifteen years of being a faithful wife and then this. Apparently her husband was the first man she had ever slept with... the only man she had ever slept with. That was another concept he couldn't somehow grasp.

'You mean Simon? Yes... well... I didn't know him so well, but he was very friendly with Paul. They used to go jogging together and that kind of thing. Why do you ask?'

'Oh,' said Michael, trying to keep the knowing tone out of his voice, 'I just wondered...'

* * *

Iris staggered across the room and sat back heavily in her armchair. All this activity had worn her out. A little sleep... yes... just a little nap. She'd find out what was happening next door soon enough. As she drifted off her mind went back twenty five years. The police were knocking on her door... hammering. It was a raid... there were girls flying everywhere... girls and men with their trousers around their ankles. Her sleeping mouth crumpled into a wise old smile. She could almost hear them hammering on the door now...

* * *

'Doesn't seem to be anyone in, sir.' The sergeant had been knocking on Iris' door and had got no answer. 'Actually, it doesn't look as if anyone lives there... but I'll try again later.' They had questioned all the neighbours and nobody had seen anything out of the ordinary the night before. If only they could just get a description... a hint. It might at least prove that the Haynes man had got it all wrong.

128

*   *   *

Michael walked down the stairs with Marcia to her flat, glad that her mood had improved a little. Helping her in her moment of need had given him a sort of buzz. He hoped she would feel she could rely on him as a friend.

Glancing at his watch, he dashed back up the stairs. The video would have to wait. He had to admit there was more than a tinge of enjoyment in the self-denial, like forcing himself not to eat a chocolate fudge cake on plain view in the fridge. Mind you, he didn't really have chocolate fudge cakes on his mind now. He had other urges. And he had a very good idea where he might be able to satisfy them.

The sun was still out as he walked down the front path and out onto the pavement. He looked over at the lush green grass of the common and thought - not for the first time - how lucky he was to be living there. Everything was fitting into place. Everything was at his fingertips. London: the ideal playground for a born-again gay man. He laughed softly to himself at the thought. He wouldn't exactly refer to himself as 'born-again', but he was certainly having more fun now than he ever had before.

Dodging a large dog turd, he turned left and walked purposefully up the tree-lined road, noting with amusement that it was possible to tell what type of people lived in the terraced houses on either side of the avenue just from their curtains. Habitat prints probably meant young newly-weds or co-habitating first time buyers. Laura Ashley would have to indicate thirty somethings who couldn't quite stretch to Colefax and Fowler but might be able to afford Sanderson next time. Next interiors were a bit of a problem. Since they had produced their bold, masculine range it had attracted the custom of the type of single man who would never previously have even considered interior design a possibility let alone a necessity. So now it wasn't only gay men who had drapes with matching borders. But when it came to swathes of white muslin and paper blinds there was no doubt whatsoever. They just had to belong to a friend of Dorothy.

He had reached another junction by now and had to wait for the lights to change before he could cross. A little old coloured woman stopped beside him and put her three large bags of shopping down, heaving a sigh of relief as she did so. Michael wanted to offer to help her carry them, but he knew there was no point. Nobody trusted anybody on these streets. How would she know he wasn't going to run off with her shopping? Feeling helpless, he waited for the little green man to appear and then skipped across the road, nearly colliding with two inebriated Rastafarians who suddenly staggered out of a seedy looking pub onto the pavement. Whistling to himself, he spotted his destination. It was just a few yards ahead now. The small glass-fronted shop, rather like a barber's in appearance, bore the title 'Sauna' above its steamy windows.

* * *

'Tony...' Julia was feeling in the mood for a bit of fun, 'I'm just going to go and get in the bath. Why don't you come up and... you know...'

'What?' Tony looked up from his copy of the Evening Standard and frowned.

'You know...' Julia simpered, trying to look seductive as her husband stared back at her blankly.

* * *

The combined smells of sweat, pine and baby oil reached Michael's nostrils and got progressively stronger as he neared the bottom of the stairs. He pulled the towel tighter around his waist and wondered what he had let himself in for as he found himself in a dimly lit narrow corridor. There was a frosted glass door through which he could see steam swirling and another doorway leading to the showers. Shower first, he thought to himself, then a bit of steam. It had been a long time since he had been in the midst of a large number of naked men and he was feeling horny just thinking about it.

* * *

Julia sat in the foaming bath water, wondering why she couldn't get Tony interested in a bit of afternoon sex. Why couldn't he just loosen up a bit sometimes? After all, he was very good at it when he was in the mood, or at least in costume. But she had yet to find out what he was like in the sack - or the bath for that matter - when he was just being himself. Letting out a long sigh of frustration, she reached for the loofah.

* * *

As the spray of hot water gushed down on to his naked body, Michael laughed at the thought that he was probably one of the only men in London to be taking a shower for the third time in one day. His mother had always said that cleanliness was next to godliness, but what did she know? He looked up as a hulking great black man dropped his towel and stepped into the shower beside him. Unable to tear his gaze away from the cock ring he was wearing, Michael made a mental note to remember that *all* the rumours he had heard were true.

* * *

Feeling rather better since her talk with her new friend, Marcia picked up the newspaper to see if there was anything on the television. As she turned the pages, her eye caught the horoscopes and she paused. Paul had always said it was a load of mumbo jumbo. Oh, sod Paul! She was going to get on with her own life now. She scanned the page for her own birthsign.

'Although turbulent changes have recently turned your world upside down, an encouraging new aspect in your sign means that these clouds may have a silver lining. A new acquaintance or friend could be on the horizon - take advantage of what he or she makes possible. Ring the changes and enjoy them!'

* * *

Groping around for a seat in the thick steamy atmosphere, Michael sensed the sexual electricity all around him. He was sweating profusely and the musky male smell filling his nostrils sent a wave of excitement through him. Men together. There was nothing quite like it. No pretence. No inhibitions. All the men there wanted one thing. United in pure lust.

As his eyes became accustomed to the hazy gloom, he made out the shapes of at least a dozen men sitting and standing. Some were still wearing towels around their waists, others were completely naked, hands around their penises, eyes scanning the steam room for contact. Gripped with a sudden claustrophobic nausea, Michael got up to leave, scrabbling through the mass of bodies to get to the door. As he put his hand on the door, he felt a hot spurt of semen slap against the back of his leg.

* * *

Ratter poured himself a large scotch and slumped into an armchair. His wife was out at choir practice and had left his dinner in the oven. It sat on the kitchen table uneaten. His guts were still churned up after the discovery of the body. How could he eat shepherd's pie within hours of seeing what he had seen? But more than that, he was very close to despair. The responsibility for this whole case seemed to rest on his shoulders. It would be his fault if the killer was not caught. Why did people seem to think policemen were superhuman beings devoid of feelings, sensibilities and human failings? Was he more to blame for not having caught the killer than the killer was for having done it in the first place?

* * *

The warm red glow from the lantern in his living room was comforting to Michael as he ripped off his leather jacket and threw it onto a chair. He had been wrong. The sauna was not the answer. Why hadn't he stuck to the original plan?

Retrieving the video from the bookcase where he had hastily thrust it earlier on, he fed it into the machine and picked up the remote control. The curtains were firmly closed. The door was locked. No-one would know what he was watching. His mouth curled into a smile at the thought of what Sebastian would say if he knew what he was watching, not to mention the guys at work. So what... he was being honest to his urges. After all, what was life about if he couldn't do what he wanted to do and watch what he wanted to watch? He wasn't forcing anyone else to watch it, was he? Why should he feel ashamed? To whom was he answerable to other than himself? He had ordered it, collected it and brought it home. A memory of some magazines in a brown envelope hidden under the chest of drawers in his bedroom at home brought with it a rush of guilty pleasure. He pressed the button and watched the screen burst into life. As he loosened his belt and stretched out on the sofa, the title appeared: *'Jilly Cooper's RIDERS'*.

CHAPTER EIGHT

The well-manicured fingers turned the pages of the Saturday newspapers as the eyes scanned the reports. A smile came to the lips. Three front pages. It was even better this time around - maybe it would last longer...

'... *the man found murdered yesterday afternoon in Battersea has not yet been named, but police sources say there is evidence to suppose that he is a victim of the same killer who struck earlier this week in Maida Vale. The man killed earlier this week has been named as Eric Hefford, a fifty three year old known homosexual...*'

The smile broadened into a grin. He had made them sit up and take notice. Nobody could push him into the background now. He was in control...

'... *precise details of the murders have yet to be released, although they are known to have been of a violent nature and sadomasochistic equipment was apparently found at the scene of both crimes. Gay men are being urged to be on their guard and not to take strangers home with them...*'

Soon the whole country would know about his work, but that was just an added bonus... an unexpected pleasure. He would have them all guessing, pointing the finger, accusing each other. But the finger wouldn't be pointed at him... oh no... he was too clever for them...

'...*enquiries are being made at several pubs and clubs in the capital known to be frequented by gay men, but so far no common link has been established between the two dead men. The appointment of Detective Inspector Gerald Ratter to lead the hunt for the killer has led to growing speculation that the killer is the same one who struck more than two years ago, killing three gay men in similar circumstances. Ratter, who headed the unsuccessful enquiry into these murders, declined to comment. A press conference has been arranged for later on today...'*

He turned to the middle of one of the papers to read an article by a well-known gay rights activist claiming that the police could have done more to prevent the latest murder.

'... why wasn't the connection made sooner? Why wasn't the gay community warned that the killer could be on the loose again? When a middle-class white woman is murdered, the country is up in arms and all the stops are pulled out to find the killer...'

It got worse.

'... just because the victims are gay men, the crime seems somehow justified in the eyes of the police; the focus is shifted to the sexual practices which led up to it...'

But they were missing the point.

'... as the Operation Spanner case proved, the public is fascinated with anything sexual, particularly if it is of a somewhat unusual nature. Who is in a position to judge what we may or may not do in the privacy of our own homes? There has been a far more lethal killer in our midst - the Aids virus - for a long time and the blame for that has been laid at our door too...'

The newspaper was thrown to the floor. How could people be so stupid? How could they not see what he was doing? Had it all been for nothing?

In an instant he was back there. More than twenty years melted away as he heard the bedroom door open and shut quietly in the darkness. Nothing was said. Not for the first time, he wondered if he was imagining it - then he felt the rough hand on his flesh as it slid under the bedcovers and he knew all too well that it was real. The frisson of guilty pleasure was no longer there - not after the first time. He could smell the whisky on the rapid, heavy breaths of the man who was getting on top of him, prising his legs apart. He wanted to scream out. The room was spinning, there was a buzzing in his ears and he wanted to vomit, but he knew that he couldn't do anything about it. It was at this point that he always came close to unconsciousness - as if his mind was trying to shut off to protect him from the terror of reality. But he always had to hang on... had to know what was happening to him... He knew that he had to endure every painful, excruciating, disgusting moment of it. It was obvious that he had done something to deserve it... or was going to. Nobody must know. Never. 'Let this be our secret... no need to tell *anybody*! Remember God punishes little boys who can't keep a secret.' And just as quickly it was over. There he was in a damp patch on the bed. Alone in the dark.

But that was all in the past.

* * *

Julia slipped down into the hot bubbling water and closed her eyes. She was having the whole day at Champneys with Serena, who was beside her now in the jacuzzi. She intended to leave all the pressures of the show behind her and concentrate on getting her body into shape again. Serena was there for the weekend, but Julia had got to go home that evening because they were having Sunday lunch with Tony's mother the following day. She begrudged having to give up her free time. Who gave a shit about families anyway? It would also have done her good to spend another day being pampered. There was no denying that it was getting harder all the time to look attractive.

'Has Tony mentioned the dreaded baby question again?' Serena purred, hardly opening her mouth as she spoke, relishing in the all-pervading warmth that almost took her mind off the fact that she hadn't had a drink yet, even though it was nearly midday. 'Perhaps you should reconsider - just think of all the eating you could do without having to feel guilty...' Her voice trailed off as a large jet of bubbles continued to stimulate a part of her she had almost forgotten existed.

'Don't be so stupid! I have enough trouble keeping myself in trim without having to worry about stretch marks....' Julia stopped herself just in time from saying 'again'. How fortunate it was for her that one-piece swimming costumes were in fashion.

* * *

'You want to open a new account? If you'd just like to fill this in.' The girl behind the counter at the bank handed Michael a form. 'And we'll need some form of identification.'

'Will my passport do?' He felt for it in his jacket pocket, having become accustomed to carrying it with him all the time on his travels. Damn! It must have been in the jacket he left at Bruce's. 'How about a credit card?'

'Yes sir... no problem.'

Marcia was patiently waiting behind him. She had looked so lonely and lost when he had called in on the way out that he had urged her to come with him. He was working in the bar in the afternoon and then a late shift on the dating line, but he intended to spend an hour or two wandering around the shops.

'Sorry... I won't be long.' Michael looked round at her and smiled apologetically. 'Where are we going to go first? Do you fancy a coffee somewhere?'

'Oh, yes... that would be nice.' Marcia smiled agreeably. He was amazed at the way she left all the decisions to him, as if she had totally lost the ability to make any of her own.

* * *

'...Remember that the aspects of the planets are extremely powerful in your sign this week and you must be ready for sudden changes. Events may seem to be haphazard and erratic, but their overall purpose will become all too apparent in the near future.' Marilyn's voice once again caressed the microphone as Max smiled to himself behind the mixing desk. 'Therefore, even though you may be inclined to be wary of what is new, trust instincts which tell you to at least try what is on offer.' She stopped and looked up

137

anxiously.

'Good... very good. I don't want to be patronising, but you really sound as if you mean it.'

'Well... I do.' She looked serious for a moment. 'This isn't something I just dabble with.'

'I can see that.' The more time he spent with her, the more he found himself identifying with what made her tick. Suddenly realising that he was allowing his thoughts to wander into uncharted territory, he snapped himself back to the present. 'So... there's just the sample tarot reading now. How would you feel about reading mine?'

*   *   *

Sebastian groaned and rolled over in bed. Why did he have to get so disgustingly drunk every time an audition went badly? Every hangover gave rise to a sworn declaration that it would be his last, but then the depression and rejection would set in and one drink would inevitably lead to another. He couldn't even remember how he had got home the night before. It was mornings like these that made him seriously consider whether or not he really had a purpose in the world.

A gentle knock was followed by the head of his youthful flatmate peering around the bedroom door.

'Did you know there'd been another murder?'

'What?' This wasn't really the kind of conversation he wanted to have in his present state.

'Another gay murder. That's two in one week! The papers are full of it. They reckon it's the same bloke that killed those guys a couple of years ago. Mind you, I wasn't "out" then.' The boy was genuinely excited about it. He had even thought about ringing his mother, but had decided it might be more advisable to wake Sebastian and share the news with him. 'Oooh... it makes you wonder who's going to be next.'

Sebastian leapt out of bed, his hangover forgotten. How could something like this have passed him by? He had suddenly realised

138

that he *did* have a purpose. Michael. He had to make sure Michael was alright. The news could bring it all back to him...

* * *

'You're trying to tell me that this telephone dating is a multi-million pound industry? I can't believe it... especially about the married couples and all that.' Marcia watched her teaspoon as she propelled it around the coffee in her cup.

'Didn't you ever look at other men while you were married?' Michael asked incredulously. They were well into their third coffee and the shopping spree had been forgotten.

'No!' Marcia was taken aback by his directness - particularly at having her marriage referred to in the past tense - but then paused to think. 'Well... er... not seriously anyway.' Her frown broke into a smile as she saw Michael grinning. 'I wouldn't have dreamed of being unfaithful.'

'Wouldn't have?' He felt he had achieved something. She was at last coming out of her shell a bit. 'Anyway, I wasn't talking about being unfaithful. I meant just looking.'

'Doesn't that amount to the same thing?' She was confused and intrigued at the same time.

'No... not at all.' He looked pensive for a moment. 'I was with a guy for three years and we regularly went window shopping together.'

'Is that what you call it?' Marcia was shocked.

'No, I was just being camp. But it doesn't have to threaten a relationship - looking at other men I mean.'

'What happened then?'

'With me and Peter?' Michael looked straight ahead for a moment.

'Yes,' Marcia replied quietly, realising that she might have touched on a delicate subject.

'It all ended a bit suddenly... that was one of the main reasons for me going away.' He looked very sad and she wished she hadn't been so inquisitive. 'Anyway, we'd better get a move on. I've got to

139

be at work soon.' He smiled as he spoke, but there was a clouded look in his eyes.

* * *

Max felt more than a little uncomfortable as he listened to Marilyn calmly recounting his destiny into the microphone.

'But despite the strong influence of money, stability and material possessions in your past and present, your future influence is going to be the Wheel of Fortune...' She paused and looked up at Max to see whether or not the reading was having any effect on him, '... which means that you are going to actually take some uncharacteristic risks... or at least leave more to chance than you ever have in the past. It could also mean that you will trust your instincts more. As you can see, your immediate goal is the World... you have a definite image of what you want out of life... and you're not afraid to dream. But there is a definite obstacle.' Max swallowed as she continued. 'The Two of Swords is your obstacle... and swords signify a fight or conflict of some kind. It's not necessarily a physical fight... but being an even number - a two - it's evenly pitched and there could possibly be a stale-mate situation...'

* * *

'Can I come into town with you?' Marcia asked suddenly as they walked up the garden path to the front door. 'I haven't been to the West End for ages.'

'Of course you can... you don't have to ask.' Michael looked at her and smiled, his lips parting to reveal even white teeth. 'You can come and see the bar where I work. I hope it won't be too much of a shock to your system! When are you going to put this advert on the dating line then?' He had made her promise to try it and didn't want her to back out. In his opinion, she needed to launch herself back into life in the same way that he had. 'Why don't you come up to my flat and do it now?'

'Oh... er...' Marcia prevaricated for a moment and then made a decision. 'Alright then... strike while the iron's hot as they say!'

* * *

'This card signifies the way you are at the moment... not yesterday... not tomorrow... but right now.' Marilyn turned it over, revealing the Hanged Man. She heard Max draw in his breath sharply, so smiled to reassure him. 'The Hanged Man is a very good, if much-maligned, card which is often misunderstood. The man is hanging by his foot, not his neck, so is still very much alive. He's able to see the world from a totally different perspective... in a new light, so to speak. You can see coins falling out of his pockets because in his new condition - with his fresh insight into the world around him - he doesn't need the material trappings he previously thought were essential.'

* * *

'Is Michael working today?' Sebastian had tried telephoning the flat but couldn't get a reply. He knew he had to see his friend as soon as possible and hoped he would be able to track him down at the bar. It was busy, despite the fact that it was early afternoon, and he had to shout to make himself heard

'Yes... he should be here any minute,' the barman answered. 'Do you want me to give him a message?'

'No... I'll wait. ' He bought himself a drink and leaned on the bar. It was only then that he noticed the two police officers.

* * *

'And this card tells you what the final outcome of the present chain of events will be...' Marilyn's hand hovered before turning the card as she looked again at the previous two. 'The High Priestess represents the environmental factors affecting you at the moment... obviously a strong but wise feminine influence... and the Hierophant shows that deep inside you have started to think about things... and consider your position... a lot more than in the past. Now for the final result...' She flipped the card over and smiled as she saw the Lovers.

* * *

The young police officers making enquiries in the bar had

obviously been instructed to be open-minded, unbiased and understanding. Despite the seriousness of the matter in hand, the barman couldn't help smiling at the obvious apprehension they were feeling at being vastly outnumbered by gay men.

'Now they know what it feels like,' he muttered quietly to Sebastian. 'It's strange to think that the "twilight world of the homosexual" can be investigated at lunchtime!'

Their conversation was brought to a halt by one of the policeman who, having bravely finished interviewing the motley bunch of customers, politely asked if he could have a word with the barman. Sebastian, who had always had a penchant for men in uniform, raised his eyebrows and pursed his lips in mock jealousy.

'I'm sorry to interrupt your work, sir, but I just wanted to ask if you'd noticed any suspicious-looking customers over the last week or two?' The young officer looked at him earnestly.

'Er...' the barman looked thoughtful for a moment as he surveyed the customers in their many and varied modes of dress. 'You mean like a man in a pinstripe suit?'

* * *

'Hello. My name's Marcia... reference F353. I'm 37, quite tall and recently separated. I'm looking for a man around the same age for fun and friendship. Once again, my name's Marcia, reference F353.'

'No... do it again,' Michael whispered. 'Remember the things I told you to say. Sell yourself!' Marcia made a face and obeyed.

'Er... I'm sorry... can I do it again please? Right... yes... I'm ready.' She took a deep breath. 'Hello. My name's Marcia... reference F353. I'm an attractive, shapely brunette in my mid thirties living in South London. I have many interests, enjoy theatre, cinema and eating out and am looking for men in their late twenties or early thirties who would enjoy my company and be able to live up to my high expectations. If you think you're up to it, my name's Marcia... reference F353.' She grinned nervously as Michael beamed at her proudly.

* * *

Darren had spent all morning in the First Out coffee bar, his mood alternating between morbid fascination and absolute horror at the prospect of there being a serial killer on the loose in London. Most of his friends had different views on the killer. All, without exception, denied that they were at any great risk since they never took strangers back home with them. One friend had been so vehement about this that Darren had been unable to resist taking the matter further.

'But what about Robert?' he had asked. 'You told me yourself...'

'What do you mean... we've been seeing each other for nearly eight months!' The anger in his friend's expression had been apparent.

'But,' Darren continued, 'you told me you took him home with you the night you met him at "Bang" and had the best sex you'd had since...'

'Well... that's different. Anyway, murderers don't look like Robert, do they?'

Darren suddenly felt much older and more responsible. At twenty one years old, he seemed to be far more capable of dealing with this threat than any of his peers. He knew only too well that a vast proportion of the gay community was at risk from such a killer. The current publicity would frighten them all for a week or two, but what if the killer wasn't caught? What if any new man he met had to be viewed as a possible psychopathic murderer?

But he didn't want just any man. He had had enough of casual encounters which led nowhere... and he had set his sights on a man he had thought was out of reach. Perhaps that had been the initial attraction. After all, anything forbidden was immediately more attractive, especially when in the form of a man like Tony Barkworth. Ever since he had spotted him on Tuesday night at the Fridge, Darren had been in turmoil. Had Tony seen him there? Is that why he had left so abruptly? There had certainly been no evidence of this over the last few days at the studio. Why would a man like that risk being seen in a well-known gay club? Perhaps he hadn't realised that it *was* a gay club. Yes... that was it. He must have been out looking for a place to get away from that dragon of a wife of his and, on realising his mistake, had beaten a hasty retreat. There really was no hope. But there was still room to fantasise... fantasise about having a man like Tony to protect him and look after him.

A tear of desperation welled up in Darren's eye as he gathered up his things to go shopping. Spending money never failed to cheer him up.

* * *

'Michael... I've been waiting for you.' Sebastian was relieved the police officers had gone. 'I wanted to see if you were alright.'

'Alright? Of course I am. Why shouldn't I be? Marcia this is Sebastian... Sebastian this is Marcia.' He looked enquiringly at his friend who began to wonder how to phrase the next question.

'The murders... you *have* heard about them?' He saw the bemused look on Michael's face. 'Two men have been killed this week in circumstances that lead the police to believe that they are the work of the same killer who struck two years ago...' He stopped as he saw the colour drain from Michael's face.

'I see...'

* * *

Gerry Ratter looked around the room again and felt the bile threatening to rise in his throat. Murder was a nasty business, whichever way you looked at it. He felt helpless in his sterile shoe covers as personnel from the forensic department bustled around him taking samples, lifting fingerprints, sifting through the contents of the flat searching for any clues to the murder which had been committed there less than two days earlier. The smell of death lingered. It angered him to think that the man they were hunting had been right here, here where he was standing, but might as well be on the other side of the world by now as far as they were concerned.

144

He had left no helpful clues. So far they seemed to have unearthed nothing of significance to the enquiry.

Nothing of significance. The cupboards had spewed out piles of magazines depicting leather-clad men whipping subservient dog collar-wearing 'slaves', inserting foreign - but familiarly shaped - objects into every imaginable orifice. The murder victim's video collection had revealed similar scenes captured on film. People spent their lives making and distributing this stuff, making it available to those who wanted it by whatever means. But it was nothing of significance.

* * *

'Do you ever feel guilty about what you do for a living?' Marilyn had difficulty asking the question, not least because she too profited from involvement with Diamond Communications. 'I don't mean to be hypocritical, but...'

'I know... I know,' Max sighed as he reached over to fill her glass with mineral water. They were having lunch out in the courtyard and, until this question had arrived out of the blue, he had been thoroughly enjoying himself. The smoked salmon quiche had been delicious and the lemon sorbet he was about to taste looked equally tempting. Marilyn's recordings had been exceptional. He was sure Harvey was going to go ahead with the idea. It would be a good venture for all of them. 'Don't think for a moment that it isn't something that concerns me, but...' Marilyn watched his brow furrow in thoughtfulness as he continued, '... if you take the stuff we recorded the other day, for example, I think you'll agree that it was pretty tame. You can find far worse stuff on the shelves of any bookshop. I must admit that I don't particularly like being involved with Barry Sugden and his Daily Nation, but that's more to do with the kind of man he is than the moral aspect of it. Sally Beauman and Jackie Collins make my so-called "explicit" sex lines sound like "Listen With Mother". Only the other day I was at a meeting with the advisory committee who monitor and censor us with a rod of iron. They also, incidentally, have the power to have any lines they find offensive disconnected. Whilst agreeing with the need for such a committee, I do get a bit fed up with their prissiness. It's as if we're the evil enemy in their moral crusade.

Anyway, this woman on the committee was saying that it was sometimes very difficult to decide whether or not they found something "offensive". I asked her whether a line featuring extracts from, for example, "Lady Chatterley's Lover" would contravene the code of practice. Do you know what she said?' He looked at Marilyn, who was amazed at the way he had come to life... as if he had to justify his existence. 'She said that if I played extracts from "Lady Chatterley" and then discussed sentence structure and use of alliteration, there could be no objection, but if it was read in a "lascivious"...' he grinned as he mimicked the lady barrister '...fashion, it would *definitely* be deemed "unsuitable". It's the stratifying of sex and the issues surrounding it that annoys me... and I'm sure it's the cause of a lot of the problems in the world. There must be some reason for the demand for telephone fantasy lines. What do you think makes people pay through the nose to listen to you or someone else talking about things that shouldn't be out of anyone's reach? I genuinely think it's because sex and its associated mysteries have been blown out of all proportion in this country...' he paused to take a sip of water '...but I've got past the stage of feeling guilty about it. After all, I don't force anyone to pick up the telephone and dial 0898...' He stopped and smiled at her. His white teeth caught the light from the sun and Marilyn, not for the first time, realised she might be falling in love with him.

'But what about all that dating... you know... couples wanting single bisexual females and men looking for transvestites?' Marilyn, while being quite familiar with the services for which she had recorded intros, still didn't feel totally happy about them.

'It's the same story, really. People seem to find it easier to talk about their sexual preferences anonymously over the telephone than face to face. Our society seems to expect so much of people, or a certain standard of behaviour anyway, that the majority are too frightened to differ from the norm even if they want to. That's why some supposedly straight men get married and find that they're not quite as straight as they thought they were. The reality of sex with a man frightens them... threatens their masculinity I suppose... so they go for the next best thing - a man dressed as a woman.' Max paused again. 'I'm sorry, I'm on my soap box again, but it really does fascinate me. Like the way nobody admits to actually calling any of the lines, but I don't need to tell you how many people do.' He looked around him at the house, the courtyard with its Italian fountain, the stable block. 'But for goodness' sake don't think you're corrupting anyone. Just think of it as massaging the pent-up frustrations of a nation who like to be as boring as possible in public, but aren't averse to putting on their wife's Marks and Sparks underwear in private or ringing one of my lines and being told to "sit in the corner like a naughty little boy" by Matron Whip or Sister Spank!'

* * *

'Are you happy?' Serena shot the question at Julia as they sat swathed in towels and dripping with sweat in the steam room.

'Happy about what?' Julia asked, wondering what colour to have her hair tinted that afternoon. 'Do you think dark ash blonde would be too young for me?'

'Don't change the subject! I mean are you happy? You know... life...Tony... the show. Last time we were here it was all about to happen. How do you feel now? What sense of achievement have you got?'

Serena stopped, realising that she might have hit upon the root of her own problems.

* * *

'It had never really occurred to me before, but how did you get into this business?' Marilyn was savouring a mouthful of lemon sorbet. Her spoon hovered in mid air as she waited for the answer.

'Oh... it's a long story. I never even intended to be a businessman at all... let alone one in *this* business!' Max, feeling at

147

ease with Marilyn since he knew Serena was away for the whole weekend, went into a detailed history of his entry into the somewhat veiled world of premium rate telephone lines. Marilyn, in turn, felt very relaxed since Zoë was spending the whole day with a friend and listened in fascination as Max explained his initial hopes and dreams as a journalist, his rapid disillusionment, his desperation for money leading to writing scripts for some of the first premium rate services in the country. '...of course, I'd met Serena in the meantime and - I'm ashamed to say - fell for her charm and...' he stopped briefly and laughed, but it was a laugh of irony and frustration. He had missed out any details of his childhood... a childhood deprived of virtually everything except a public school education - his main influence an absentee father who'd let his wife die broken hearted and penniless. '... sexuality. Yes, she used the oldest tricks in the book - as far as women are concerned - and she caught me in her web. She had always been accustomed to getting exactly what she wanted. Her beloved father always saw to it that she did. She decided she wanted me and there wasn't anything I could do about it. The long and the short of it was that we got married, her parents were killed in an accident and we inherited this place...' As he paused, Marilyn looked a bit disappointed. She had assumed the house belonged to Max in his own right. She didn't want to accept the possibility of it being some sort of dowry which would chain him to the wife she had never met but could envisage from the brief moment she had almost been run her off the road by her Jaguar. The sorbet on her plate had melted - her appetite had been diminished by the story. Max continued 'Call it naivety if you like, but I had always assumed that the family had lived here for years. I'd only visited the place once or twice and Serena always referred to it as "home" and made out it was the ancestral seat. It turned out that the old man had only bought it a few years before. He was a big gambling man and had a lucky streak on the horses enabling him to move his family from their semi in Surbiton, but he'd had a subsequent run of bad luck on the stock market and the place was mortgaged up to the hilt. We'd not only inherited the house, but a string of debts far exceeding its value.' Marilyn felt relieved and then wondered why. 'I'd already fallen in love with the place - and out of love with my new wife - and didn't want to lose it. It might sound silly, but it was like a sign, a chance to prove that I could do something, that I could achieve something... and I did. I did it and it's all mine.' Max stopped, exhausted by this sudden unexpected reminiscence.

Marilyn smiled. He suddenly appeared to her as a child seeking praise for his achievement... like Zoë bringing home her pottery bowl from school, desperate for Marilyn to give it her seal of approval.

'Have your aims and ambitions changed now you've succeeded?' she asked, interested to know what made him tick.

'In what way?' Max looked different in her eyes now, much more human. 'If you mean would I do it all over again... yes, I would. But I'd hopefully have a different woman to do it with...' his voice trailed off as his eyes met hers. 'It all came back to me the other day when we were having dinner with some friends of Serena's and it transpired that the host was a journalist who tried to dump a load of scandal on my company a couple of years ago. I'd never name drop, but he's quite a celebrity now. Tony Barkworth... does some naff mid morning show on telly. Coincidentally, it's one of Harvey Wolfenden's productions. Anyway, he was drivelling on about his so-called greatest achievement as a journalist, when I suddenly twigged that it was the same story that nearly finished me. He bribed some of my staff to say that the recordings on my dating lines weren't genuine. I got the paper to print an apology in the end, but it still could have finished me. To the contrary, though, it gave me something to fight against. After all, whether we admit it or not, we all like something to fight for don't we? Poor sod didn't realise he was making a fool of himself until he asked me what I did for a living. You should have seen his face!' Max suddenly realised that the colour had drained from Marilyn's face. His story had made her realise how much her hopes and ambitions had changed since having Zoë to take care of, but the mention of the chat show host had taken it further.

'Did you say Tony Barkworth?' she asked.

'Yes,' Max replied, getting up and standing beside her. 'Are you alright?' He felt a bit foolish for talking about himself for so long. 'Do you know him?' She continued as if she hadn't heard him.

'So... you met his wife then... at the dinner party?'

'Yes, it was at their house. Marilyn, what is it? Is it *her* you know?' Max was really concerned now. Marilyn looked pale and drawn.

'Well... I used to... I used to work with her seven years ago in the States on one of the network stations. I did continuity... she presented a show. She was Karen Valente then; no talent and definitely no charm, but she used her Englishness to bluff her way into a lucrative little niche. She... married my best friend.' The memory seemed painful to recount.

'Oh... a love rival?' Max kicked himself as he realised he'd jumped to a typically male conclusion. 'I'm sorry... that was insensitive of me. It's none of my business.'

'No... really. It's something I've been wanting to get out of my system since I had the shock of seeing her on television the other day. She married my best friend... my flat mate... had a child... spent his money... ruined his career... and then left him for pastures new. He was destroyed, mentally and physically.' She paused, the memories vivid in her mind 'He rang me at work one day to say he was going to kill himself and... and I told him to pull himself together.' Max saw a tear trickle down her cheek. 'I found him when I got back that night.' Marilyn sank back into her chair.

Max awkwardly broke the ensuing silence.

'But... but you said she had a child. Julia hasn't got any children...' Max was puzzled. Serena had made a point of recounting the Tony and Julia baby argument to him, despite the fact that he was not remotely interested.

'No,' said Marilyn quietly, 'but she had a lovely daughter...'

* * *

The press conference had gone according to plan, but Gerry Ratter couldn't help feeling that it was a bit like shutting the stable door after the horse had bolted. After all, the press had managed to make quite a meal of the few facts to which they had had access already. His pleas to them not to sensationalise the murders in case it encouraged the killer to continue had predictably been ignored. The press had a living to make and this was an opportunity not to be wasted. Coupled with the emphasis they had given to the sado-masochistic aspect of the attacks and, subsequently, the rather sinister side of the homosexual world, the coverage so far had portrayed the police as having been reticent to release facts and warn the public - in this case the gay public - about there being a killer on the loose.

But all this paled into insignificance when the matter of Clive Haynes reared its ugly head. What if - and as far as Gerry Ratter was concerned it was a very big 'if' – the man was right. He had a hunch that there were going to be developments on that front before long.

* * *

Iris had had a bad day. She hadn't even had the energy to get out of bed until the afternoon. A cup of tea and a few biscuits had revived her a bit, but all she felt like doing was going back to bed. Old age - she wouldn't wish it on anyone. She sat propped up on her pillows and wondered how much life she had got left. And then she suddenly remembered about the police activity outside the day before. She never had found out what was going on. Perhaps it was time for some fresh air...

* * *

'Why on earth do you blame yourself? How could it have been your fault?' Max put his arm tenderly around Marilyn's shoulders. He had brought her into the house and made some coffee. It was obviously the first time she had talked about it to anyone. Her slim form seemed lost on the huge sofa. 'I never seem to be in the right place at the right time.'

'Would you rather be somewhere else now?' he asked cautiously.

'No.' Marilyn realised that there was nowhere else she would rather be. 'Look, Max, I'm sorry if I'm burdening you with my problems...'

'That's what I'm here for! I don't know if this is the right time to tell you, but you've made me realise that there might be some hope of happiness in my life...' His voice trailed off as Marilyn looked up at him and their lips met.

* * *

The young police officer outside the front door of Trevor's flat looked up disinterestedly as Iris came out of her house and peered over the fence at him.

'What's happened?' she asked brusquely.

'Haven't you heard?' the policeman asked, wondering how anyone in the neighbourhood could have possibly missed all news of the murder. He had seen enough morbid sightseers to last him a lifetime. 'Are you having me on, madam?'

'Don't get funny... just tell me what's happened? Why are you standing outside Trevor's door?'

'Er... there's been a murder.'

'No! Here? When?' Iris was suddenly flustered.

'Two nights ago. Do you mean to say you live right next door and didn't know anything about it?'

'I haven't been well.' Iris had a terrible feeling of foreboding. 'Who's been murdered?'

* * *

Marilyn opened her eyes and stretched out in the big bed, the crisp white sheets caressing her naked flesh. Max walked in wearing a white towelling robe. She ran her eyes over his broad tanned chest and strong thighs. She couldn't help grinning to herself at the thought that the head of a sex-based empire could make love in such a gentle and innocent - though still masculine - way. He smiled a little nervously and sat down on the bed.

'I thought I'd leave you to sleep for a while. I hope you haven't had regrets about...'

'No Max.' She put a finger to his lips. 'No regrets at all.'

*   *   *

The night shift on the telephones was dragging. It was even more humid and close inside the office than it was out in the street. Michael could feel rivulets of sweat running from his armpits and his palms felt clammy. He shouldn't have had that third drink before he left the bar.

He made his excuses to John and dashed out to the toilets and locked himself in a cubicle. Sitting down, he tried to pull himself together, but his head was spinning and he could feel the cloud of depression that had descended on him earlier getting heavier... weighing down on him. In the days when he had been ambitious and frustrated, alcohol had helped to slow him down and quell the inner anger. Now that he had supposedly got himself together, drink seemed to take away his contentment. It changed his view of the world.

He looked at the cold white walls around him. They seemed to be closing in on him...

*   *   *

'You sure you won't have a little drink with me?' Iris looked up at the policemen. It didn't seem possible that Trevor had been murdered. Her mind seemed unable to catch up with reality. She took a gulp from the glass in her hand and made another attempt at taking in what she had just been told. Two police officers in her house! The last time any members of the police force had been in a house of hers they certainly hadn't been invited. But that was twenty five years ago. Chuckling, she remembered that what had annoyed her most was the damage to her mahogany front door. If only they'd knocked, they wouldn't have had to force the locks! She poured herself another measure of brandy from the dusty old bottle and hobbled back over to her armchair.

Gerry Ratter shifted uneasily on the old sofa. He had had another long day and wasn't sure what this old bird was going to tell them. He just wished she'd get on with it. To think that they'd almost missed this potentially vital witness who lived right next door to the scene of the second murder! 'Right... where were we? Oh yes... I was just about to say how I always watch that "Family Values" show because she was one of my girls.' Ratter's ears suddenly pricked up. 'And it was him I saw outside here the other night.'

'Who?'

'Her husband!' Iris shook her head at him and tutted. 'That Tony Barkworth. I always thought he was far too good for the likes of her, but now I'm not so sure...'

CHAPTER NINE

Marcia looked at the front page of the Mail on Sunday and shuddered again at the thought that a gruesome murder could take place just a few streets away in Battersea. London: always in the news and not always for the right reasons. It made her wonder whether or not it was safe to go out on her own. She jumped as a knock came at the door and nervously put the chain on before opening it. A sigh of relief escaped from her lips as she saw Michael's smiling face peering through the gap.

'Well? Are you going to let me in or carry on staring?'

'I waited up for you to get back from work last night to see that you were alright.' Marcia looked at him with a sort of sisterly concern. 'I'm afraid I must have gone to sleep, though, because I didn't hear you.' She opened the door and stood back to let him in.

'It was probably just as well. The mood I was in, I'd have kept you up all night talking.' He sauntered past her, his jaunty manner showing no traces of the distressed state in which he had been the last time she had seen him. She was relieved, but still felt she had to say something.

'That's what I'm here for. Look... I didn't like to pry yesterday, but would it help to talk about it now?'

'What is there to talk about?' He sat down on a stool in the kitchen. 'Any coffee going?'

'Don't be so flippant! I saw your face when you heard about the

155

murders. You can't just shrug something like that off. Sebastian told me...'

'Sebastian told you what?' he interrupted. 'I expect you heard all the ins and outs of my private life. Is there anything else you'd like to know?' Seeing Marcia's face fall, he realised he had gone too far. 'Look... I'm sorry. I didn't mean it. I was just taking out my frustration on you. It's bad enough just knowing that the man who killed your lover is still on the loose, but when he starts killing again...'

*　*　*

Kathleen Barkworth had gradually worked herself into a near frenzy. The recipe said to 'bake until well risen and golden brown', but the tart was still sadly flat, looked a rather sickly yellow colour and had been in the oven for nearly twice the recommended time. Why did things always go wrong when it really mattered? All her life she had tried to get things right, to do what was expected, to bring her boys up right. What on earth would Tony's new wife think if she served up a flat tart?

*　*　*

'I suppose - more than anything - I miss having someone to come back to after a night out. I used to tell Peter everything. We'd gone past the lovey dovey sort of stage. He used to see other men and so did I, but what we had was so strong that it wasn't threatened by that. It was way above all that, in fact. He was quite a bit older than me and I suppose he was responsible for my development... although I didn't realise it at the time.' Michael paused thoughtfully.

'I think I know what you mean,' Marcia said quietly. 'My whole life revolved around Paul. In fact, you were the first person to make me realise that I might be able to carry on without him.'

'Yes... it's a lot easier to give advice than it is to take it.' Michael stood up suddenly. 'Just remember that the important thing is to stay in control.'

'Are you going?' Marcia was hoping he would stay a bit longer.

Sunday was not a day she wanted to spend alone.

'Yes. I'm going up to Northampton for lunch with my mother. My brother and his new wife are going... it'll be the first family reunion since I got back.' He frowned as he spoke.

'You don't sound exactly thrilled about it.' Marcia was still secretly impressed that she knew someone whose twin brother was a television personality. It had crossed her mind that Michael's flippancy about it was tinged with jealousy.

'I'm not, but duty calls I suppose. Anyway, I'm going to go for a jog around the common first to try and put myself in a good mood. See you later.'

* * *

'I suppose you think I'm looking forward to meeting your mother and having a polite chat over roast beef and Yorkshire pudding?' Julia was propped up in bed with the Sunday Mirror and a cup of Nescafé and wasn't going to hurry herself for anybody, least of all a mother-in-law she hadn't even met. 'Can't you go on your own?'

'No, I can't! This means a lot to her. Please try to be a bit enthusiastic.' Tony had a terrible sense of foreboding about the day ahead. The last thing he wanted was for his mother to think they had marital problems. Desperate to get Julia in a good mood, he appealed to the only side of her nature that was always reliable. 'I'll make it up to you. What do you want?'

'To know where you've been disappearing off to into the early hours...'

* * *

Gerry Ratter was regretting the day he had ever heard of 'Operation Sparkplug'. It was the kind of case that could prove all their suspicions right and get him promotion... but it could also backfire and finish him. For a start, any case involving kinky sex was, by its very nature, going to be tricky to deal with. Although it had been proven time and time again that an alarmingly large proportion of the population indulged in all sorts of weird sexual

157

practices, when it came to anything of the sort being made public there was inevitably a stampede to pillory those involved. The actual matter of the murders would no doubt be usurped by the circumstances in which they had taken place. Straightforward murder was one thing, homosexual murder another, but sadomasochistic homosexual murder...

As if this wasn't enough, the prime suspect was a celebrity. The old woman's statement the night before had confirmed his worst suspicions. The likelihood was that Clive Haynes had been right all along. If he went to the press, they would have a field day. Accusations of police procrastination were to be avoided at all costs.

What worried him more, though, was the fact that - taking past history into account - the murders they knew about could be just the tip of the iceberg.

* * *

'Ooh... this is going to be the best day ever!' Zoë beamed at Marilyn as she helped her pack the picnic basket. 'You really mean we're going to spend all day together? All day?'

'Yes Zoë. All day.' Marilyn felt a warm tide of contentment wash through her as she realised that she could make the little girl happy just by being with her.

* * *

Kathleen had a headache now and didn't really feel like going to Mass. Surely God wouldn't mind if she missed it just once? She couldn't convince herself, though, and went to get her coat and hat.

* * *

Michael looked at the happy family groups walking and playing on the common as he jogged past. It was a warm and sunny morning and he wanted to make the most of it before going home to shower and change. Lunch with his mother wasn't top of his list of favourite Sunday pursuits, but he did feel that he ought to make the effort since she had gone to the trouble of organising it. Not that she ever followed up any of *his* invitations - not since he had told her that he was gay - but she was his mother after all.

A small boy ran unsteadily into Michael's path and he changed course, narrowly missing him. The father ran up and, apologising to Michael with a smile, swept the child into his arms. As the little boy giggled excitedly, the father hoisted him onto his shoulders and carried on walking. A long forgotten feeling of regret descended on Michael. His father had died years ago and, although he didn't miss him, he missed the kind of intimacy that was meant to exist between father and son - an intimacy he had never known. What made it worse was that he knew his father was capable of such feelings. He had tried so hard to impress his father, to make him proud, to make him notice him.

*   *   *

The thought that Michael was going to spend the day with his family made Marcia strangely pensive. He hadn't been very enthusiastic about it, admittedly, but the fact remained that he did at least have a family. Her own parents had emigrated to Australia more than ten years earlier. They still rang at frequent intervals, but it wasn't the same as being able to go and see them when she wanted to. She had no brothers and sisters and her aunts and uncles were too far flung to count. Paul's parents had been really good - more like friends than in-laws - but she didn't feel like calling on them now. It would probably make them feel awkward.

A thought suddenly struck her. There *was* someone she could go and visit. She wasn't family in the strictest sense of the word, but Marcia had always called her 'Auntie'. The old girl would probably be glad to see her, even if she was a bit intimidating at the best of times.

Feeling a new sense of purpose, Marcia set about getting herself ready to go out.

*   *   *

The police car drove almost noiselessly into the drive of the large Georgian house and came to a halt. Gerry Ratter, accompanied by two uniformed policemen, got out and strode up to the large front door. He drew in his breath as he surveyed his surroundings.

'Phew! They live in another world don't they...' His voice trailed off as his mind wandered to the dingy house in Battersea where he had interviewed Miss Devereux the night before. To him, that had been more real. Its shabbiness made it less fragile.

He pressed the heavy brass bell push and waited.

* * *

Marilyn steered the mini between the large gateposts and watched Zoë's mouth drop open as the house came into view,

'Oh, Mummy Marilyn! Do we know someone who lives here? It looks like a house a queen would live in!' The child was clearly impressed.

'Well Zoë,' Marilyn laughed, 'I can assure you Max isn't a queen!'

Max was out on the lawn waiting for them and rushed over to the car as they drew up in front of the house,

'Hello ladies...' he leaned over and kissed Marilyn as she got out of the mini '... and you must be Zoë. I've heard an awful lot about you. I'm Max. Come on over and have a glass of lemonade. I've got the boat all ready. How do you fancy having our picnic in the middle of the lake, Zoë?' He could see that the little girl, beautifully dressed in a Laura Ashley print summer frock, was almost bursting with excitement. 'Of course, if you don't want to...'

'No, no, please... I'd *love* to!' Zoë unselfconsciously put her small hand in his large one and skipped as she walked with him over to the table and chairs on the lawn. Marilyn followed, happier than she had felt since returning to England. She knew that in Max she had found a real friend... but she also knew that he needed her friendship as much as she needed his.

* * *

'Mr Anthony Barkworth?' Gerry Ratter stood firmly on the doorstep, registering the look of surprise on Tony's face.

'Yes... what's the matter? Has something happened?' He looked around as Julia came up behind him. Realising they had got an audience, he went into television mode, remembering to portray the image of a perfect marriage. 'It's the police... darling.'

'Mr Barkworth,' Ratter continued, 'I wonder if you would be so good as to answer a few questions for us?'

'Certainly... but I haven't got long... you'd better come in.' Tony was agitated. If they didn't leave soon they'd be late for lunch at his mother's.

'I'm afraid that won't be possible, sir. We'd like you to accompany us to the station. I think it would be in your best interests not to refuse.' The firmness of his tone got the message through.

'What the bloody hell's going on?' Julia, annoyed at the intrusion and even more annoyed at not knowing what was going on wasn't going to let them cart her husband off without a fight. 'How long's this going to take?'

'That,' said Ratter gently, 'depends on Mr Barkworth.'

* * *

The large old rowing boat moved silently across the mirror-like surface of the lake as Max effortlessly but powerfully handled the oars, the muscles in his arms flexing. Marilyn couldn't help admiring his bronzed torso, visible through the opening at the front of his loose cotton shirt. Zoë sat mesmerised, taking in all the details around her. The huge lake was surrounded by weeping willows. Swans swam regally by, cheeky little moorhens skipped in and out of the reeds at the edge of the water and a wild duck watched over its young as they swam together. The whole picture was surmounted by an almost cloudless cerulean blue sky. Marilyn smiled to herself. To an outsider, she thought, they would look like the perfect family group...'

'Oh... I almost forgot,' Max said casually, 'Harvey was more than impressed with your tapes. I think he'll be getting in touch with you soon.'

* * *

'Hello... could you possibly get a message to Serena Hesketh? Yes... she's with you for the weekend. Yes. Could you ask her to ring me... Julia... yes, she's got the number. Tell her it's really urgent!' Julia was worried. The police hadn't told her anything, apart from the fact that they had got some questions to ask Tony. She couldn't really imagine him having done anything illegal... but what if he had? What about her career?

* * *

The fields shot past the train as Michael gazed blankly out of the window. Somehow he never realised quite how busy London was until he was faced with something with which to compare it. There were cows calmly grazing, birds hopping about in the hedgerows and sheep oblivious to the fact that their close relations were right at that very moment being basted in ovens around the country. The track ran beside a housing estate - lots of little houses all slightly different but basically the same. He caught sight of children playing in the gardens and fathers washing their cars in the drives: happy people, content in their obscurity.

What was it that made him different? There was his sexuality, of course, but that was by no means the basis of his life. He had always felt different, that the world was somehow his for the taking, but that he would get nothing without striving for it. Life had always been a challenge and today was no exception. He put his hand on the small holdall on the seat beside him and braced himself for the day ahead.

* * *

Iris grumbled at the nagging pain in her old bones as she hobbled to the door. Today she felt old - old and alone. Trevor had gone. She would never see him again. The one flicker of fun in her life had been cruelly snuffed out and she felt more alone than she would have ever thought possible. Why had it happened? The poor sod had been HIV positive anyway. Somehow, the fact had bound them together. It had given him a new outlook on life. His ability to live each day for what it was had impressed and touched her. But for it to end like that...

Was it really that Tony Barkworth chap who had done it? The policeman had said he would keep her informed. She had always done her best to co-operate with the police - as long as there was something in it for her - but being a key witness in a murder enquiry was not something she had ever envisaged. She heard the door knocker again as she put her hand on the handle.

'Alright... alright... I'm coming!' She didn't bother with the chain. If someone had come to murder her as well it would be a merciful release. She pulled the door open and exclaimed in surprise as she saw a familiar figure on the doorstep. 'Well! Bugger me if it ain't little Marcia!'

* * *

The doorbell chimed and Kathleen scuttled to answer it.

'Hello Mum. You look well!' Michael smiled at her, taking in the careful cotton print dress, the sensible shoes and the rather too clumsy string of pearls. Somehow his mother had never managed to do anything casually.

'Michael... how lovely to see you.' She didn't even try to keep the disappointment out of her voice as she stooped to let her son kiss her cheek. She had been expecting it to be Anthony, and for a split second had thought it was. But Anthony never had the carefree air that Michael seemed to carry around with him. She looked him up and down, taking in the black Levi's, loose white shirt. He wasn't even wearing a tie! Anthony would never come to lunch dressed like that. 'Did you have a good journey?' Not even waiting for a reply, she turned to go back to the kitchen and left Michael wondering whether to follow her or go into the lounge. He felt stifled already.

* * *

'Serena! Thank God it's you!' Julia screamed down the telephone. 'Can you come over? I'm beside myself. Tony's been taken to the police station for questioning. I don't know what he's

163

meant to have done. Oh please, come over... I need you!'

'Oh darling, how awful for you!' said Serena, thinking how wonderful it was. Silly little sod had probably been caught shoplifting or something. 'I'll be right over!' This was definitely worth missing a colonic irrigation session for.

*　*　*

'Where on earth do you think Anthony's got to?' Kathleen was marching around the lounge with her glass of medium sherry. Michael had managed to find a small can of light ale in one of the cupboards and was sitting quietly sipping its warm contents. 'He's never late. He's always punctual. Do you think he's had an accident? Oh Michael, do you think...' Michael watched his mother work herself up into a state of near hysteria and vehemently wished he hadn't bothered to come. It was as if he had only been invited as a foil to Tony's success; in his mother's eyes, he was a pale shadow of his twin. The telephone rang and Kathleen dashed to answer it.

'Hello? Yes... oh!' Her face took on a look of extreme puzzlement. 'Thank you. Goodbye.' Michael watched her brow as it creased into a frown. She replaced the receiver, walked to the sofa and sat down gently, staring ahead, not looking at Michael. 'That was Julia - your brother's wife. She said that Anthony's been called away suddenly so they won't be able to come... and then she hung up before I could even say goodbye properly. It was a bit abrupt. I've never even met her... well except on the telly... but that's not meeting really is it? So... I'm not going to see Anthony today...' Her voice trailed off and Michael thought she might cry.

'Never mind, Mum, at least there'll be more for us to eat!' Michael wished she would at least make the effort to make light of the situation. It surely wasn't too much to ask for her to pretend that she was looking forward to having lunch alone with him? But she didn't.

*　*　*

Gerry Ratter was trying to remain calm, but this Barkworth chap was the coolest customer he had dealt with in a long time. He had calmly answered their questions, once his solicitor had arrived, and they hadn't managed to catch him out on one single point. If he was telling the truth, there was no way he could have committed the murders.

'So... last Tuesday night you say that you had a dinner party at home and then stayed in...' Ratter stopped and lit another cigarette '...all night.'

'Look, I don't know what you're trying to get at. In fact, I wish you'd tell me what it is you think I've done.'

* * *

'Whatever made you want to come and visit a washed-up old bag like me then? How's that dishy husband of yours? Heard from your mother lately?' Iris had suddenly come alive as she led the way into the house. The barrage of questions was a bit overwhelming, but made Marcia glad that she had come.

'I hope I'm not intruding...'

'Lord no! Come and fill me in on what's going on in the world. Mind you, I've been in the thick of the action lately without realising it. Did you hear about that murder?'

'Yes. Terrible wasn't it. To think that that kind of thing can go on around here!'

'I know.' Iris suddenly felt young again. 'It was right next door!'

'No!'

'Yes! I knew him. He was my friend.' Trevor, she felt sure, wouldn't mind her getting a bit of mileage out of this one. Marcia felt a thrill of guilty pleasure at knowing someone who knew a murder victim.

'Don't you feel frightened that something like that can happen? Aren't you worried that it might happen to you?'

'Marcia, my love, after the life I've had I'm ready for anything. Anyway, I think the murderer will be behind bars before long.'

'What makes you say that?'

'Well,' Iris remembered Detective Inspector Ratter's orders not to tell anyone about her sighting of Tony Barkworth and smiled knowingly, 'let me just say that the police are working on a very strong lead at this very moment.'

'Oh, Auntie Iris! Don't get all mysterious. You know something, don't you?'

'Ask me no questions and I'll tell you no lies... and knock off the 'Auntie' - it makes me feel old!'

* * *

Serena's black Jaguar screeched to a halt behind the police car in Julia's drive and she leapt out in a cloud of black silk and Salvador Dali. If there was going to be any publicity about whatever was going on, she wanted part of it. She tripped up to the door and rang the bell.

The door was opened a fraction by a policeman who politely told her that Mrs Barkworth was busy.

'I'll come in and wait!' Serena barked, attempting to push the door open and enter. 'Let me in! I'm her best friend!' The constable didn't find that hard to believe. They made a good pair, this one and the offensive old bag his colleague was currently trying to interview in the library. Whatever made people think that having money made them any different in the eyes of the law?

'I'm sorry Madam... you'll have to come back later. We shouldn't be too long.'

* * *

Michael and Kathleen sat on either side of her carefully polished teak dining table and ate their meal in virtual silence. Michael made initial attempts at conversation, but his mother made no effort to follow them up. Any mention of his travels or social life aroused no interest on her part other than the occasional frown or remark referring to his sexuality. The only point at which she became animated was when she spoke of Tony and his recent marriage.

'Of course, they wanted it very quiet and private... what with being famous and all that.' Michael didn't like to mention that neither of them had been heard of at that point. He was also too

166

kind to elaborate on the reasons for Kathleen not being invited. Although she was totally oblivious to the fact, Tony didn't like his mother.

His last meeting with his brother was still fresh in Michael's mind. He had wanted advice and support at a time when his world had been in turmoil and Tony had as good as brushed him aside. His sexuality was apparently a 'phase' and his lifestyle 'immoral'. In Tony's eyes, Michael seemed to deserve everything he got, particularly if it was unpleasant. The fact that his long-term lover had just discovered he was HIV positive - an obvious source of distress - produced a reaction dangerously close to smug satisfaction from his twin.

'I suppose there's no harm in discussing the matter of the cottage with you... since I probably won't see you again for a long time.' Kathleen broke the embarrassing silence and then created another one. 'I know it's a long way for you to travel up here to Northampton. Don't worry... I'm not complaining... even if I sometimes don't see anyone for days on end.' She picked daintily at her food in an attempt to appear delicate. It was unfortunate that the reality of her rather ample frame collided with the possibility. 'Anyway, the cottage has got to be sorted out.' She stopped to have a big mouthful while she thought her son wasn't watching.

Michael, who had not thought about their holiday home in Norfolk for years, was suddenly reminded of the weeks spent there in his childhood, of the days when his father and Tony had gone out sailing in the dinghy, hunting for crabs in the rock pools, bird watching... His mother had always waited patiently for their return, making sure there was a meal ready. Michael had always been left to his own devices. 'Michael doesn't like sailing... can't stand the pace,' his father had always joked, cutting him to the quick as he desperately wished that he could at least have had the chance to decide for himself.

'... so I thought Anthony might as well have it,' his mother's words brought him back from his reverie, 'since you never liked it

167

there anyway.' Michael once again would have liked the chance to make up his own mind on the matter. 'It needs a lot of work done on it. At least Anthony has the money to do it now he's so successful. It'd be nice for him anyway... he always used to go up there to write those things he did for the newspapers. I think the fresh air used to inspire him.' Michael privately thought that there was nothing particularly fresh or inspired about anything his brother had written.

*   *   *

'Yes, officer, I'm absolutely positive that my husband was at home every night this week. We're a blissfully happy couple. We love each other's company.' Julia was worried. Whatever it was that Tony had been up to, she needed to cover it up. Nothing was going to destroy her television career. *Nothing!*

*   *   *

'Can we get an identity parade organised for tomorrow?' Ratter was exhausted. The interview with Tony Barkworth had so far given no hint of his guilt. He had even agreed to them taking a blood sample, which was currently being processed in the laboratory. If they could get Clive Haynes and Iris Devereux to pick him out of a parade, there would at least be grounds to arrest him. The blood sample genetically matching the traces of sperm they had found at the scene of the first murder would be the icing on the cake, but that would take a bit longer. He needed an arrest... and the sooner the better. 'We can? Go ahead then. Yes. Contact the witnesses.' A light was appearing at the end of the tunnel. 'As soon as possible!'

*   *   *

Serena poured another glass of brandy for the distraught Julia and, for the third time, tried to find out what the police had been questioning her about. All this sympathy was wearing her out. She wanted something to show for it.

'Did they tell you how long they're going to keep him? Have they charged him yet? Has he got a solicitor there?' This was

168

delicious... even more so than when Max had been dragged through the mud about his smutty telephone lines. 'What did they want to know?'

'They kept asking if I could vouch for his whereabouts every night last week.' Julia was frightened. 'So, naturally, I told them I could. But...'

'But you told *me* that the gorgeous Dr Leslie came round on Thursday and...' Serena never missed a trick.

'Serena! That was between you and me. Please... forget I ever told you!' Forgetting juicy gossip, unfortunately for Julia, was not in Serena's repertoire. Julia put her head in her hands. 'Oh God! I forgot about Leslie...'

*   *   *

Michael did his duty in the silent ritual of the washing up and watched his mother as she put everything back in the cupboards - everything meticulously arranged and painfully tidy. Not for the first time, he wished he hadn't come. Why did family matters always make him so edgy? Why did he let his mother get to him?

*   *   *

'We'll keep him in until tomorrow morning. There's an identity parade organised.' Gerry Ratter was annoyed. Barkworth still hadn't given an inch... and didn't look as if he was going to. The solicitor was starting to get on his nerves. He would have considered releasing Tony that night, but this officious little man with his leather brief case had made him determined to keep him in as long as the law would allow.

*   *   *

'What? How can a simple signal failure prevent any trains getting to London?' Michael was incredulous as the British Rail official shrugged. 'How long is it likely to take to put things right?'

'Dunno... and it *is* Sunday.' He shrugged again and scurried off to the sanctuary of his office, leaving Michael wondering what to do. The last thing he wanted to do was to go back to his mother's, but there might not be a train for hours. Northampton wasn't his idea of the ideal place to spend a Sunday evening. Unless, he suddenly thought, the seedy old bar he had frequented once or twice in his youth was still in existence...

* * *

Marcia put the magazine back on the coffee table and sighed. She had run out of things to do. Weekends used to be something to look forward to. This one had been a void to be filled, a quantity of time to be used up. Admittedly, Michael had helped her realise that there was more to life than being married. In reality, though, she hadn't quite come to terms with it yet. She looked at the telephone, silent as usual on the sideboard, and smiled at the thought that she had actually recorded a message on the telephone dating service. It had taken more courage than Michael would ever know. Goodness only knew if anyone had left a reply for her. There was only one way to find out...

* * *

The big old pub appeared to be closed, but as Michael walked closer he realised that a gentle hum of voices and music was just audible through the closed door. All the ground floor windows were boarded up and painted over. A few overgrown window boxes hinted at the fact that someone had made a half-hearted effort to brighten the place up in the past. The encroaching green slime on the canopies blatantly stated that they had since given up.

He couldn't help grinning as he gingerly knocked on the door. It brought back distant memories of his first forays into the mysterious world of the provincial homosexual. He had somehow thought that things would be different now, that there wouldn't be a need for boarded-up windows: the barricades against the heterosexual world he remembered only too well. A face appeared in a little square cut out of the door and he felt a pair of beady eyes looking him up and down. Shifting from one foot to the other, he felt as if he had accidentally travelled back in time.

'This is a private members' club.'

'Er... is there any chance of coming in?'

'D'you know what kind of club it is?'

'Yes,' Michael said, feeling that it would be better not to voice his true opinion, 'and I have been here before.' Stepping backwards and glancing up at the canopy over the door emblazoned with the name 'DOROTHY'S' he grinned. 'I think we've got a mutual friend.'

*   *   *

'Hello, London Love Lines. Brad speaking. How can I help you?'

'Er... I'm calling to see if I've got any replies. My reference is F353. My name's Marcia.'

*   *   *

Looking about himself in amused incredulity, Michael realised that the thing that made 'Dorothy's' so precious was not its dated shabbiness, its dralon banquettes, patterned carpet and pictures of old screen stars on the wall, but the fact that it didn't realise what it was. Like an old matron who had seen better days, it clasped its children to its bosom and hung on for dear life, closing its eyes to life in the outside world.

'It could do with a lick of paint in here, couldn't it?' The owner of the face behind the hole in the door had eventually let Michael in, revealing a bulky body dressed in baggy trousers and a silk shirt. 'I'm Steve... but everyone calls me Steph. I'll sign you in as a guest. D'you want to check your bag in?' Michael handed over the holdall and his jacket, paid the cloakroom fee and wandered over to the bar. He was well aware that his arrival had caused an inordinate amount of interest and was amused. Many years ago, he had plucked up the courage to come to this place and had looked up to its inhabitants as experienced gay men. Now the roles were reversed. He knew that the life he had carved for himself had far exceeded his expectations in those days. Now he had returned, bringing with him a worldliness rare and attractive to the fifteen or so pairs of eyes focussing on him.

'A pint of Budweiser please.'

171

'Haven't seen you around here before. New in town, are you?' the petite barman chirped.

'Just here for the day.' Michael decided not to give anything away and make the most of this unexpected and rather amusing interlude. He leaned on the bar and surveyed his surroundings again. This, he realised, was the only glimpse of gay life the men in this town ever had. If this was what they did for enjoyment, what did they do the rest of the time? There was a group of about five men sitting around a table behind him and he knew that he had become the subject of their conversation. Further along the bar there was an old man of about sixty standing alone. In a corner behind an incongruous palm tree was another little huddle of what he supposed were regulars. He couldn't help noticing that they all had a similar look, even though he normally hesitated before gen-eralising. They seemed perfectly at home in their surroundings. For a moment he felt like an intruder. He wondered if his arrival was seen as a threat to their world rather than a diversion. He paid for his pint and walked towards the darker end of the room, hoping to blend into the background.

'Hello.' A deep voice spoke from the shadows. 'It's good to see a new face around here.' Michael jumped as he came face to face with a heavily built man in a leather biker's jacket. For an instant he was reminded of Peter and his heart skipped a beat. It wasn't so much the guy's looks as his overall appearance. He was about forty, a little over six feet tall with broad shoulders and a very masculine aura. His strong jaw line, adorned with a day's growth of stubble, completed the image. 'I'm Ian. Do you want to come and join me over here?' He motioned towards a bench in the corner.

'Alright... yes. I'm Michael, by the way.'

'Pleased to meet you Michael.' Ian looked him straight in the eyes as he shook his hand firmly.

* * *

Marcia looked proudly at the name and telephone number she had jotted down on the pad. She had got a reply! Michael would be so impressed. She couldn't wait to tell him.

*   *   *

'Do you want another drink or do you fancy coming back to my place?' Ian's forwardness added to his masculinity. 'It's not far away.'

'Since you put it like that, I think you'd better lead the way.' Michael found himself unable to refuse. They got up and walked towards the door. As Michael collected his jacket and bag, the doorman winked.

'I hope you'll stay longer than an hour next time!' He opened the door for them and enviously watched them go out into the night.

'So that's your local is it?' Michael asked as Ian led the way down the road.

'Well, it is now. I used to live in Earls Court, but I had to move out here about five years ago for work. In a strange way, it was a good move. When I was in London, everything was available, but it meant I expected more. Out here the pace of life is slower. You come to expect less, so you're disappointed less often.'

'Oh... so it's not good to have high expectations?' Michael frowned.

'It depends what your chances are of fulfilling them.' Ian paused as he led the way into a street of red brick terraced houses. 'It's not much further.'

'But,' Michael was struggling to keep up, 'don't you ever hanker after a bit of London action?'

'Not really... I manage with what comes my way!' He grinned down at Michael. 'Here we are.' They had come to the first in a row of houses that opened straight onto the pavement. There was a warm red light glowing through the drawn curtains at the front window. He took a key from his pocket and unlocked the front door, which led into a dark hallway. Michael followed him in, clutching his holdall, a feeling of expectation growing in his loins. Ian opened a door and walked in, throwing off his jacket as he went. Michael followed, slightly taken aback to find that there was

173

another man in the room.

'Look what I've brought back for us! His name's Michael.' Ian sounded proud. The other man, similar in looks to Ian but older, smiled and got up.

'Er... look... I think you got the wrong idea.' Michael backed out through the doorway. 'I'm sorry, but it's not my scene.' He turned and headed for the front door, not waiting for a response from Ian.

* * *

Tony focussed his attention on the light bulb hanging from the ceiling of the cell and wondered how Julia was handling the situation. They were apparently keeping him in until the next morning. As far as he was concerned, the setting was different, but the feeling of imprisonment was nothing new.

* * *

Michael woke up as the train was pulling into Euston station. London beckoned to him as he thanked his lucky stars that the trains had started running again. Spending a night on the streets of Northampton might just have finished him off. Looking at his watch, he realised he had got time to get into the West End and have a drink before the bars closed. For once, he really needed one.

* * *

Darren, too depressed and lonely to stay at home despite the threat of there being a serial killer on the prowl, had decided to have a few drinks in town. 'Substation' was located in a basement in an alley off Tottenham Court Road and stayed open until one in the morning. As he walked down the stairs into the club, he wondered if he was about to meet his ideal man. The optimistic streak in his nature put a spring in his step and a smile on his face.

As he stepped into the semi-darkness, though, his smile faded; the industrial look of the place, complete with corrugated tin walls and link chain fencing, had more to do with cold hard reality than dreams and ideals. He wondered for a second as he approached the bar whether he would have been better off staying at home after all. Suddenly his eyes were drawn to a familiar-looking man sitting on a bar stool a few yards away from him. He thought his mind was playing tricks on him as he looked closer. His heart began to beat faster and his mouth dropped open.

'Tony?' he virtually whispered. His mouth had gone dry.

'No.' Michael laughed and Darren's heart skipped a beat. The voice was similar, but somehow different. 'My name's Michael.' He watched the boy flush crimson. 'Look... can I get you a drink? I think you're confusing me with my twin brother. To be quite honest, I didn't think any of our lot watched daytime television...'

CHAPTER TEN

'Looks like we'll have a result before the day's through then.' Gerry Ratter sat back in his chair cradling the receiver under his chin and allowed himself a smile for the first time in several days. 'Even if only one of the witnesses picks him out, we can arrest him.' He wished that they could have scheduled the identity parade for an earlier time. As far as he was concerned, the sooner the arrest was made and the press informed the better. 'And the results of the DNA profiling on the blood sample should be ready by this evening? Thanks.' He replaced the receiver and sat back in his chair. If things carried on in this direction, his promotion would be inevitable.

* * *

'... and last but not least, our very own cookery expert Diana Hennessy will be showing us how to make a wonderful goose terrine!' Julia's fixed smile didn't succeed in hiding the fact that she was tired. She had been up most of the night drinking with Serena, desperately hoping that Tony would be brought back from the police station in time for the morning's show. The brandy had given her a headache... but that wasn't what worried her. In her distraught state she had told Serena rather more than she should have done about Tony's late night sorties, not to mention intimate details of their rather strange sex life. Oh God, when would she ever learn? Now she was burdened with the extra strain of hosting the show on her own. 'So let's go straight into our first item, which concerns the problem of infidelity in marriage.' Smiling was getting more and more difficult. 'Our first guest is Marcus Langham from the Marriage Guidance Council.' Camera two homed in on the smartly dressed young man sitting on the sofa. 'Now, Marcus, you deal with people's marital problems every day of your working life. Just to enlighten those of us not familiar with such things,' Julia swallowed and fought the temptation to clear her throat, 'can you reveal the extent to which infidelity features in the breakdown of marriages today?'

'Well, Julia, I think it would be safe to say that lack of communication - in the sense that many married couples seem incapable of telling each other what they really want, both physically and emotionally - is more of a problem than actual infidelity itself. Of course, the former tends to lead to the latter in many cases.' He could see from the vacant look in her eyes that he had lost her already. 'Often it may be a simple thing like a private fantasy that someone may have - I'm talking about the sexual side of things now - and a failure on the part of the spouse to satisfy or at least go along with this can often lead to satisfaction being sought elsewhere...'

'Can you be more specific?' Julia asked, soon to wish she hadn't.

'Well,' Marcus began, 'one couple came to me a little while ago and they had stopped sleeping together, were barely able to carry on living in the same house and had started initial divorce proceedings. They only really came to me as a last resort.'

'And,' Julia butted in, suddenly interested now someone else's problems were in the limelight, 'what was the matter?'

'It was exceedingly simple, really. The husband had a fantasy about seeing his wife dressed as a maid - mainly because she had been a waitress when he first met her - but had never dared mention it...'

'Oh... really.' Julia wrinkled her nose in disgust.

'...and the wife, believe it or not, had written her husband off as

177

being boring in bed. Once they talked about it - and visited the Ann Summers shop - their relationship was completely rekindled. She said it was like starting their courtship all over again!'

'Well, that's a lovely little success story,' Julia said without much feeling, 'but surely this weird sex thing doesn't apply to *normal* people? I mean, when I first met my husband...' she stopped for a moment, looking at the empty space on the sofa beside her '... I was at a fancy dress party dressed as a nun. Are you saying that I've got to put on a wimple and habit to rekindle our relationship? Not, of course, that it needs it.' She gave a silvery laugh and waved her hand in the air. 'Of course, we're devoted to each other. Really, Marcus, I think you're being a bit extreme! Perhaps you'd like to discuss the medical causes for infidelity with our very own Dr Leslie McManus...'

* * *

'My God, love,' Iris Devereaux chortled at the screen, 'you've changed your tune. You were the best little lollipop lady I ever had on my books!' She wondered again how much Julia knew about her husband's nocturnal activities. The press, she knew only too well, would gleefully rip her apart when the story broke. A policeman had contacted her that morning to ask if she would be available in the early afternoon for an identity parade. It looked as if an arrest was imminent. She looked again at the woman on the screen and couldn't help feeling some sympathy for her.

* * *

Tony looked at the cold grey walls of the interview room and wondered what he was paying his solicitor for. Why hadn't he got him out of this already? He had hardly slept a wink on the hard bunk and he couldn't help wondering if Julia would back him up on his account of his whereabouts during the week. Only the day before she had been desperate to know what he had been up to. God... wasn't a man allowed a bit of space? He looked again at the grey featureless walls and thought he would rather die than be locked up. But how could they lock him up? They hadn't even told him what crime he was meant to have committed. The door opened and Detective Inspector Ratter strode in.

'Good morning Mr Barkworth. Sorry you've had to miss your show. I'm sure your lovely wife will be coping admirably on her own. Now, we just need you to sign your statement. Shall we go over it again?' Tony's clammy hands didn't go unnoticed as they fidgeted under the table.

* * *

'When we come back after the news break, we'll be talking to a sex therapist who uses hypnotism to find out what really turns her patients on,' Julia gabbled, eager to get a chance to talk to Leslie McManus in private, 'so stay tuned if a session on the couch is just what your sex life needs!' She breathed a sigh of relief as soon as she was off the air and looked around again for the doctor. He was ambling back to the green room. Julia was almost out of breath as she intercepted him.

'Leslie! I didn't get the chance to talk to you before the show. Look... this is a bit embarrassing but....' she stopped as Darren, armed with a clipboard, walked past annoyingly slowly. When he was at a safe distance, she continued '... your little visit on Thursday. It... it didn't happen okay?'

'Sure thing sister!' Leslie grinned, his smile almost evaporating the feeling of dread that was gripping her stomach. 'To think I was just on the verge of telling my wife...'

'Leslie! It's not a laughing matter. Look, I'll tell you why another time...' her voice trailed of as Darren came rushing back along the corridor.

'Miss Daley! There's someone waiting to see you in your dressing room. Apparently it's urgent.'

* * *

'London Love Lines... Troy speaking. How can I help you?' Michael felt that his life was on an even keel again now that he was back at work. The events of the previous day had thrown him slightly off balance. His chat with Darren had reminded him of his

179

own youth - the constant and largely fruitless search for a man - but had also made him realise how far he had come. The boy hadn't actually said as much, but was clearly obsessed with Tony. Why was the unattainable always so much more attractive?

'Yes... I'd like to get in touch with Marcia... reference F353.' Michael smiled. At least Marcia was going to get a bit of what she deserved at last.

* * *

Marcia jumped as the telephone rang.

'Hello?'

'Hello Marcia. It's Iris. Look... I hate to have to ask you... but would you come to Scotland Yard with me this afternoon? I don't really feel up to going on my own. I wouldn't ask but...'

'Of course. What time do you want me to come over?'

'I've got to be there at one.'

'Iris,' Marcia was curious, 'is this about...'

'I don't want to talk about it on the phone, love. I'll tell you later.'

* * *

Clive nervously chewed his nails and wondered how he was going to fill his morning. He had received a call asking him to be at Scotland Yard at one o'clock. The police seemed to have suddenly changed their tune. It wasn't long ago that they had made him feel that *he* was the criminal. He almost expected to be arrested any minute for wasting police time. He had been intrigued to see that Tony Barkworth was missing from his place on the sofa that morning... and no explanation had been given. The suspense was almost too much to bear.

* * *

'Mrs Barkworth?' The solicitor didn't watch daytime television.

'Oh, for goodness' sake call me Miss Daley! I might be married to him, but I'm a woman in my own right!'

'I'm sorry, I didn't mean any offence. The reason I'm here is to try to explain what this business is all about. I'm quite sure you've got no idea why your husband has been detained for questioning. There is a distinct possibility that the police will want to ask you a few questions...'

'Too late... they already have!' Julia spouted, keeping a close eye on the time. She didn't want to mess this show up: her first attempt at hosting it without Tony.

'Oh... did they want to know his whereabouts at certain times during the week?'

'Yes,' Julia was starting to feel rather sick, 'and I naturally told them that he was at home with me.'

'Oh... er... well that's good.' In a way, the young solicitor felt he had been overridden. 'But I think in future I ought to be there during any questioning.'

'In future? How long is this likely to go on? We *have* got the show to consider.' Julia was tired, irritated, impatient and more than a little worried about the lies she had told the police. What if Tony really had done something when he was out in the middle of the night? 'What are they questioning him about anyway?'

The solicitor took a deep breath and looked straight at her.

'Murder.'

* * *

'No news about this serial killer, then?' John was sitting on the edge of Michael's desk. 'They'll probably never catch him... you know how efficient the police are! Just think... it could be anyone. One minute, a nice bit of rumpy pumpy... the next you're bound and gagged doing an impression of a shish kebab. Oh well, it all makes life a bit more exciting!'

'I think that's a bit tasteless, don't you?' Michael was still slightly subdued from the day before. 'And I do think the police are doing all they can.'

'Why haven't they made an arrest yet, then?' John sneered.

'They can't just go around arresting people out of the blue, can they?' Michael did sometimes get a bit exasperated with his colleague.

'What about me in the toilets in Hyde Park, then?'

* * *

Darren's head was nearly bursting. His brain had been working overtime and he didn't know quite what to make of it all. The chance meeting with Tony's brother the night before had both raised his hopes and dashed them: Michael had quite clearly not been into younger guys. Consequently, his morning had been spent in a reflective haze. But now he had suddenly been forced to arrange his thoughts and work out what to do next. His habit of listening at the dressing room door had become addictive and, even though Tony wasn't there, he had been unable to resist the temptation to press his ear against the door when Julia had gone in to speak to the smart little man with the briefcase.

He jumped suddenly as the floor manager shouted at him. Shit! He had forgotten the coffee! He leapt over to the coffee machine with seconds to spare and ran over to the table where Julia was arranging her legs into a suitable position for discussing the use of hypnotism in sex therapy.

* * *

Kathleen sat on her dralon sofa surveying her collection of china flowers on the mantelpiece. She had spent the whole of the previous evening waiting for a telephone call from Anthony to apologise for having missed lunch. All night she had waited. It had quite spoiled her enjoyment of 'Lady Chatterley's Lover'. And still he hadn't telephoned. On top of that, he wasn't on television this morning. There was something wrong. She could feel it.

Just as, many years earlier, she had known there was something intrinsically wrong with her family, she knew now that something was happening: something that could threaten the very core of her comfortable existence. Only this time it might not just go away if she ignored it...

* * *

'...what you're saying is that a problem of a sexual nature,' Julia had resorted to repetition again, 'can be quite simple to solve

182

once the cause has been found.' The sex therapist viewed her sadly. 'But do you really think quoting this case history involving an ex-prostitute is really *relevant?* I mean, normal everyday people don't know much about prostitution and that kind of thing,' Julia gulped as she found herself running out of breath, 'so don't you think it would be a bit more appropriate to deal with more regular topics?'

'Such as?' The therapist had had enough of her work being brought into question and wanted to see what this rather odious woman could come up with on her own. 'I'm open to suggestions.'

Julia paused, wishing that Tony was there to make some inane comment for which she could criticise him afterwards. At least it would have filled this embarrassing silence.

'Maybe,' the therapist continued, having proved her point and wanting to draw attention to another, 'you mean something like the problems encountered by a mature woman married to a much younger man.'

* * *

'Serena! That bill from Champneys is completely over the top. Much as I enjoy seeing you going away...' Max had decided to put his foot down and had found his wife in a deck chair by the swimming pool with a large Pimms. It had only just dawned on him what a drain on his resources his wife was. She seemed to spend more on incidental fripperies than most women earned. But then Serena had never had to work for a living. Everything had always been provided for her. '... I really think it's time you learned that money doesn't grow on trees.'

'Oh, Max, don't go on. You know I've got a headache. Just because I got a taxi back from Julia's last night...'

'You did *what?*' Max was incredulous.

'Oh... so you want me to risk losing my licence do you? I had to have a drink with her to calm her nerves what with... her problems and... well, as I said... you wouldn't want me to risk losing my licence would you?' At that particular moment, Max would have gladly risked her losing anything that was vital to her continued existence.

'How much did it cost?'

'Darling... you know I can't abide meanness. Anyway, the driver was a dirty old sod. He made improper advances!'

'You should be so lucky!'

'What? Are you trying to say I'm not an attractive and vulnerable woman? You should be concerned about your wife being out alone in the middle of the night - out on a mission to help a friend in distress.' Serena tried to look helpless and hurt. 'But you needn't worry about the money. I told him I'd report him to the police for attempted rape if he charged me more than forty quid.' She looked pleased with herself. 'You know I have this way with men.'

'Well,' Max felt rather ill at the thought that he was married to this woman, 'enough's enough as far as I'm concerned. I've just cancelled your credit cards and your housekeeping will be brought into line with reality as from now.'

'Oh... I see... it's like that is it? Well, we'll see how you change your tune when your little Percy Flonker decides he wants a little trip up Serena's Slippery Slalom...' realising as the words left her mouth that it had been well over six months since they had engaged in anything remotely sexual, she changed her tune. 'Oh... look... I'm sorry darling! Let's be friends. I didn't mean it!'

'Well I did!' snapped Max with a finality that quite surprised her. 'And just in case you were in any doubt about it whatsoever, I find you about as sexually appetising as a lump of braising steak with a hole in it!'

* * *

'And now we move onto the somewhat different topic of eating disorders in men. All too often we hear stories of women who have become victims of anorexia nervosa or bulimia - the Princess of Wales being the most highly publicised case in recent months - due to the extreme pressures put on us to be slim and shapely.' Julia breathed in and pushed her bust forward before continuing. 'But now, apparently, it has come to light that men, too, suffer from similar disorders.'

'Yes Julia,' Leslie McManus took over calmly, 'the most common being an excessive need to feel in control of the body - its intake and its appearance. A dramatic increase in the use of the male body in advertising - as well as the forced emergence of the "new man" - has led to an increased feeling of inferiority in the male mind.' He smiled sympathetically, perfectly confident of his own outward appearance. 'Consequently, many men now virtually starve themselves, whilst attempting to build up their bodies in the many gymnasiums which have become noticeably more popular over the last decade. It's a rather sad sign of the male species striving for control...'

* * *

'Max... hello... it's Marilyn. I just want to thank you... and so does Zoë... for a lovely day yesterday. You really made me think life's worth living again.' Max smiled to himself. The sentiment was mutual.

* * *

Feeling like a naughty schoolgirl being called up in front of the headmaster, Julia knocked on the door of Harvey Wolfenden's office. She didn't know how to explain Tony's absence, but she was sure something would spring to mind. Telling the truth had never been her speciality, nor an habitual practice, but she knew she had handled the show well on her own and would bluff her way out of it somehow.

'Come in.' She felt herself shaking slightly, her self-confidence suddenly fleeing just when she needed it most, as she pushed the door open.

* * *

'Well,' Gerry Ratter paused again, 'it's just that we need to make *absolutely* sure that your version of the events of this week tally with your wife's...' Tony tried to keep his face expressionless and, purely by chance, detected a subtle wink from his solicitor.

'I think you'll find no irregularities,' he said, his confidence regained. So that was why this guy was so expensive. Ratter sighed. At this rate, they weren't going to be able to keep him much longer. If only they had one more hint of evidence to work on...

* * *

'The thing is, Julia, you've been sailing a bit close to the wind, lately - what with some of your rather unsubtle comments and your "open mouth put foot in" approach to interviewing. And now you decide to turn up without your husband with the excuse,' he paused on the word and watched her shift slightly in her chair, 'that he's had a sudden attack of diarrhoea.' Julia wished she had chosen another illness... any other illness. But what do you say when you're desperate? How could she tell him that Tony was being questioned about a string of murders? 'Just make sure he's back here with you tomorrow or we might have to reconsider a few things... like your contract for instance.'

* * *

'Now, Miss Devereux, I'm sure you've seen this kind of thing on the television, but I just want to assure you that the men behind that screen can't see you at all.' The Inspector was younger than she would have thought possible. He took her arm gently as he guided her along the glass wall. 'As you'll see, they're each holding a number. I want you to take your time and if, and only if, you recognise the man you saw leaving your neighbour's home in the early hours of Friday morning, I'd like you to tell me.

* * *

'I'll see you tomorrow then,' Michael shouted to John as they parted at the tube station, 'I'm off to the gym.'

* * *

Gerry Ratter watched the seconds ticking by on the clock as he waited in his office for the results of the identity parade. The was still a feeling in the pit of his stomach that everything wasn't going to go quite as smoothly as planned. Perhaps there *was* more to this case than met the eye after all. The telephone rang. Having

186

particularly asked not to be disturbed, he picked it up and barked angrily into the receiver.

'Yes? Ratter speaking!'

'Sir... I know you didn't want to be disturbed, but there's somebody on the line who refuses to speak to anyone but you. He says it's about the gay murders. We've traced the call to a payphone at Waterloo Station.'

'Alright... put him through.' The line clicked as he wondered what kind of crank he was about to speak to.

'Hello... er... the man you've been questioning about the gay murders...' Darren's palm sweated as he clung to the receiver.

'I beg your pardon?' Ratter was perturbed. He had given strict instructions for a total press ban on the case until an arrest was made.

'I think you should know that he has an identical twin brother who's gay.' Darren's heart was in his mouth as his courage evaporated and he hurriedly replaced the receiver.

'Hello... hello...' Ratter angrily got back to the switchboard. 'If you get any more calls like that, you can keep them!' A knock at his door calmed him down. 'Come in!' It was the young inspector who had been conducting the identity parade. He looked pleased.

'Both of them picked him out, Gerry. Both of them!'

* * *

'Look, Iris, you did what you had to do.' Marcia had brought the old lady back to her flat for a cup of tea. The ordeal seemed to have taken a lot out of her.

'But... but I've never been responsible for incriminating anyone before.' Iris paused and then thought of what Trevor must have been through. 'No... no... I suppose you're right.' She still hadn't told Marcia who the suspect was. She would leave that to the media. The girl had been good enough to accompany her to the police station. She didn't want to burden her with more secrets to keep. A knock came on the door and Marcia ran to answer it.

'Michael! You were late back last night... what happened to

you? Come in a moment.' She stood back to let him into the flat, simultaneously letting the old lady catch a glimpse of her friend.

'No thanks Marcia, I'm in a bit of a hurry... and I've got to clean up the flat. I just wanted to let you know you've got quite a few replies to your...' He suddenly realised that she might not want the news broadcast. 'I'll see you later anyway.' He turned and leapt up the stairs two at a time as Marcia closed the door.

'Iris! What's the matter?' The cup had fallen from the old lady's hand and she was staring blankly in front of her as the hot liquid ran over the sofa. 'Iris... are you alright?'

'Yes... yes... I just had a funny turn.' Her composure returned swiftly as she tried to pull herself together and think about what she had just seen. 'Ooh, look at your sofa. I am sorry!' She hobbled to her feet. 'Find me a cloth and I'll mop it up.'

'No, don't worry. I'll do it later. Are you sure you're alright?'

'Yes, of course I am! Who was that nice-looking young man, dear?'

'Just a friend. And you might as well know he's gay before you try to pair me off with him. Strangely enough, you might have seen his brother on the television. He does a mid morning show.' She smiled, proud that she knew someone interesting. 'They're identical twins.'

'Could you take me home please, dear? I suddenly feel very tired.' Far from feeling tired, Iris' mind was working overtime.

* * *

The realisation that he had actually solved the murder was just sinking in to Gerry Ratter's mind. The DNA of the sperm sample found at the scene of the Maida Vale murder had matched that of the blood sample taken from Tony Barkworth. On top of that, both witnesses had picked him out straight away from the identity parade. Seldom had there been such a clear-cut case. Now he was going to have the pleasure of arresting the smooth-talking creep. The only thing marring the otherwise perfect picture was the fact that his wife had given him cast-iron alibis for the two nights in question. Silly cow must have been lying after all.

The telephone rang.

'Ratter speaking!'

'Sir... the lady who identified the suspect from the identity parade is on the line. Yes. Miss Devereux. She says it's very important...'

* * *

He had done it! Clive sank back into an armchair pleased with himself. He had actually come face to face, albeit through a piece of one-way glass, with his attacker. The police had told him they would keep him informed of any developments. An arrest was evidently just around the corner. If only they had listened to him a bit sooner, at least one life could have been saved.

* * *

'You mean that identical twins have an identical DNA profile?' Ratter had suddenly realised the full implications of what the forensic scientist was trying to explain to him.

'Of course. One sperm fertilises one egg which then splits and makes two babies.'

'So a sperm sample from one twin could match a blood sample from the other one?'

'Of course.'

CHAPTER ELEVEN

'Well... how about that then?' Ratter's eyes had scanned the living room of Michael's flat and come to rest on the large machete hanging on the chimney breast. 'I think we've found our murder weapon!'

'What about this, sir? I think you'd better have a look in here,' the officer called from the bedroom. Ratter followed the source of his voice and saw his colleague carefully holding a cupboard door open. Inside, hanging neatly in rows, was a collection of black leather harnesses, masks and whips.

* * *

The telephone rang. Julia jumped. She must have dozed off. Her mouth felt dry and there was a dreadful taste left by countless large brandies. Trying to drag herself back into consciousness, she looked at her watch. It was nearly eight o'clock. Eight o'clock and drunk already. The telephone was still ringing. But what if... no... it couldn't be. With a shaking hand she reached for the receiver.

'Hello?'

'Mrs Barkworth?'

'Yes... speaking.'

'Scotland Yard here. We're very happy to tell you that your husband is on his way home. He's been eliminated from our enquiries.'

'And about bloody time too!' she snapped, slamming the receiver down. The cheek of it - keeping him in there all this time, putting the fear of God into her and getting Harvey annoyed. And not so much as an apology! How *dare* the police pick on innocent people? She would show them. They would wish they had never tried to intimidate the Barkworths!

She groped around for the telephone book and, picking up the receiver again, dialled a number. This would show them! 'Hello... news desk please.'

*　　*　　*

'Look... I don't know what you're talking about.' Michael was beginning to feel victimised. He had been in the interview room for what seemed like hours and they still hadn't told him what he was meant to have done. But he had a fair idea. 'What do you want me to say?'

'Well, for a start, let's talk about your movements on the evening of last Tuesday.' Ratter spoke slowly and clearly. He knew it would only be a matter of time before they got a confession. They had already made the arrest - the search of the flat had provided enough evidence for that - but a confession would just round it off nicely and make it a lot more straightforward. The press would have to know sooner or later and he wanted to have it all sewn up first. He couldn't afford to be portrayed as anything short of totally efficient. If only they hadn't brought in the celebrity brother for questioning. Ratter could feel it in his bones that there would be repercussions.

*　　*　　*

'I think we could come to some sort of agreement for exclusive rights.' Julia was proud of herself. This would clear Tony's name before any hint of it leaked out. He would be made into a hero for withstanding all those hours of police questioning. Perhaps they could do a piece about it on the show. 'Perhaps you'd better send someone over to discuss the figure... I think it's so vulgar to talk about large amounts of money on the telephone. But don't take too long about it. Remember... the early bird catches the worm.'

*　　*　　*

191

'So, let's run over this again.' Gerry Ratter paused and paced the room. So far this guy hadn't come up with an alibi for the times during which the two murders had taken place. 'You left this... club... in Brixton in the early hours of Wednesday morning and *walked* home to your flat in Clapham. Don't you know how dangerous it is to walk alone at night? There are some strange people around...'

* * *

'Tony!' Julia flung her arms around her husband as he stood in the doorway looking frail and tired. Slightly taken aback by this uncharacteristic show of emotion, he was nevertheless past caring and simply wanted a long hot bath and a good night's sleep in his own bed. 'What have they done to you?' She grabbed his hand and pulled him inside. 'Thank you!' She dismissed the policeman who had brought him home and slammed the front door.

* * *

'Let me take you back two years.' Ratter had changed tack. His rapid research into Michael's recent past had confirmed his view that he had, without a shadow of a doubt, got the right man.

'Look, I've already told you I've been away in Greece for the last two years...' Michael began.

'Yes.' Ratter paused and leaned towards his suspect. 'You left at the beginning of April. Which *happened* to be just after the mutilated body of the third victim was found.' He paused again, using the silence. 'Now that's convenient isn't it? *Had* to get away did you? Perhaps you'd like to tell me about it... what you thought you needed to get away *from.*'

* * *

Julia looked down at Tony's sleeping form and smiled. He needed his sleep. Tomorrow would be a long day. And now she was in for a long night. She had telephoned Harvey and organised the show for the next day. It was short notice, she knew, but they couldn't waste an opportunity like this. The proposed item on cot deaths had gone out of the window. This was far more important. It

192

was their duty as a 'caring' show to let the public know about the tactics used in police questioning. The fact that she hadn't discussed any of his ordeal with her husband didn't occur to her - there would have plenty of time for Tony's side of the story tomorrow. She wondered whether she ought to have told Harvey a bit more. No, in her experience it was better to be a bit vague and mysterious. He would find out soon enough how brilliantly she had handled the whole business.

The journalists would be arriving at the house any moment. She was wearing a loose silk kimono and a doleful face to let them see what a dreadful experience she had been through. She smiled at her own cleverness as she walked down the wide staircase. Almost on cue the doorbell rang.

* * *

'And you use these telephone dating lines on a regular basis do you? I mean, you just think "I'll pick up the phone and find a new man" do you?' The Detective Inspector looked again at copies of gay newspapers and magazines found in Michael's flat. Many of them carried advertisements for chatlines and dating agencies on the premium rate network. Some of them had been underlined and there were names and reference numbers scrawled by the side of them. The duty solicitor wrinkled his nose in disdain as he continued taking notes. 'And you don't think this is in any way unusual behaviour?'

'Look... I've told you... I work for a company that runs some of these lines.' Michael, far from being daunted by this policeman, was getting indignant. 'Telephone dating is big business and it's been going on for years. Thousands of people use those lines every day. It's a very efficient way of meeting the type of people you're looking for.'

'Oh... I see!' Ratter's mind was making rapid deductions... and it all fitted in with Clive Haynes' account of the attempted murder. He made a note to contact all the dating companies to see if the two recent victims had advertised on any of their lines. He felt sure they had. 'And that's where you found your other victims was it? Very clever. No chance of being seen with them in public. Perhaps there were more? How many more *were* there Michael? Where did you dump the others?' He was getting excited now. Perhaps he had caught another Nilson or Lupo! He had always suspected that this thing might be a lot bigger than they had previously thought. According to psychologists, a killer was getting towards the end of his 'career' when he started killing in the victims' homes and left the bodies to be found. Thank God they had caught him before he did any more. 'What have you got to lose, Michael? It'll be a lot easier if you tell us all about it now.'

* * *

'... I don't mind telling you that they were some of the worst hours of my life,' Julia lowered her voice and put her fingers to her temple, 'but I didn't doubt his innocence for a moment.' She moved a little in the armchair and crossed her legs, allowing the kimono to part slightly. Thankfully she had shaved her legs all the way up. 'You see... we're devoted to each other.' She smiled sweetly at the reporter in the chair opposite who was secretly beginning to feel rather nauseous. 'My one concern,' she purred, thinking of the figure on the agreement she had just signed, 'is that other innocent members of the public are made aware of the fact that at any time they could be pounced on by the police and put through gruelling hours of sheer hell.'

* * *

'I think you're being very foolish, Michael.' Ratter drummed his fingertips on the desk. Things were not going to plan. The boys from the forensic department, who were still going through the flat with a fine tooth comb, had so far turned up nothing new. The machete on the wall had not been ruled out as a possible murder weapon, but there were no traces of blood or human tissue on it. He needed a confession and he needed it now, before the press conference he had hastily organised. There was still just about enough time to get it in the following day's papers and get the public off his back. At the very least they would be able to report that there had been an arrest. He looked at the clock and then, looking straight at his suspect, got up to leave.

Michael looked back at him calmly. He had telephoned Sebastian when he had first been arrested and was confident that he would have found him a decent solicitor. Paying for it would be another matter, but he would cross that bridge when he came to it. So far he was confident that he had said nothing to incriminate himself.

*　*　*

Julia opened a new bottle of brandy and smiled. The reporters had gone and she was alone with the prospect of even more money to spend. She poured herself a large tumbler full of the brown liquid and downed it in one gulp. She belched loudly and poured another. Tony would be so impressed when he found out. She took another mouthful. They could afford a Ferrari now. Maybe two Ferraris.

As she drifted into a drunken sleep, the glass fell from her hand and the contents spilled onto the Aubusson carpet.

*　*　*

'Mr Hunt?' Ratter was not in the most patient of moods. He wanted to carry on trying for a confession, but the duty solicitor had advised him to give the suspect a respite. Now this 'close friend' of the accused had turned up with some flashy solicitor and wanted to speak to him.

'Yes... Sebastian Hunt. Are you Detective Inspector Ratter?'

'Yes.'

'I feel that I ought to speak to you for a moment if I may. The whole matter of Michael's arrest is causing me great concern.' Ratter tried not to smile. The power of understatement in the upper classes never failed to amuse him. 'I take it that your chief reason for suspecting him is the fact that his lover had the misfortune to be one of the victims?'

'I'm sorry?' Ratter realised that he had missed something somewhere.

195

'His lover... Peter Harlow. He was murdered two years ago...' Sebastian's voice trailed off as he saw the look of bewilderment in the Detective Inspector's eyes changing to a triumphant gleam.

'Thank you Mr Hunt. I think your 'close friend' omitted to fill me in on that little detail.'

'I...' Sebastian was thrown totally off balance. 'I just thought that you might have been jumping to false conclusions and...' Too late, he realised that he had done his friend no favours.

CHAPTER TWELVE

'*A thirty year old man was arrested yesterday in connection with the murders of homosexuals Eric Hefford and Trevor Bainbridge. He has not yet been named but will appear in court tomorrow morning to face charges...*' Julia switched off the car radio and breathed a sigh of relief.

'Thank goodness they got him! How on earth did they think it could have been you anyway? I think the Metropolitan police force has got a lot to answer for.'

'I'm just going to pull over and get the papers.' Tony felt better after a good night's sleep and was quite looking forward to getting to the studios. He was wearing a new light grey Balmain suit and felt that, somehow, the happenings of the day before had made him more worldly. Hopefully the viewers would pick up on that; maybe they would notice that he was more than just his wife's sidekick.

'No!' Julia looked at her reflection in the mirror on the sun visor and wondered how the photographs accompanying the story had come out. She hadn't had the opportunity to tell him about her newspaper deal yet and, in the cold light of day, couldn't deny the fact that she was starting to get cold feet. She ran her fingers over the pleated silk of her skirt, thinking how old and wrinkled her hands looked in comparison to the smooth delicate fabric. 'We'll see them later anyway. We really ought to get to the studios as soon as possible to run through this new stuff.'

'What new stuff?' She hadn't told him about that either.

'Oh... Harvey decided to replace that cot death feature with a piece on the methods used by the police when questioning suspects.'

'What!' Tony nearly went through a red light. 'I don't bloody believe it! The cold-hearted bastard. How fucking insensitive can you get?'

* * *

'Now Michael,' the solicitor had arrived the evening before and was going through Michael's side of the story for what seemed to his client like the hundredth time, 'the thing is that you haven't got an alibi for either of the nights when the murders were committed, not to mention the fact that a machete was found in your flat along with a collection of leather... er... appliances.'

'Look, I've told you. They're not mine... they belong to the guy who owns the flat. How many times do I have to tell you? You *do* believe that, I didn't do it, don't you?'

'*My* opinions don't come into it. The point is that it's my job to get you off.'

'Get me off? But I haven't done anything!' Michael's nerves were beginning to fray. 'What do I have to do to persuade you?'

'It's not me you have to persuade.'

* * *

Max sighed and replaced the telephone receiver. Once again the nature of his business was being brought into question. This time the police wanted access to the records of his various dating companies to see if the victims of the recent murders had advertised on the lines. The man arrested the night before apparently worked in his Brixton office. It was all he needed. If the press got hold of the story, they would be swarming around him all over again.

* * *

'Come on Michael. How could you have forgotten to tell me something as important as that?' Ratter was determined to get a confession before the end of the day.

'I didn't forget. I just couldn't see how it was relevant that my

198

lover was murdered two years ago. Do you know what I went through at the time?'

'No,' Ratter flicked through the pathologist's report on the table in front of him, 'but I've a fair idea of what *he* went through! Why did you do it? Did it start of as a bit of fun?'

'Fun?' Michael was stunned.

'Yes... all this role playing. Did it get out of hand? Maybe it was a mistake. Maybe you didn't mean to kill him. Yes. Perhaps it was all a game that got out of hand...' he was sure he was on to something '... and then you found you enjoyed it... *needed* it. Was it like a drug Michael?'

* * *

Kathleen rushed to her front door as the doorbell chimed again.

'Oh... I'm glad you're in. Have you seen the papers?' It was Marjorie, breathless but excited. 'Your Tony... they had him in for questioning about those gay murders!' She was quick to note her friend's shocked expression. 'Didn't you know? They've done a big interview with his wife about the ordeal she had to go through when he was hauled off by the police. I know they let him off, but it makes you wonder, doesn't it?'

* * *

'Mr Barkworth,' Darren was overjoyed to see Tony back at the studios, but frustrated that he couldn't tell him that he was responsible for him being released, 'I've got a message for you. Can you ring your mother immediately? It's very urgent.'

'Oh bloody hell... that's all we need!' Julia scowled,

'I didn't ask for your opinion... I think you've said far too much already!' Tony felt that life was closing in on him again. The whole studio had been buzzing that morning with the news of the arrest. Every paper carried a front page story about it and, no doubt, London's gay community was breathing a sigh of relief. A 'thirty year old man' was apparently 'helping the police with their enquiries'. Nobody would have been any the wiser if it hadn't been for Julia. Now his name was being bandied about in connection with the murders thanks to her loose tongue. He could almost hear the speculative comments. 'There's no smoke without fire'. 'He's a dark horse... who'd have thought he knew anything about the gay scene?' 'I wonder where the police picked him up?' Even if he couldn't hear the comments, he could see them in people's eyes. He couldn't believe that Julia could be so stupid as to talk to the press... and nor could Harvey Wolfenden. He had made it blatantly clear that he was immensely displeased and had made a point of telling them, none too subtly, that he was meeting with his lawyers later on that day to go over their contracts.

* * *

Kathleen said three Hail Marys and took a valium. Why hadn't Tony rung her yet? She sat looking at the telephone. If only he would ring and tell her everything was alright.

* * *

'You've obviously got it into your head that I did it, so I don't see any point in discussing it further.' Michael put his head in his hands and hoped, not for the first time, that it was all some terrible nightmare from which he would wake up soon. 'Peter meant more to me than you'd probably even understand. I was going to lose him anyway. Why would I want to bring the day any closer?'

'Lose him? You mean he was going to leave you?' Ratter was excited.

'No.' Michael swallowed and looked reflective for a moment. 'He had been diagnosed HIV positive. He was already showing signs of developing full-blown Aids.' He stopped. The pain of the memory was too much.

'I see.' Ratter's memory had been jogged. 'Well, I think we'll take a break now...'

* * *

Max looked at the newspaper and grinned. He didn't normally read the tabloids, but one of the girls in the office had left it lying around. Julia's face, bearing a doleful 'wronged' expression, stared out at him. He couldn't believe the lengths some people would go to

200

get a bit of publicity. So Tony Barkworth had been questioned about this gay murder business. While not wishing that on anyone, he couldn't help feeling that Tony might be getting a taste of his own medicine. As he knew only too well, the truth and tabloid newspaper stories didn't always go hand in hand. The telephone rang.

'Hello. Max Hesketh.'

'This is Detective Inspector Shadwell from Scotland Yard. I'd just like to thank you for your co-operation this morning.'

'Oh... did you find what you were looking for?'

'I'm not at liberty to say at the moment, but if we need your help in the future we'll be in touch.'

* * *

'Good morning and welcome to "Family Values". I'm Julia Daley and this is Tony Barkworth...' Julia simpered at the camera as Tony chipped in.

'Yes, I'm back with you after my absence yesterday. I'm sure a lot of you will already know why I couldn't be here.' He smiled dangerously at his wife who wriggled in her chair and re-crossed her legs. The powder blue of her flimsy blouse seemed to reflect the ice-blue of his eyes which were boring into her. 'Our first guest today is Rachel Hills from the Citizens Advice Bureau who will reveal some surprising facts and figures about the number of innocent people - like myself - who are subjected to hours of rigorous and often *gruelling* questioning at the hands of the police. I was lucky because I was able to get a good solicitor, but what about those people...' he looked straight at the camera with large 'caring' eyes '... who can't *afford* to do that?' He paused, looking at their guest. 'Rachel, what can people in this situation *do?*' She moved to open her mouth and then shut it as he continued, gesticulating wildly with his hand, exposing the gold Rolex on his wrist. 'Why should someone's poverty affect their ability to prove themselves innocent?'

* * *

201

Clive Haynes' mouth dropped open at the sight of Tony Barkworth on his television screen. The relief he had felt at reading the newspaper reports of an arrest being made evaporated in an instant. How had he been released? Maybe his mind was playing tricks on him. Not wanting to take any chances, he rushed to make sure his front door was bolted.

*　*　*

'Revenge.' Ratter was pulling out all the stops. 'What does that word mean to you Michael?' He knew he was nearly there. He had checked the records and three of the five victims had definitely been HIV positive. The other two cases were being investigated. 'You wanted revenge for your lover infecting you with the deadly virus... and then you took your need for revenge further...'

'I wish you'd make your mind up.' Michael was getting near the end of his tether. So far it had been a sex game gone wrong and now it was retribution for passing on a virus. Ratter picked up on the tone of his voice.

'Touched a nerve did I? Are you HIV positive Michael?'

'No! Well, not that I know of anyway...'

'So you don't know? That's rather convenient. I take it then that you wouldn't mind us taking a blood test?'

'What conclusion would you draw if I refused?'

*　*　*

'I still can't believe that he did it.' Sebastian was sitting in Marcia's kitchen. 'He didn't do it, did he?'

'Well, there's obviously some doubt in your mind if you put it like that.' Marcia didn't know what to think either. 'From my experience, I know that people you think you know very well sometimes do things that seem completely out of character.' She thought for a moment about the way Paul had suddenly left her. 'How can anyone know what's going on inside someone else's mind?'

'Oh God! What are we going to do?' Sebastian had never been good in difficult situations. He wished he could make it all just go

202

away. The fact that his friend might be guilty was not a possibility he wanted to face.

* * *

'So now it's up to you, our viewers,' Julia smiled patronisingly 'to phone in with your questions. Our switchboards are open and Rachel is here to answer your questions about what to do if you are ever questioned by the police.' Harvey had insisted on this 'human angle' and she wasn't in a position to argue with him. 'I think we've already got Sharon from Surbiton on the line. Hello Sharon. What's your question?'

'Well, it's not really a question.' The voice was high and forced. Poor thing, thought Julia, she's terrified at being on the air. She couldn't, however, help detecting something familiar about it. 'It's just that the other day my... friend...'

'Yes Sharon.... your 'friend'?' Whoever fell for that one, she thought tiredly.

'Well, my friend was interviewed by the police who wanted to know where her husband had been on a certain night last week. She actually didn't know where he was... and he'd been out on his own a lot lately... but she panicked because she'd been in bed with another man at the time and she lied and told them her husband had been at home with her.' Julia's face lost all its colour. 'I was just wondering if she could get into trouble about it. You know... I mean... I was worried... since she's my friend.'

'This is a tricky one,' Rachel took over, 'because giving false information to the police is a very serious matter. I think your friend probably acted on the spur of the moment, but she really ought to reconsider her position. I don't know what the police were making investigations about, but there is always the possibility that her husband could have been involved...'

'Well, thank you Sharon.' Julia was trying to stay calm. 'I'm afraid we've got to move on to our next caller...'

* * *

Serena put the receiver down and laughed. Suddenly she began

203

to cry. She had no motive for what she had just done and had gleaned no satisfaction from it. Now Julia would hate her as much as everyone else did. Well, it was her own fault. The silly bitch believed everything she said... hung on every word... every bit of advice. She reached for the vodka bottle and took a large swig. The liquid burned her throat as it slid down, taking away the hurt. Another mouthful followed its course. All she needed was a little sleep, then she would be her old self again, then she wouldn't care. She dragged herself to her feet and walked up the heavy oak staircase to the bathroom. She opened the cabinet. Just one sleeping pill. Well, maybe two. Oh fuck it, she might as well have a handful - she wanted a nice long sleep. Clutching the pills in her hand, she dragged herself back down the stairs and plonked her body on the antique leather again. Another mouthful of vodka sent a feeling of wellbeing on its way around her system. Stuffing the pills in her mouth, she took another swig from the vodka bottle. The fiery potion dribbled from the corners of her mouth, taking the remnants of her peony red lipstick running with it in red rivulets down her smudged chin as she greedily gulped from the bottle again. Who cared that her father had left her without a penny, stripping her of her dignity? Who cared that she had no purpose in life? The reality dawned on her. No purpose.

She lay back in a broken heap and, fighting to keep her eyes open, surveyed the ceiling. The plaster mouldings moved in blurred patterns as her eyelids became heavier and heavier. Darkness moved in and she somersaulted into oblivion.

* * *

'You can do what you like. I've told you that I didn't do it, so what objections could I have?' Michael was tired. He had let them take a blood sample which had since been whisked off to the laboratory. If he was HIV positive, he was soon going to know about it. A day or two ago he wouldn't have wanted to know. Now he was feeling that he had totally lost control of his life. The suggestion of hypnotherapy came as a pleasant interlude in what

204

was fast becoming a very bad dream. 'When do we start?'

Ratter was surprised. In cases like these, the suspect usually guarded the privacy of his mind ferociously. Who knew what an exploration of the criminal mind could reveal? Perhaps this guy genuinely believed he was innocent. His solicitor was obviously at least pretending to believe him or he wouldn't have gone along with the hypnosis idea. Innocent! A smile crept over the policeman's features. They would soon see about that!

* * *

'And our next caller is John from Edmonton.' Tony attempted to regain control. He knew something was wrong. Julia had gone totally to pieces after the first caller and the truth, much as he hated to admit it even to himself, was that he couldn't cope without her. She gave him something to fight against... a reason for existing. 'Hello John. What's your question?'

'Hello Tony.' The voice was deep and coarse. 'I'd just like to say... if it was you... thanks for killing all them queers.'

* * *

'Now, Michael, there is nothing dramatic about this process. There won't be a watch swinging in front of your eyes and you're not going to tell me anything you don't want to.' Michael listened to the hypnotherapist from his comfortable position on the couch. It really was comfortable. And he really was tired. 'Now I just want you to relax.... let your body relax... close your eyes and concentrate on the lovely warm orange light that's surrounding you. Feel your body melting... let everything go... let the couch support your weight... you have nothing to do except listen to the sound of my voice...'

* * *

At last the show was over. Tony wiped his brow as he walked into the dressing room. Julia was slumped in a chair, looking suddenly years older. The lines around her mouth had deepened and the dark bags under her eyes were showing through the heavy make-up. The veins in her temples were visibly pumping. She looked up at him and he sensed a vulnerability in her. He had always suspected it was there, but now her defences were down and she wasn't even trying to hide it.

'Harvey's not taking this matter lightly...' he began and then decided to leave it. It would be better to hear it all straight from the horse's mouth. The producer wanted to see them in an hour's time. Tony thought about their house, their show, their marriage. Julia just gazed straight ahead.

* * *

Iris just couldn't cheer herself up. She had watched "Family Values" and noted the strained expressions on the faces of both presenters. She knew she ought to have felt some kind of satisfaction at knowing she was responsible for Tony Barkworth's freedom, but there was a nagging doubt at the back of her mind. Had she been right?

* * *

'You're five years old, Michael.' The hypnotherapist looked down at the heads turning on the cassette recorder. He had been through the earliest memories his patient could recall and was now gradually building on them. It would take time if he was going to uncover things. That was something the police always had trouble understanding. There was no magic formula for making suspects admit to crimes. It would take time. 'Can you hear me?'

'Yes... I can hear you... and I can hear Mum.' Michael spoke softly.

'Where are you? What are you doing?'

'I'm in the garden... in the garden at the cottage... playing with Mr Barnacle...'

'Mr Barnacle? Who is he?'

'He's my friend... my best friend... but no-one else can see him. He's all mine.'

'So your mother can't see him?'

'No. She says I like to be on my own. But she doesn't know...'

'You said you can hear your mother. Is she calling you?'

*　*　*

Kathleen crawled across the hallway to answer the telephone to avoid being seen through the window. The neighbours would all be dying to know why Anthony had been suspected of those terrible murders. She had always seen herself as a cut above the likes of Marjorie with her young man and coarse language! Why did this have to happen to *her?* She lunged at the receiver. This would be Anthony. He would know what to do.

'Hello?'

'Mrs Barkworth?' It wasn't Tony. It was a strange voice. Blind panic flooded her system.

'What do you want? I don't know anything! Who gave you my number?'

'I'm ringing from Aluplast Windows. We're doing a special summer offer: forty per cent discount on four or more double glazed windows. Would you like one of our fully trained consultants to come and discuss your requirements in the comfort of your own home?'

'No! I'm perfectly well insulated thank you!' She slammed the receiver down angrily and then slumped back against the telephone table. Why didn't Anthony ring?

*　*　*

'Michael... is your mother calling you?'

'No... never me. She's calling Tony... she wants Tony... but he's with Daddy. They're fixing the boat. Mummy wants Tony with her...'

'But he's with your father?'

'Yes. Tony's Daddy's favourite. Daddy says Tony will be successful one day just like him.'

'Are you jealous, Michael?' The patient on the couch was silent as a tear rolled down his cheek.

*　*　*

'You may think that you're successful and in control.' Harvey paused as he moved around the office. He came to a standstill behind the two chairs on which Tony and Julia sat, side by side. 'But to me you appear about as responsible and successful as two naughty schoolchildren who can't resist stealing the limelight by disrupting the class. And - may I remind you - *you* revolve around the show, *not* vice versa!' He paused again, letting them sweat for a few moments. Let them think the worst, he thought, let them squirm. *They* didn't have to carry the can at the end of the day. 'Anyway, your services will not be required for the rest of the week. If you read the small print on your contracts, I think you'll be in no doubt as to why. It will be better for all concerned if you're not in the public eye. In fact, I would advise you to stay as far away from it as possible. I'll speak to you again on Saturday.'

Not a murmur, not a squeak, he thought as they left his office. It was always the way. The mouthy ones were the easiest to deal with in the long run. Now he had got to find someone to replace them - and pretty damn quick too. He reached for the telephone.

'Max? It's Harvey Wolfenden. Look... I might need to follow up the matter you mentioned the other day. Yes... the paper did make a meal of it, but they couldn't exactly turn it down when that silly cow offered it to them on a plate. Is there any chance... no... tonight. Of course it's urgent... see what you can do. I'm relying on you. Do your best Max... I'm over a barrel here... Right... I'll be waiting for your call.'

* * *

Max replaced the receiver on his car phone and a broad grin spread over his face.

'Cinderella,' he muttered under his breath, 'You *will* go to the ball!'

* * *

Conversation was noticeably lacking during the journey home from the studios. Tony looked at the road ahead: the long road he had thought was planned and measured and marked out for him. And Julia looked at nothing. Beyond the show there was nothing. This was the pinnacle of her career, the zenith of her achievement and the culmination of a long journey through life. Her supposedly clever move with the newspapers had backfired, her one friend had betrayed her trust and the future of their contract was now in jeopardy. Surely nothing else could go wrong?

* * *

'Are you jealous, Michael?' The hypnotherapist continued calmly. 'How do you feel?' Silence. 'How do you feel about your parents? Your brother?' He waited patiently, realising that Michael could hear him, knowing that he would get a response eventually. The barriers were gradually coming down. 'How does it make you feel when they don't notice you'?' He watched as Michael moved slightly and clenched his fists. His mouth was set in a firm line as he spoke.

'Angry.'

'Angry?'

'Yes... I want them to notice me. When I'm bigger they will.'

'Why, Michael?'

'Because I'll do something that'll *make* them notice me. *Then* they'll know I'm important...'

* * *

'What do you *really* think, Sebastian?' Marcia had reached no conclusions in her own mind. The reality of Michael's arrest had hardly had time to sink in. 'You knew him when he was with Peter. What kind of relationship did they have?'

'Well... it was strange really. At first, they couldn't get enough of each other. Michael's always gone for the older type - Peter was in his early forties - and they were both apparently into a bit of M and S.'

'M and S?' Marcia risked appearing ignorant. She was sure it was nothing to do with shopping.

'Master and slave role play.' Sebastian forgot that it wasn't everyday terminology - not in public anyway. 'Michael always liked to be dominated. Mind you, he was by far the stronger of the two when it came down to it.'

'How do you mean?'

'It was Michael who always made the decisions. I think he made the first move when they met, actually.'

'And all this role playing stuff... how serious does it get?'

'From what I can tell, it's essentially a game. To be quite honest, it frightens the life out of me!' Sebastian grimaced. 'All that sweaty leather and being tied up. I just can't bear pain.'

'Can anyone?' Marcia was confused.

'Oh yes. Michael used to say it hadn't been a good night if he hadn't got any bruises to show for it.'

'Bruises?'

'Yes. He had a brief fling with a gym instructor once. His backside was black and blue for weeks!'

'So... you mean he enjoyed the pain?'

'Well... that's what I could never work out. I don't know whether it was the pain or the feeling of being dominated. Or maybe it was the fact that he could deal with it all...'

'You've lost me.' Marcia's eyes had been opened, but now she was confused.

'He had a big thing about always being in control.'

'Yes.' She thought for a moment. 'He said something to me once about always being in control. But doesn't that contradict his desire to be dominated?'

'It's beyond me.' Sebastian was suddenly glad that his sex life was virtually non-existent. It certainly made things more straightforward.

* * *

'So what's your conclusion?' Ratter looked eagerly at the hypnotherapist.

'Conclusion? I can't draw one that quickly.'

'What do you mean?' The Detective Inspector was impatient.

'It's going to take quite a while. I've already broken down a lot of his barriers and he's just beginning to tell me how he *feels*. I'll continue tomorrow. With time, I might be able to get closer to finding out if he's capable of committing the crimes he's been charged with.'

'Oh... he committed them alright. It would just be a lot easier if he pleaded guilty at the hearing tomorrow.'

'Easier? For him or for you?'

CHAPTER THIRTEEN

'Would it be possible for someone to tell my mother about this before she hears it on the news? The shock might be too much for her...' Michael had heard that he was going to be named by the media now that he had faced the charges at the hearing. Despite his mother's faults, she didn't deserve to hear that her son had been charged with murder without being prepared for it - if anyone *could* be prepared for news like that. The whole of the country would be hating him now - him specifically rather than the nameless maniac previously in their imagination. He had heard them, or thought he had, from beneath the dark sanctuary of the blanket that had been put over his head to get him into the court building.

'Yes... I think we might be able arrange that.' Ratter wasn't happy. Michael had stuck to his guns and pleaded 'Not Guilty'. 'We'll have the results of your HIV test soon.' He smiled knowingly. 'And you've got another session with that hypnotherapist later on... if you can fit it in!'

Michael didn't feel up to rewarding Ratter's sarcasm with a smile as the cell door closed behind the policeman. What had he got to smile about? In the last two days he had lost more than his liberty. Since the hypnotherapy the day before, the way he thought about himself had changed. He had expected to go into some sort of trance and wake up feeling refreshed. Instead, he had remained completely lucid throughout the session. He had felt that at any time he could have sat up and opened his eyes... except that he was so relaxed the inclination to do so wasn't there. But he had seen things from his early childhood that he wouldn't have remembered otherwise. Little things, unimportant things... and unexplainable things...

*　*　*

Tony rolled over in bed and awoke with a start. He had been dreaming that he was in the cell again staring up at the light bulb. It had suddenly sprouted a face... and it was his father's face. The face had smiled at him and then laughed as it smashed into a thousand pieces. He had never been so glad to wake up, until he remembered that his life had also been fragmented. His head pounded and all he could feel ahead of him was a featureless expanse of time trapped in their huge perfect house. Groaning to himself and trying to ignore Julia's snoring, he rolled over and closed his eyes.

*　*　*

'Mrs Barkworth?' The young police officer had begun to think there was no-one at home, but Kathleen had eventually opened the door a crack and peered out with small frightened eyes.

'What is it? What's happened?' Anthony still hadn't rung her and she felt neglected and stranded. She could almost hear the gossip going on in the houses around her. What had she done to deserve this?

'Could I come in, please. I'm afraid I've got some rather distressing news for you.' He followed her inside and she closed the door, hoping desperately that none of the neighbours had seen the policeman coming in. She silently motioned for him to sit on the sofa as she perched on an armchair opposite. Seeing that she was waiting for him to speak, the young man proceeded with his thankless task. 'Your son...' Kathleen drew in her breath. 'Your son... Michael...' A puzzled look came over her face. 'We've been asked to inform you that he has been arrested and charged with murder.' Things were suddenly beginning to add up in her mind. 'He has hired the services of a solicitor, so you needn't worry about

213

that. You may make arrangements to see him, or I can see to it that he gets any message you may wish to…'

'Let him rot,' she hissed through clenched teeth. 'Let him rot!'

*   *   *

'Mum… it's Tony.' Sitting at the breakfast table nursing a monumental hangover, he had just remembered about the message to call his mother. It had been the last thing on his mind the day before and then in the evening he had got completely drunk on his own. Julia had refused to talk to him. It was clear that she was putting the blame for the whole fiasco on him and him alone. Silly cow. Let her sit and stare at the sick-coloured walls in her precious dining room.

'Anthony! I've been waiting and waiting for you to call… oh… it's so terrible…'

'Calm down Mum… calm down… it's alright… they just wanted to ask me a few questions and Julia overreacted a bit.'

'I can't believe this is happening to me!' Kathleen, lost in her own despair, wasn't listening. 'If your father was alive… it would have killed him!'

'Look… Mum… it was a mistake!'

'How can it be a mistake? The policeman told me he's been arrested…' As his mother twittered on, it suddenly occurred to Tony that they had been talking at cross purposes.

'Arrested? Who?'

'Michael! Michael's been arrested for murder!' Kathleen was astonished that he didn't already know. She had assumed that everybody knew. 'Anthony? Anthony? Are you still there?'

'Yes… yes… it was just the shock. When was he arrested?' Tony listened as Kathleen repeated what the policeman had told her. He had gathered that his own elimination from the enquiries was due to an arrest being made, but he had imagined some faceless homosexual, some monster they had picked up in a shop doorway, some unfortunate who fitted the description of the man they were looking for. But Michael!

'What have you done about it so far?' he asked his mother, who just remained silent. 'Mum?'

'I... I... I was waiting to see what you said. I knew you'd know what to do.'

'Has he got a solicitor?'

'Yes... the policeman said he'd got a solicitor. Oh Anthony... I don't think I could bear it if this got in the papers...'

'I think Michael should be our main concern at the moment. Leave it to me.'

* * *

Julia wretched for the third time into the toilet bowl and then wiped her mouth with the back of her hand. She felt terrible, but would only have been deluding herself if she had pretended it was due to the drink or something she had eaten. It was a feeling she had had so many times before, she couldn't mistake it now.

'Oh fuck!' she screeched, throwing a perfume bottle at the mirror. 'I don't want to be pregnant!'

* * *

'Michael... I came as soon as I heard!' Tony rushed into the room and took his brother's hand and looked around himself awkwardly. He wasn't sure how twin brothers meeting for the first time in more than two years were supposed to react, but he was doing his best. Putting on a concerned expression, he lowered his voice. 'Has it been awful?'

Michael was surprised that his brother had come to see him at all. He had thought that the relationship between them had broken down completely. He was touched that Tony had managed to swallow his pride and risk adverse publicity by coming to the police station.

'It'll be on the news today, you know. I mean... they're going to name me. I'm sorry if it's going to cause trouble for you...'

'Don't be stupid.' Tony wondered what further trouble could possibly be caused. 'I hate to have to ask, but...'

'Did I do it? Is that want you're trying to ask?'

'Yes... I suppose so.' Tony looked upwards to avoid having to meet his brother's gaze. He shuddered as the light bulb overhead loomed into view.

'When they first brought me in, I thought it was all some terrible mistake and that I'd be out in no time, but now...'

'What?' Tony looked at his brother: so defenceless, so unsure of himself. This wasn't the Michael he knew.

'I don't know... Tony, I really don't know if I did it or not!'

* * *

Julia sat at the Elizabethan oak breakfast bar in the kitchen in a pink fluffy dressing gown. There were dark rings under her eyes and her hair was matted and straggly. She lit a cigarette and inhaled deeply, relishing in the long-forgotten sensation as the smoke filled her lungs. Thank God the cleaning lady had left a packet of Benson and Hedges in the utility room. Running a shaking hand through her hair, she shuffled over to the kettle. Where the hell was Tony? There had been no sign of him when she had woken up. Useless man! It was all his fault. She tried to convince herself that Harvey would soon be begging for them to go back to the studios as she stubbed out the cigarette and then reached for another. God only knew who he had got to stand in for them. Well... she'd soon find out. It was nearly ten o'clock. She groped around for the remote control for the kitchen television.

* * *

'I'm afraid it looks as if he's guilty.' Tony spoke softly into the receiver in case anyone was within eavesdropping distance. He looked around himself at the dingy telephone kiosk adorned with cards inviting him to call 'Madame Zeta' or 'Schoolgirl Sally'. It seemed ironic that he was talking to his mother and looking at these at the same time. 'I think it would be better if you didn't go to see him. It would only upset you.' Kathleen smiled on the other end of the line. She had known that Anthony would sort things out. Now she could blank Michael from her mind and get back to everyday life.

'I've been thinking,' she mused. 'I was going to tell you on Sunday...' she stopped, unable to resist bringing up her ruined Sunday lunch '... that I'm going to give the cottage to you. There's no point in me keeping it. I haven't even been there for years... and it probably needs a lot of work done on it. What with you having the wherewithal to do it up a bit...' Tony hadn't told her about the cloud hanging over his future at that very moment '... and you being so fond of it, I thought it would be better off in your hands. I remember all that time you used to spend up there writing...'

'But I think there are more important things to think about at the moment...' Tony marvelled at his mother's ability to let trivial matters take precedence over anything she didn't particularly want to think about.

'Yes... but what I was going to say is that I think I'll go up there for a few days... you know... get away from it all...'

'No!' Tony shouted, unable to stop himself. 'No...' his tone softened, 'it'd be better if you came and stayed with us... me and Julia. I'd hate to think of you going up to the cottage on your own.'

'No... my mind's made up. I'm leaving in the morning.'

* * *

Sebastian drank his third coffee at the bar and wondered what he ought to do. He had found Michael a solicitor, but what should he do next? Despite knowing, or at least being fairly certain, that his friend wasn't guilty, he couldn't help feeling a degree of perverse excitement at knowing someone accused of brutal sadomasochistic murders. He had tried to make arrangements to see him, but hadn't got very far. The problem was that he had actually felt relieved at not being able to see Michael. He didn't know what he was meant to do or to say. It wasn't really like visiting someone in hospital was it? The temptation to tell someone was nearly killing him. He was well aware that it was no laughing matter... but it was so *thrilling*. No. Sebastian corrected himself and felt ashamed. He had got to pull himself together and make a positive move.

'Another cappuccino please, Pierre...'

*   *   *

Having lit another cigarette as she watched the opening credits of "Family Values", Julia stared at the screen, blinked and dropped her coffee.

'Fucking bitch!' she screamed as the slim, well groomed, immaculately but casually dressed woman on the sofa introduced the show. Marilyn smiled back at her: competent, together and professional. Still stunned, Julia realised that the telephone was ringing. She automatically picked up the receiver and immediately wished she hadn't as she heard the familiar gravely voice on the line.

'How the mighty have fallen! I think you'll soon be back in the gutter where you belong...' The line went dead.

*   *   *

Max felt exhilarated as he sat beside Harvey and watched Marilyn on the monitor.

'Looks as if you were right, Max,' Harvey said, 'and I must admit to being damn glad that you were!'

'No problem, Harvey. I don't think you'll regret it, even if it was a bit of a stab in the dark on your part.' He yawned. The night before had been a long one. It had taken a long time to persuade Marilyn that it was a good idea. She had been flattered, shocked, stunned... and anxious about getting a babysitter all at once. He grinned. That was what he found so appealing about Marilyn. She was attractive, intelligent, but still down-to-earth... a *real* woman. Unlike some he could mention. He suddenly felt a heavy sadness descending on him as he remembered that he was chained to Serena. God only knew why, but he had even bothered to ring her the night before to tell her he would be out all night. There had been no answer. She was probably drunk again. Oh, stuff Serena! This was Marilyn's day... and she was certainly living up to the high hopes he had for her.

*   *   *

'Yes... this is Julia Daley. I want to speak to the officer who came to my house the other day.' She tried not to slur her words and betray the fact that she had just had a large scotch... far too large for the morning. 'What do you mean? I'll wait then... of course it's of vital importance!' Feeling offended at being put on hold, she reached for the bottle again. 'Hello... yes... are you the one who was asking me all those stupid questions the other day? Well... I helped you with your enquiries... now it's your turn to help me.' She cleared her throat and tried to remain calm. 'I have just had the latest in a long succession of threatening telephone calls. I think someone is trying to ruin me. Of course it's relevant! It's probably the same person who put you on to my husband in the first place...'

* * *

'I'm going to take you back through the days, Michael.' The hypnotherapist spoke softly as he watched his subject surrendering himself to relaxation. 'Can you see the days on the calendar? Good...' His voice got softer as the barriers between them became more and more penetrable. Slowly and gradually he talked Michael back through the week, watching him closely, gently coaxing him to remember every detail. As he came to Sunday - three days earlier - he saw a flicker of discomfort pass over Michael's face. 'What's the matter, Michael?' He watched as his patient's face puckered into a frown.

'I... I want her to notice me... to be interested in me... but she isn't!'

'Who, Michael, who isn't interested?'

'Mum. She's hardly spoken to me... she wants Tony to be here... it's always Tony...'

'How do you feel, Michael?'

'Angry!'

'It's alright, Michael,' he spoke steadily, slowly, eager to delve further into his patient's recent past, confident that he was at last getting somewhere. 'Let's go back a little further. Can you still see those days on the calendar? Good... right... we're going back.' He watched Michael closely, ready to detect even the slightest flicker of an eyelid. 'Saturday... Friday...' He paused. 'It's Friday... how are you feeling?'

'Good. I'm feeling very good. I've just had a good work out at the gym. I'm getting my body into shape but...' Michael stopped and his face became momentarily expressionless '...but a man noticed the bruises...'

'Bruises? Where are the bruises, Michael?'

'On my backside, of course!' He was half smiling, half scowling. 'I was trying to forget about last night... it reminded me.'

'What happened last night?' The hynotherapist's palms were beginning to sweat. 'What were you trying to forget?'

'Oh... the usual. Just when I thought I'd got myself together...' Michael paused again and became totally motionless. The only sound in the room was that of the spools turning on the tape recorder. '...just when I thought I'd got myself together, I gave in to my urges again.' Feeling a mixture of sorrow and excitement, the therapist continued. The last murder had taken place sometime during Thursday evening and he suspected that he was about to see his patient relive the whole thing...

'Can you see the days again, Michael. We're going back further... back another day...'

* * *

Marilyn still felt as if she was walking on air. She looked over at Max beside her in the driving seat and smiled at him. He sensed that she was looking at him and smiled back.

'How does it feel to be a star?' he laughed.

'Oh, don't exaggerate! I just did the best I could. I can't help feeling it's ironic, though, that it was Karen... I mean Julia... I was standing in for.'

'Yes,' Max smiled as he spoke, 'there's some sort of poetic justice in that, isn't there?'

'Yes,' Marilyn carried on smiling, 'isn't it funny how the things you want most of all in life often only happen after you've decided that you might have to live without them?'

* * *

Julia lit another cigarette, stubbed it out almost immediately and then decided to have a bath. Bloody police! It was fine when *they* wanted something, but as soon as she had a problem they didn't want to know. She picked up her glass of whisky and walked unsteadily towards the stairs.

* * *

'What do you mean, you can't push him any further? You were nearly there. That was the closest we've got to an admission of guilt!' Ratter was agitated. The hypnotherapist had just played him the tapes from that day's session and was now telling him that it would be the next day before he could pursue the hypnosis. The HIV test had proved negative. One of his theories had failed and the nagging doubt at the back of his mind needed to be eradicated. He wanted an admission of guilt.

'He was starting to hold back. There's no point. I'll be back tomorrow.' He excused himself and left the room. Ratter sighed. On top of this, he had got Tony Barkworth's demented wife hounding his officers to do something about some threatening telephone calls. It wasn't even their department... but it might have some relevance. The faint possibility of there being a vendetta against the television couple began to germinate in his mind. He knew someone who might be able to shed some light on the matter...

* * *

Max smiled again to himself as he turned into his drive. Life really seemed to have a purpose now that he had taken Marilyn under his wing. Fiercely independent and admirably capable, she didn't actually need his help and protection; that was what made their friendship worthwhile. They had picked Zoë up from school together before he had driven them home and had tea with them. The little girl had been too excited for words. 'Were you *really* on television?' she had asked, wide-eyed with disbelief. They had brought a video tape home to show her and she had sat quietly

221

taking in the aura that her guardian projected on screen. 'Oh, I can't wait to tell the others at school!'

Now, thought Max, back to reality. He pulled up on the gravel drive and surveyed his house with wonder and pride. It was all his. He had earned it… and had to put up with the consequences.

'Serena!' he called as he opened the front door. 'Serena, are you here?' He half hoped she wasn't, but had spotted her car at the side of the house. He might as well face her now rather than later.

He wandered through the hall and opened the door into the drawing room. 'Serena, where are…' His voice trailed off as his eyes came to rest on his wife's form slumped on the floor in a pool of vomit.

*   *   *

'Miss Devereaux?' Gerry Ratter cleared his throat and held the receiver away from his ear in anticipation of a harsh reply. He wasn't disappointed. If anyone knew who was likely to have it in for the Barkworths, this old girl did.

'Who wants to know?' her gravely old voice enquired. 'Who is it?'

'It's Detective Inspector Ratter. I spoke to you about…'

'I know who you are… d'you think I'm senile or something?'

'Well, the reason I'm ringing is that I couldn't help noticing the particular interest you had in the wife of the man we were questioning the other day…'

'Karen, you mean? Or Julia… or whatever she tries to call herself? I could tell you a thing or two about her…'

'You did, Miss Devereaux, you did.' Ratter was already beginning to regret making this call. 'The thing is, you've obviously got some sort of grudge to bear…'

'Well, you would have if she'd left you in the shit like she did me! And not only once either…'

'Well…' he cleared his throat again, 'she has just reported a series of threatening telephone calls and…'

'And she's trying to put the blame on me, is she? Well, I always knew she had a nerve!'

'No!' Realising he may have disturbed a proverbial hornets' nest, Ratter wished he could turn the clock back a few seconds and start again. 'No. What I meant was...'

'Well!' Iris fumed, 'you can tell her she'll live to regret the day...' She slammed the receiver down, leaving the policeman feeling helpless and somewhat foolish.

CHAPTER FOURTEEN

Kathleen parked her little Nissan in front of the cottage and frowned at the knee-high weeds in the garden. The place really had become run down. It would be just as well if she made it over into Tony's name as soon as possible. There must be so many happy memories for him here. She delved in her handbag for the key and stepped out of the car. For a moment, twenty years melted away and she was with her husband and the two boys. The perfect family group. Except... no... she didn't want to think about it... it was all a long time ago. They *had* been happy, she was sure of it.

She put the key in the lock and struggled to turn the old mortice. The door creaked as it swung open and the musty smell of neglect wafted out to meet her. Suddenly, as if from nowhere, a feeling of fear seized her. Perhaps she shouldn't have come all the way out here on her own. Somewhere at the back of her mind, warning bells were ringing. Maybe she was just overreacting again. 'Silly old bat,' her husband would have said, 'imagining things again!'

At least the telephone was still connected. She would be in touch with the outside world. She fumbled around in the broom cupboard to turn the electricity on and wandered in to see how Anthony had left the place the last time he had been here. Boys! It wasn't like Anthony to leave things untidy. Michael was a different matter. But she would have to forget Michael... forget he ever existed. Walking towards the kitchen, she wrinkled up her nose. A dreadful smell pervaded the room. Perhaps the cellar had flooded again... or maybe it was the drains. Never mind, she had brought her rubber gloves and some Domestos.

*   *   *

Tony dialled his mother's number and listened to the ringing tone. Damn! She must have left already. Or maybe he was panicking. Perhaps she had just gone shopping.

*   *   *

Michael sat in his cell and wondered how his life, which had at last been the way he wanted it, could suddenly be revealed as a total shambles. The hypnotherapy had left him feeling weak... but also strong. It had relieved him of a burden he had been carrying for years: the burden of feeling inferior, at least in the eyes of his parents. Inferior to Tony. But he still couldn't believe that he had murdered those people, still couldn't allow the possibilty to enter his mind. His mind: was he in control of it?

He looked at the grey walls and then closed his eyes and lay back on the bunk. Stop the world, he thought, I want to get off...

*   *   *

Suddenly remembering that the telephone was still connected at the cottage, Tony picked up the receiver again. His fingers shook as they dialled. The ringing tone continued and he started to relax... and then his mother's voice came on the line.

'Hello? Hello? Is there anybody there? Hello? Hell...' He replaced the receiver and sat staring at the watered silk wallpaper.

*   *   *

'Good morning and welcome to "Family Values". I'm Marilyn Mitchell, standing in for Tony and Julia this week. As usual we've got a wide range of topics to discuss, starting with the ever increasing problem of alcoholism. We will then be looking at the sometimes overwhelming effect the arrival of children can have on our lives.' She smiled confidently. 'Dr Leslie McManus will also be with us talking about hormone replacement therapy and we have the first in our series of fashion make-overs, starting with the singer Verity Violet.' The director smiled to himself. It was a treat to have

225

a host who followed the script. 'Our first guest this morning is Dillie Montague, a lady with whom I'm sure you're all familiar...' The camera moved back to reveal the smiling - if slightly lifted - face of the best-selling novelist. 'Now, Dillie, you were telling me earlier on about the overwhelming and almost disastrous effect your meteoric success in the late seventies had on your life.'

'Yes, Marilyn,' the middle-aged woman smiled before continuing in her huskily sexy voice which still carried more than a trace of a Scottish accent, 'and I'd also like to say that I'm glad you're not patronising me and telling me how "brave" I am to come on the show! It wouldn't take a genius to deduce that I've just written another book. What's daytime television for after all?' Her face crinkled a little as she laughed. 'I always prefer to be honest about these things, don't you?' Marilyn didn't even attempt to interrupt her and calmly let the old prima donna continue. 'The thing I'd like to get across to all your viewers, though, is that fame, fortune and all it entails is vastly overrated. Perish the thought that anybody actually envies me, but they probably do. Well, all I'd like to say to them is that *they* are the lucky ones, not me. Be happy with your lives... don't let the curse of ambition fire you on to greater things.' Marilyn privately wondered who was being patronising now. 'I had it all. I had a huge house in Chelsea, holiday homes in Italy and France, six cars, countless lovers...' her eyes sparkled for a moment, 'but I wasn't *happy*. I was still searching for something more... still searching for that elusive factor missing from so many lives. The one place I seemed to find solace was in the murky depths of the bottle...'

*   *   *

Max stared at the television in his kitchen watching Marilyn coping with her situation calmly and efficiently and wondered if he was capable of doing the same with his. He had tried to revive Serena when he found her, but she had been dead for a long time. Seeing her lifeless form slumped on the floor had reminded him of the time in his childhood when his father had forced him to watch a pig being killed back at the farm. One moment it had been alive - kicking and squealing - the next, a lifeless carcass on the floor. But somehow it was different. The pig's death had had a purpose. Its life had been a means to an end, but Serena was in death as in life: useless.

He felt guilty, but not because he could perhaps have come home and saved her in the nick of time. It wasn't because he had been engineering Marilyn's break into the world of daytime television when his wife had been drinking herself into oblivion. Nor was it because he had done his best to totally ignore her of late anyway. No. He felt guilty because of the wonderful sense of relief he felt at being free from her. He was actually glad that she was dead.

* * *

Seeing the needle on the fuel gauge teetering dangerously close to empty, Tony pulled into the next filling station. Without having to think what he was doing, he filled the car with petrol and walked into the kiosk. He was tempted to scowl at the rosy-faced, overweight woman behind the cash desk who had obviously recognised him, but smiled blandly instead. She took his credit card and beamed warmly.

'I don't believe a word of it anyway. The papers'll print anything to sell a few more copies, won't they?' He tried to grin at her as he signed on the dotted line, assuming that she was referring to the humiliating 'wrongful arrest' story of two days earlier, until she added, almost as an afterthought, 'who's to say there's anything wrong with being a prostitute anyway?' His eyes wandered to the news stand in front of the counter.

* * *

Julia rolled over in bed and then realised that it was the telephone that had woken her. Shit! Bloody nuisance. At least while she was asleep she didn't have to dwell on what had happened. The ringing continued. Where was Tony, anyway? Why couldn't *he* answer the phone? Maybe it would stop in a minute. It didn't. But

227

then it suddenly occurred to her that it might be good news. After all, things couldn't possibly get any worse...

'Hello?'

'Hello, Julia...' The gravely voice taunted her down the line as she froze, unable even to drop the receiver as her fingers closed around it in fear. 'I think you'd better have a look at the papers today. The shit's well and truly hit the fan!' The line went dead.

* * *

'Welcome back to "Family Values".' Marilyn smiled at the camera, at ease with her new-found confidence, which stemmed from knowing exactly what the show was and not trying to pretend it was anything more. 'I'm talking to freelance journalist Eamonn Fleming who unreservedly defends the right of the press to report on anything which is likely to be of interest to the public, even if it does sometimes encroach on the privacy of those involved. Eamonn, what is your opinion on the recent ruling in favour of the Duchess of York against a member of her domestic staff who was going to divulge secrets about her lifestyle. Don't you think the Royal family has a right to privacy?'

* * *

Julia tied the headscarf tighter under her chin as she stood on the pavement outside the newsagents surveying the headlines: 'DAYTIME TV QUEEN'S SORDID PAST', 'JULIA DROPPED 'EM FOR CASH', 'DALEY DID IT DAILY FOR A LIVING'. She began to ask herself what she had done to deserve such public humiliation, then decided it wasn't a good line of thought.

* * *

'We're going back through the days again.' The hypnotherapist calmly proceeded with the session, well aware of the pressure that was on him to get results. It wasn't a task he relished. 'It's Thursday evening Michael. I want you to picture exactly where you were last Thursday evening. It's exactly a week ago.' He paused as he saw the expression on his patient's face changing. 'Where are you?'

'In a room... it's spinning. I've had too much to drink...'

Michael shifted uneasily on the couch and then fell silent.

'Descibe the room to me, Michael.'

'It's quite dark... it's dirty... sinister. I wish I hadn't come...'

'Why do you wish you hadn't come, Michael?' The hypnotherapist was getting a prickly sensation up and down his spine.

'I shouldn't be here... I promised myself I wouldn't do it again!' Michael was becoming agitated, beads of sweat dotting his forehead.

'What didn't you want to do again?'

'I couldn't help it. When I got the urge I telephoned him. I should have stayed at home, but something inside me makes me want to do it...'

* * *

Tony kept his eyes on the road, but his mind was racing elsewhere. He had pulled into a quiet lay-by a while back and read every word about his wife's steamy past, mentally calculating how old she must really be. He had thought his investigations in the recent past had revealed all her secrets, but even *he* hadn't imagined anything quite so sordid. He wasn't old enough to remember the Iris Devereaux case, but it rang a bell somewhere in his memory. Her name must have popped up in some of the stories he had covered over the years. She was apparently notorious in the sixties for publicly and openly flouting the laws regarding prostitution, culminating in a much-publicised raid on her house in Muswell Hill in 1968 when, among others, an alarming number of public figures were caught with their pants down. It was said that Miss Devereaux mercilessly used her connections to get away with a surprisingly short sentence. In fact, it was rumoured that the reason for the longevity of her business in the first place was her convenient friendship with certain high-ranking members of the police force. Her downfall was due to her underestimation of a spurned employee who made sure the police couldn't ignore her tip off. The old girl had waited twenty five years to get her own back... and what a way to do it! But now he had to get his mind back to the matter in hand...

* * *

Iris chortled to herself and poured another glass of champagne. She had read and re-read the stories in the paper and felt strangely proud. The reporters had lapped it up and she certainly hadn't held back. Old habits die hard after all. If they were willing to pay the money, they'd get what they wanted! They had certainly managed to get down everything she told them, starting with Julia first coming to her as a sixteen year old runaway in 1960 and being enlisted as a showgirl in one of her troupes.

'I always knew she wouldn't make it as a dancer...' they had quoted her as saying *'... no natural sense of rhythm and style...'* Iris smiled. Some things certainly hadn't changed! *'... but she did show a natural ability to get what she wanted where men were concerned. If she hadn't suggested it herself, I'd never have brought her over to the other side of the business. I supplied hostesses in several gentlemen's clubs in town...'*

The whole story was there for the nation to read and it served Julia right. She was glad they had included the bit about the rugby team. Let them know what an old slapper she really was, despite all her eye shadow and coloured tights. Once was too many times to cross Iris Devereaux, but twice! Somehow she had managed to forgive her running off with an MP and leaving her short of girls for a big job at the embassy. After all, she was young and impressionable and didn't know what they were like. The second time had done it... having it off with the chief of police and then using photographs to blackmail him into raiding the house in Muswell Hill was too much. Oh yes. Anyone who crossed Iris Devereaux lived to regret it... even if they had twenty five years of thinking they had got away with it!

* * *

Gerry Ratter walked around the interview room for a third time and came to a standstill behind Michael's chair.

'Look, you've had time to recover from that session. I don't see what the problem is. You as good as recounted Thursday's murder!'

'No... no... I didn't...' Michael spoke slowly and clearly. 'I've already told you, I was drunk on Thursday night. I couldn't remember exactly where I went... who with... what I did. Not until the hypnotherapy brought it back, that is. We all do things we want to forget...'

'What... like murdering people?' Ratter was getting more impatient by the second. This had gone on far too long for his liking. Michael's silence prompted him to continue. 'Well, if you've got no objections,' the sarcasm in his voice was heavy, 'we'll have another go at it tomorrow. We need to get to the bottom of this matter once and for all.' He turned to go. 'By the way, the result of your HIV test was negative...'

* * *

'Max... it's Marilyn. What's the matter? I got a message this morning to say you wouldn't be able to come with me to the studios. Are you alright?'

'Yes... look... something's happened, but I don't want to talk about it on the telephone. I'll come and meet you at the studio after the show tomorrow.' Max had spent all day trying to gather his thoughts. Above all he had decided that he wasn't going to lose the one chance of true happiness he had glimpsed in years.

'It's not to do with Julia, is it?'

'Julia? No... why?' Max hadn't seen any newspapers.

'Oh... the papers were all full of her scandalous past today. Haven't you seen them?'

'No. Oh God, did they mention...'

'No,' Marilyn said calmly, 'there was no mention of Zoë.'

* * *

Having scrubbed the kitchen from top to bottom, Kathleen took off her rubber gloves and put the kettle on. She had poured bleach down the drains, disinfected the fridge and put a fresh bowl of pot pourri in the loo, but there was still a dreadful smell lingering. It was almost bad enough to make her reconsider staying there. She thought about going home again, but didn't really relish the prospect of all that driving. No. She would have a nice cup of coffee and a Hob Nob and then she would find out where the smell was coming from.

*   *   *

Julia drew all the downstairs curtains in case there were any photographers hiding in the bushes and poured herself a large scotch. She had been wandering around Barnes for hours, unaware of the time, oblivious to everything except an overwhelming feeling of self pity. She had sat on a park bench, still with the headscarf tied firmly under her chin, and read the papers. It was all more or less true... and if it had been about someone else she would have loved it. But it wasn't. It was about her.

It had been quite a shock to find out that Iris Devereaux was still alive. She had assumed that the silly old bag had died years ago. At least they hadn't delved into her more recent past in the States. She tried to imagine how *that* would read if it was plastered across the tabloids: 'EX-TART BLACKMAILED AMERICAN PRODUCER TO GIVE HER TALK SHOW SLOT', 'CARING TV PRESENTER DROVE HUBBY TO SUICIDE', 'HEARTLESS DALEY DESERTED BABY DAUGHTER'. It hadn't seemed that bad to her at the time, but neither had the Iris Devereaux chapter in her life. Now it seemed different. Perhaps it was because she had, for the first time, been viewing it through the eyes of an outsider... through the eyes of a woman sitting on a park bench reading about the scandalous past of a television presenter.

The stories about her had totally overshadowed the accounts of Tony's brother appearing in court to face the murder charges, except in the Daily Nation. It was ironic, really, that the paper that prided itself on covering every sleazy story on offer had plumped to concentrate on Michael's arrest. Only brief mention had been made of the fact that he was Tony's brother, but people had probably already put two and two together. Barry Sugden, in his 'Bazzer

Speaks' column, had made a big joke about the whole thing. *'All this nonsense about the gay community breathing a sigh of relief now the killer is behind bars,'* he had written. *'What are they relieved about? It seems ridiculous to me when all they're ever after is a stab up the bum anyway!'*

She took a large mouthful of whisky and swilled it around her mouth before letting it trickle its fiery way down her throat. She thought about her husband and wondered how he was dealing with the sudden expulsion of skeletons from her closet. Oh well... she had lost her career so she might as well lose her husband as well. For the first time in her life Julia minded the fact that she was alone: alone with no dreams, no ambitions, no friends, no hope...

* * *

Michael looked at the grey walls in a new light. They were still holding him captive, but he was free from the lurking doubt that he wasn't in control of his own mind. He had relived the blank patches in his memory and now could assure himself that he had done nothing to reproach himself *for*. Ratter's casual mention of the HIV test result had lifted another burden from him. He knew he wasn't alone in having cause to worry about it, but hadn't been able to bring himself to be tested since Peter's death. It had almost been like a time limit hanging over his life... telling him to live for the moment... make the most of every minute. He now knew that it was the pressure of this that had driven him to drunken binges like those of the week before.

Never again would he get so drunk that he truly couldn't remember what he had done. Never. Coming back to his senses, he realised that unless he could prove his innocence, he wouldn't ever have the chance to.

* * *

Kathleen panted a little as she rolled the carpet back to reveal the trap door. She had to find out where the smell was coming from and the cellar was about the only possibility left. It wasn't really a cellar as such, rather a storage space under the floorboards and it

233

had been known to flood in the past. Perhaps the drains had overflowed into it. Well, if they had she would be on the telephone to the council. How dare they let their effluent upset her life?

The trap door was large and heavy. She could feel all the blood rushing to her head as she tugged at the iron ring. It was stuck. Kathleen frowned at her own limitations and sat down to get her breath back. The sound of a car pulling up outside reached her ears. Rushing to the open door her face broke into a wide smile.

'Anthony!' she whinnied. 'Fancy you coming all this way just to see me!' She flung her arms around him as he came towards her. 'It's been so long since I saw you. You really shouldn't have bothered to come all the way up here! I just wanted to get away from all the fuss.'

'Yes,' said Tony, looking over his mother's shoulder at the exposed trap door, 'all the fuss.'

* * *

Julia rooted through the kitchen cupboards for another bottle of whisky. There had to be one there somewhere. Damn! Why hadn't she bought more? She couldn't go out shopping in the state she was in. There were bound to be photographers and reporters waiting for her. God, she needed a drink. Maybe there was some in the utility room. The daily woman sometimes rearranged things. Lighting another cigarette, she went to investigate. Crouching down on her knees, ignoring the cracking sound they made, she opened the door of the cupboard under the sink. She smiled to herself as she found a bottle of sweet sherry tucked neatly behind the washing powder. So, Mrs Finneron liked a bit of a tipple, did she? Julia hoped and prayed that the old girl had stashed a bit of the hard stuff as well. Please let there be some. Please. Her frantic hands came to rest on a small holdall she didn't recognise. She lifted it out. It was heavy. Perhaps it was Mrs Finneron's. Perhaps she used it to smuggle booze home with her. Bloody cheek! She unzipped the bag and looked inside. A frown crept over her face as she reached in and pulled out a knife - a large broad-bladed knife. She dropped it as the smell of old blood and excrement reached her nostrils. She barely reached the sink in time to vomit.

*   *   *

'I've cleaned the place up a bit. Did you notice?' Kathleen felt like a young girl again. Anthony - her favourite son - had driven all the way up here to be with her. 'But there's still a funny smell. I was thinking that it might be coming from the cellar. Do you remember it flooding once years ago?'

'No... and I can't smell anything.' Tony tried to sound nonchalant. 'I don't know what you're fussing about.' He swallowed and looked around the room for another topic of conversation. 'We should be talking about Michael!' His mother pretended she hadn't heard the last remark.

'I'm not fussing... I just don't like this smell. Look, I'll put the kettle on while you get the trap door open...'

*   *   *

'Hello... this is Julia Daley... yes... please put me through to Detective Inspector Ratter.' She tried to remain calm. The truth was beginning to dawn on her in its awful entirety. She had to tell the police before she dug herself in any deeper. What had she got left to lose? 'No, it's not about the nuisance telephone calls. It's rather more serious. Please send someone over here as soon as possible...' The officer on the end of the line sighed, wondering what she was going to waste their time with. 'I think I've found the murder weapon.'

*   *   *

'Oh, come on Tony. I'm sure you can do it. Pull!' Kathleen wasn't willing to let the matter of the smell rest. 'Go on... it moved then!'

'Mum, I'm sure there's nothing down there... and what are you going to do about it if there is?' Tony was stalling for time.

'If it's those drains overflowing again, I'll get the council to come and sort them out. Let me help you... that's it... look... it's moving!' The trap door thumped loudly back onto the bare boards

235

and her suspicions were confirmed as a nauseating stench seemed to billow from the dark hole in the floor. Reaching for her torch she put her foot on the first step down.

'I'll get to the bottom of this!' she muttered to herself... and a split second later felt a firm push from behind, missed her footing and fell. The last thing she heard was the trap door clanking shut as her head hit the bottom step and she passed out.

*   *   *

Ratter arrived at the house in Barnes, cursing the Daley woman for having insisted on him coming in person. He had been about to carry on with Michael's questioning. He was sure he was as near to a confession as he had ever been. It was only ever a matter of time...

'Oh... thank God you've got here...' Julia had been half expecting Tony to arrive home at any moment. She didn't know where he was and she didn't know what to believe now. She was well aware of the fact that she had lied to the police about her husband's whereabouts on the nights of the murders. 'Come through here... look!' Ratter looked down at the machete which was still where she had dropped it on the floor.

'Where did you find it?' He was puzzled.

'Under the sink... hidden behind everything. I was looking for... something.' She hoped she wasn't slurring her words,

'And,' Ratter frowned, 'could your brother-in-law have easily put it there without you knowing?'

'No...' Julia stared at him in incredulity '...I've never even met my brother-in-law and he certainly hasn't ever been here. I don't think you realise what this means...'

*   *   *

Kathleen opened her eyes and thought for a moment that she had gone blind. Then, along with the dreadful smell and a splitting headache, it all began to come back to her. Tony had pushed her into the cellar and shut the door! Why? She pulled herself up onto her knees and felt around for the torch. It had to be there somewhere - she was been holding it when she fell. The earth floor

236

beneath her was damp and clammy, soaking her skirt and coating her hands with thick slime as she scrabbled around in the foetid darkness. The search for the torch took all her concentration, protecting her mind from the dreadful reality of the situation, protecting her nostrils from the nauseating stench of sewage... sewage and something much worse. The reasons and possibilities faded into insignificance as she frantically groped around at the bottom of the stairs. At last her fingers closed around the hard plastic and, heaving a sigh of relief, she flicked the switch.

Her mouth opened to scream as the light revealed the secrets of the cellar and the source of the smell. Within feet of her was the decomposing body of a man... nearly naked... studded leather straps wrapped around the rotting skin of his torso. Dark, murky indentations -deep purple in colour - were filled with hundreds of thin red worms gorging on the putrid flesh and blood. She moved the torch closer, unable to tear her gaze away, and watched the little creatures burrow deeper, their vampire tendencies being confirmed as they shied away from the light. The smell seemed to have become worse the instant she knew what was causing it, but still she shone the torch on the body. Inches away from it was another one... or at least parts of it. She wanted to look away... to faint... to somehow get away from this dreadful scene that was thrusting itself at her. She could see a head... a severed head... festering holes where its eyes should have been. And the smell! Her stomach heaved and she put her hand up to cover her nose, swallowing her acid regurgitation and dropping the torch. Her body froze as she realised she was shut in... trapped... within inches of death.

Just feet above her head, Tony sat in the armchair he had stationed on top of the trap door and stared blankly ahead. Things were closing in on him. He was no longer able to keep the different aspects of his life neatly separated. They were beginning to spill over into each other. It wasn't right... he couldn't manage... couldn't cope. He needed to be in control. He had got his mother under control at last. Let her stay there with the others. Now he had to make sure the other woman in his life was behaving. Fear. That's what kept him going - knowing that he could induce fear.

He had tried to warn Michael from the start... warn him that the man he had teamed up with would try to do unmentionable things to him. He had felt a need to protect his twin from the horrors he had endured himself as a child. But how could he have explained to him and still kept it a secret. It had to be a secret. Nobody else could know. He was fighting a battle single-handed...

* * *

'So you haven't seen him all day? Where do you think he's gone?' Ratter was confused. Finding the blood-stained knife had put his investigations in a whole new light.

'I've told you... I don't know!' Julia put her head in her hands and realised that everything had caught up with her. To think that she had lied in the first place to try and save her career! Look at it now. The telephone rang and broke the tension. 'Hello... Julia Daley speaking...'

'You're next...' the husky, threatening voice came down the line at her, but it didn't inspire the usual fear. For the first time, she recognised the voice and remained silent as it continued. '...you disgusting old bag... filthy old whore...' The line went dead as she looked at Ratter, who seized the telephone and punched in a number.

'If that was your husband,' he said, 'we've got him!'

CHAPTER FIFTEEN

Kathleen's initial horror gave way to a numbness which started to creep through her body, freezing her senses into a non-feeling, non-thinking limbo. She sat in the dark, knowing the rotting, festering bodies were there, but shutting off her mind to the fact. As the minutes ticked by, her mind wandered to the good times they had had at the cottage as a family - all those happy weeks during the summers of distant years. It had all been part of their perfect, affluent family life - so different from her childhood years.

It had been like a dream come true when she had married her husband, even if he had been a few years older than she was. 'I'll make a lady of you, Kathleen', he had said, helping her to get rid of her ugly accent and choose the right clothes, trying to guide her in the right direction when it came to dealing with people. He had been like a saviour, a knight in shining armour plucking her from a mundane life where working in a factory seemed to be her best prospect, giving her the chance to be a wife. She smiled as she remembered their first home. He had given her a budget to decorate it and she had had the time of her life. All the things she had only ever dreamed about having were hers: floral print curtains, a three piece suite, brand new bedroom furniture. Bedroom. Her smile evaporated as more memories flooded into her mind. She shuddered uncontrollably as she remembered the force with which he had tried to invade her body in a way even she knew was wrong.

As she tried to shut off the memories, she came back to reality with a jolt. She knew, whether or not she wanted to admit it to herself, that she might never get out of this cellar. What a place to die! This dark, foul-smelling hole filled with rotting bodies: murder victims... her son's murder victims. If only she hadn't come up here. But now she could see that it didn't help to ignore things and pretend they weren't happening. To think that these decomposed remnants of human life would have been down here under her pretty cottage without anyone knowing if the smell hadn't drifted upstairs. Like the memories of childhood that had obviously been haunting Tony... twisting his mind. Why oh why hadn't she done something about it at the time?

It had all started when the twins were about five. She had thought she was imagining it at first - had prayed that she was imagining it. It had happened here... here at the cottage. All the years between seemed to shrink into insignificance as she found herself back there... back in bed on a dark night... waking up to find herself alone... creeping along the landing to see where her husband had gone to... stopping horrified outside the open door of Tony's bedroom.

She had tiptoed back to bed and pretended that it hadn't happened, pretended that she hadn't seen anything. The morning daylight had made it easier for her to convince herself, but it didn't stop the recurring nightmares. She couldn't count the number of times she had dreamt of her husband's pale bare buttocks rising and falling in the dark... the pathetic whimpering coming from underneath... her child needing her... whimpering...

It was too late to do anything now - too late to make amends for being too foolish, too frightened of losing her 'perfect' lifestyle, frightened of any scandal. Like the pretty cottage with its foetid cellar filled with putrefied bodies, she was now too well aware of the rotten foundations of her marriage. To think that her family had been the envy of her friends!

This was punishment. The darkness spelt it out plainly to her. She was being punished because she was guilty. She spoke the word out loud and then shouted it.

'Guilty!' She was guilty because she knew... and did nothing about it. 'Guilty!' The pale buttocks appeared in front of her eyes... rising and falling... rising and falling. 'Guilty!' She could hear Tony crying... pitiful cries of a child in pain... physical and mental pain. 'Guilty!'

* * *

Tony put his foot flat down on the accelerator as his car sped back towards London. It had been a close shave, but he had sorted out his mother. She wouldn't be telling anyone about what she had found! Silly old bag. He had put her car in the garage and nobody knew she was there. Let her rot in the cellar...

* * *

'Shit!' Detective Inspector Ratter swore. He had driven up to the cottage with two colleagues as soon as they had traced the call. He wanted to make the arrest himself. It would give him great pleasure to catch Tony Barkworth off his guard and tie up all the loose ends. He couldn't afford to make any more mistakes. They had forced the door, but the cottage was in darkness and there were no signs of him. There were officers at the Barkworth house with Julia. They would get him if he went back there. What should he do now?

'What's that stink, sir?' the young officer was wrinkling up his nose in disgust. 'Smells like something died in here.'

'Smell?' Ratter sniffed, There *was* a dreadful smell, but he had far more important things on his mind. 'Come on... this has been a wasted journey. We've got to get back to London!'

Just a few feet below them, Kathleen stirred. She had passed out in desperate exhaustion, her head propped against the bottom of the wooden staircase, but the sound of footsteps above her head made her wake with a start. She put her hand down to steady herself and felt her fingers sink into rotten flesh as an even more vile and unbearable stench met her nostrils. Her scream reached Ratter's ears as he was about to close the door behind him.

* * *

The motorway was virtually clear as Tony joined it. He watched the needle on the speedometer creep higher and higher. His mind wandered back over the week. A week! Only a week earlier everything had appeared to be fine. Except for that stupid black bitch of a singer making him look incompetent on the show. The show. What was the situation there now? Was his career over? How could it be? He needed it. Without it he was nothing. What was the situation with Julia? Without her he was nothing...

How could life be so ruthless? It let you build up your hopes and dreams only to dash them down overnight. It handed you success on a plate and then snatched it away again. How could you be successful when you didn't know what you were fighting for or, more importantly, against...

*   *   *

Marilyn switched off her bedside light and snuggled down for a good night's sleep. It had been another long day, but she had managed to fit everything in. Didn't someone once say 'If you want something done, ask a busy person'? She smiled to herself at the way she had managed to juggle her maternal role with whatever else had come her way. She had a girl living in now to take Zoë to school in the morning. The show was over and Marilyn home before the little girl needed to be picked up. Everything was falling into place. Just one thing spoiled the picture: why did Max have to be married? She knew it was selfish, but she wanted him desperately.

'Never mind,' she sighed to herself, grateful for what she already had. 'You can't have everything!'

*   *   *

Julia poured herself another glass of whisky, but passed out before it even reached her lips.

*   *   *

Kathleen was still in a state of shock as the policemen helped her out of the cellar. She collapsed into an armchair and started to cry.

'Don't cry, love, it's alright.' The young officer put his hand on her shoulder, trying to ignore the nauseating stench that had permeated the woman's clothes. 'Everything's going to be alright... it's not your fault.'

'Yes,' she sobbed, 'Yes it is...'

*   *   *

Tony saw the metropolis looming closer and prepared himself to carry on with his life. His mother's interference had nearly blown the cover on his secret, but he had solved that problem. Now he could get back to living his life...

*   *   *

Ratter fled from the stench to the sanctuary of his car. The place was swarming with forensic scientists and coroners. Once disturbed, the bodies in the cellar had come to life again, spilling out noxious gases from their ruptured cavities. He watched, the smell still in his nostrils, as another body was brought out. The charcoal masks worn by those working in and around the cottage failed to stop the stench from working its way into their nasal passages. Nothing could reduce the repulsive impact of the scene. Even the journalists who had turned up had beat a hasty retreat having got the photographs and information they needed.

Three of the four bodies had already been identified from items found on or near them. They were all men in their forties. It was virtually impossible to tell how they had been murdered, but the signs were that they had met the same fate as the other five victims. The guys from forensics had intimated that the most recent of the bodies had been deposited there only nine months ago. The knife the Daley woman had found had been positively identified as the murder weapon. Michael Barkworth was ruled out completely, that was for sure.

And he had let the real culprit slip through the net...

CHAPTER SIXTEEN

Sebastian walked into Michael's bedroom with a tray and drew the curtains back letting the sunlight flood in.

'Come on... rise and shine! We've got a big day ahead of us!' Michael looked at his friend blankly. He was grateful that he had come to fetch him as soon as he had been released and had stayed the night to make sure he was alright, but this early morning brightness was almost too much to bear. 'Don't tell me you've forgotten,' Sebastian chirped. 'It's the Gay Pride March today!' Michael groaned.

'Oh, Sebastian! I'm not up to parading the streets proclaiming my sexuality. I've only just come to terms with the fact that I'm a free man.'

'No...you're a free homosexual!'

'Oh... look... I really don't think I'm up to it. I'm still exhausted from all that questioning. They almost made me believe I was guilty. Can you imagine what it's like to face the possibility that you are a murderer... and then there was the HIV test. The whole episode was one long nightmare. My life suddenly seemed to be over just as I thought I'd got it together.' Sebastian looked at him enquiringly. 'But I've survived... and I've made a vow to never again get drunk and go home with a stranger who wants to put me over his knee and spank me!'

'Who cares as long as you enjoyed it?' Sebastian's eyes

twinkled as he put the tray of coffee and toast on his friend's bed.

'It's not a laughing matter! I'm a reformed character...'

'Oh... sing it to somebody else!' Sebastian laughed, wondering how his friend could live with the fact that his own twin brother had murdered his lover and then been prepared to allow him to carry the can for his own crimes. He didn't want Michael's spirits to drop, but knew he had got a lot to come to terms with. 'I've brought the papers in for you to read. You're going to have to see them sooner or later.'

* * *

"Michael Barkworth, brother of top daytime chat show host Tony Barkworth, was released yesterday after the discovery of 'graves from hell' at the TV star's country cottage.

Michael Barkworth (30) was arrested by Detective Inspector Ratter of Scotland Yard after a tip off.

Tony Barkworth had previously been questioned in connection with a series of gay murders and mutilations in London; he was recognised on his show by a gay man who had escaped the Gay Slasher's clutches after agreeing to have perverted gay sex with the murderer. But when police were tipped off about his openly gay identical twin Michael, they released the daytime smoothie and captured his brother.

The shock discovery of up to SEVEN mutilated male bodies underneath Tony Barkworth's country retreat has sent a shiver down DI Ratter's spine.

Have they let the wrong man go free?

Julia Daley, recently exposed ex-call girl partner of Tony Barkworth in real life as well as TV, has fled their mansion home in London and is believed to have her small but close circle of friend around her. A spokesman for the show has exclusively told The NATION that she is '...confused and unable to understand anything...' and that she will be in '...need of psychiatric help soon...'"

Tony scanned the newspaper he had found on the park bench

and sank back into the shadow of a tree to watch the hordes of people rushing past to the Embankment tube station. They all seemed to know where they were going and what they were doing. Each stride, as he watched, seemed to hold purpose. By comparison, he was in limbo.

The police had been waiting for him at the house, but he had been too quick for them. Quick thinking had meant he was still one step ahead, still in control. He had spent the night wandering the streets, trying to gather his thoughts, wondering what he should do next. Should he give himself up and let the state decide on his punishment or should he stay on the run - free, but saddled with his own guilt, imprisoned within his own mind.

His eyes wandered back to the newspaper.

"Police today continue their gruesome search of the vile basement in Norfolk. One said '... there are wall to wall bodies all floating on a decaying sludge...' It seems likely that Tony Barkworth will attempt to flee the country. DI Ratter would like to speak to him urgently. He added that Mr Barkworth should be considered '... extremely dangerous...'.

Tomorrow The NATION have the FULL inside story and an interview with recent guest on Barkworth's network-topping show: Abbie Cadabra, TRANSSEXUAL member of the Magic Circle."

It looked as if his luck had run out. He felt dirty and tired... and vulnerable. There was no way out...

'Michael! What the hell have you been doing? You look awful!' Tony looked up blankly at the man addressing him. 'Don't say you don't remember me. Bruce... last week?'

'Oh yes... sorry,' Tony stammered.

'My God, last night must have been a rough one! I was hoping I'd see you today - it was touch and go whether I'd make it back in time for Pride. Luckily I managed to change my flight back at the last minute. I suppose you're waiting down here for the start of the march...' he gesticulated behind himself to the Embankment where gaily decorated floats were already beginning to assemble '...but, if you don't mind me saying so, you don't look in any fit state.'

'No... er...' Tony looked down at his grubby clothes and put a hand up to feel the day's growth of stubble on his chin '...you know what it's like.'

'Look...' Bruce continued, 'why don't you come home with me and have a wash and brush up? It's only just around the corner.'

'No... I don't want to impose..'

'You're not imposing. I'm just going back to have something to eat and a coffee - a bit of sustenance for the march.' He smiled, 'Come on... I won't take no for an answer!'

* * *

'I know we'll get him.' Ratter sipped at the styrofoam cup of coffee. 'Where can he hide? It's just a matter of time.'

* * *

'Michael!' Marcia rushed into the bedroom and planted a kiss on his cheek. 'I can't tell you how glad I am to see you back!'

'Did you miss me?' He laughed and then realised that he had tears in his eyes. Everyday life now appeared to him as the precious commodity it really was. 'How's the dating going?'

'That was the last thing on my mind after they took you away.' She paused for a moment and then looked at him with a glint in her eye, 'but I have got five men lined up to meet... as long as you promise to come with me to check them out.'

'Happy to be of service! What do you call the antithesis of a fag hag?'

Sebastian grinned to see that Michael was fast becoming his old self again, albeit with a slightly haunted look in his eyes. He knew he had a duty to make sure his friend thrust himself back into everyday life as soon as possible. He didn't want to see him withdraw into himself.

'Look... how about a compromise? I'll agree that we don't go on the march if you'll agree to go straight to Brockwell Park for the rally after lunch. That way we'll get the best of both worlds - we'll still see thousands of gay men enjoying themselves... and we'll have enough energy left to appreciate it!'

'Oh... alright!' Michael knew that Sebastian usually got his own way in the end, so it was easier to agree. He was glad anyway. It took the decision out of his hands. It really was the highlight of the gay year: Jimmy Somerville, Sonia, Julian Clary, Boy George, Dannii Minogue, Lily Savage, Margi Clarke – they would all be there doing their bit for gay awareness, not to mention an estimated six figure number of gay men and women proud of what they were.

* * *

'Have a shower if you want,' Bruce said over his shoulder as he put the kettle on, 'Sorry about the mess... I haven't had time to clear up since I got back this morning. Oh... you left your jacket here. It's on the back of that chair over there,'

* * *

Julia rolled over in bed and felt her head throb. At least the hangover took her mind off the fact that her life was over...

* * *

'Come on... we don't want to miss the start!' Bruce jumped down the stairs two at a time. Tony did his best to keep up, feeling much better after a shower. He had borrowed some of Bruce's clothes and felt more able to face the world. As they emerged into the street and walked back down towards the Embankment, the excitement in the air was almost palpable. Excited people bustled everywhere unravelling banners and blowing whistles. Tony looked around him in wonderment at the brightly-coloured floats lined up in the road as the infectious excitement began to grab him in its clutches. These people knew what they were. They cared what they were and, what was more, they were happy.

Bruce introduced him to the friends he had organised to meet and, for the first time in years, Tony felt that he belonged. A sense of wellbeing swept through him as he caught a glimpse of the forbidden fruit of happiness dangling in front of his eyes...

* * *

Kathleen made sure the curtains were closed and sat down on

the sofa. The subdued light matched her depression. She hadn't slept since the police had brought her back from the cottage. She was tired... so very tired. But sleep was no escape anymore. She mustn't let it creep up on her, bringing with it the nightmare vision of those pale buttocks rising and falling in the dark...

*   *   *

'I'm sorry if I kept you from the march,' Michael looked at Sebastian apologetically as they arrived at the park, 'it's just that I really didn't feel up to it.'

'No problem! Do you really think I wanted to walk all that way? It was a good excuse not to! Come on, let's get something to eat.' He led the way up the grassy slope. As they reached the top, a huge temporary settlement of stalls, stands and marquees came into view. A massive stage with thousands of people already sitting on the grass in front of it seemed to be quietly waiting for the excitement it was going to host throughout the day ahead. There were men and women everywhere - thousands of them in all shapes and sizes, all modes of dress. Michael's eyes opened wide as he took in the full impact of the festival,

'Just look at them all! Who would ever realise there were so many of us?' he murmured, newly aware of the colour of the sky, the smell of the fresh air, the quality of life.

'Yes,' said Sebastian, 'I hope the toilet arrangements are better than they were last year!'

*   *   *

Tony felt himself being swept along with the tide of bodies flowing out of the tube station. He didn't have to use his mind, he just followed. His feelings alternated between amazement at the existence of so many gay people and envy - bordering on outright jealousy - at the sense of purpose and identity they shared. He felt in the pocket of the bomber jacket and ran his fingers over Michael's passport. A smile came to his lips.

The crowd moved as one down the street, whistles blowing...

*   *   *

'And can we have a warm welcome for a lady who has just seen her hit single shoot to the top of the charts for a second time after fifteen years!' The drag queen tottered in the middle of the main stage on her thigh length stiletto boots. 'Ladies and gentlemen... the one and only... Shanelle!' The sprightly black singer skipped onto the stage and grabbed the microphone. The line of coke she had just snorted in the dressing room had sent her head whizzing and the sight of thousands of adoring faces in front of her nearly pushed her beyond the limit.

'Hi!' she shouted. 'It's good to be back! I'm delighted to see you all here despite the fear that must be gripping you all...' she had never been able to keep abreast of the news and the last few days seemed to have passed her by '...but I've got a message for the killer if he's out there among you. Stop... in the name of love!' With that she launched into a rendition of the Diana Ross hit 'Stop In The Name Of Love' amid groans from the audience. Tony lowered his head and tried to merge with the crowd.

* * *

'Hi John!' Michael shouted, having spotted his work mate across the crowded tent they were in.

'Oh... so you're speaking to me now are you?'

'What?' Michael was puzzled.

'I spoke to you on the march and you looked straight through me,' John snapped. 'I only wanted to say how glad I was the police came to their senses and let you out.'

'But...' Michael suddenly felt the colour draining from his face. 'I wasn't on the march...' He turned to Sebastian. 'Quick... I've got to find a telephone!'

* * *

In a remarkably low key manner, police armed with photographs of Tony combed the park and surrounding area. The last thing they wanted to do was cause panic. The only way they were going to catch him was by creeping up on him - wherever he was. Gerry Ratter arrived in the park just as a positive sighting had been made at one of the beer tents.

'He's sitting at a table outside the "Coleherne" tent, sir. Right in the corner...' the voice coming over the walkie talkie was like music to his ears '...we've got him surrounded.'

'I'll be there. Just make sure he doesn't get away!' This time he was going to arrest him or die in the attempt. A steward escorted him briskly to the bar tent in question, amused at the policeman's incredulity at the sheer volume of people. 'Are they all... you know?'

'Yes...' said the steward '...we are!'

Ratter's heart began to beat faster as he neared his target. Closer... closer... he rounded the corner of the tent and there he was... just feet away. Ratter homed in and was suddenly face to face.

'Anthony Barkworth.'

'Oh come on Inspector... it's me... Michael...' Ratter's mouth dropped open and the frustration showed clearly on his face. 'I can take a joke, but you've only just released me.' He stood up from his chair and realised that a small crowd had gathered. The sense of brotherhood, together with a large quantity of alcohol, had seized everyone. Despite the fact that they were not entirely aware of the circumstances surrounding the situation, they weren't in any mood to let one of their own get trampled on by the police. 'Today of all days when we - still a persecuted minority - can air our views, feel free to express our persuasions openly and publicly, when the joys - not the oppressions - of homosexuality are ours, when I am experiencing civil freedom as well as sexual freedom for the first time in a week... don't you think this is a bit ironic?' A cheer went up from his new followers as he sat down again. Almost as an afterthought, he produced the passport from his pocket and waved it at the policeman.

A momentary look of confusion passed over Ratter's face, giving way to one of relief as he looked up to see Michael approaching with the two officers accompanying him. Although torn between his duty to the community and the pain he felt at hastening his brother's capture, the trite little speech - far from moving him - had cleared his mind.

'Still a tabloid journalist at heart I see, Tony...'

EPILOGUE

The good weather had given way to light drizzle soaking the three mourners at Serena's funeral. Grey clouds hung dispassionately in the sky as the trio walked away from the grave.

Max Hesketh, feeling that a huge weight had been lifted from his shoulders, looked forward to the rest of his life with a fervour now devoid of any guilt or remorse.

Julia Daley hung her head, but the life she was mourning was not that of the woman whose body was now lying cold in the damp earth. She had already made arrangements to sell the house in Barnes and her career was over. She could feel her recently swollen nipples chafing against the black silk of her dress and wondered what she had got to offer the unborn child inside her.

Barry Sugden took her hand - licking his lips as his practised eye noticed the oestrogen ring clearly visible on her palm - and tried to look suitably sympathetic. He could feel himself hardening inside his trousers as he looked her in the eyes and mentally undressed her. A few more months and she would be ripe...

'I'm sorry it has to be in such sad circumstances, but it's good to see you again.' He motioned towards the huge black Cadillac waiting to take him back to his mansion in Essex. 'Can I give you a lift home?'

*   *   *

'Are you sure she won't mind you bringing me?' Michael looked across at Bruce in the driving seat. They were driving down to Surrey to have lunch with Bruce's mother on her birthday.

'Of course she won't.' Bruce grinned and put his hand on Michael's knee. 'I've told you she keeps asking when I'm going to bring Mr Right home to meet her!'